❖

"ONE CAN NEVER HELP BEING born into perfection," I whispered.

He came close, wrapping an arm around my waist so that we faced each other. His nose tickled mine. He ran his fingers across my cheek so gently it seemed he was afraid I would break.

"No, I don't suppose you can," he breathed.

With his hand holding my face toward his, he lowered his lips to mine and gave me the faintest whisper of a kiss.

Something about the tentativeness of it made me feel beautiful. Without a word, I could understand how excited he was to have this moment, but then afraid at the same time. And deeper than any of that, I sensed that he adored me.

❖

THE SELECTION

KIERA CASS

An Imprint of HarperCollinsPublishers

HarperTeen is an imprint of HarperCollins Publishers.

The Selection
Copyright © 2012 by Kiera Cass
www.epicreads.com

Library of Congress Cataloging-in-Publication Data
Cass, Kiera.
The Selection / by Kiera Cass. — 1st ed.
p.   cm.
Summary: "Sixteen-year-old America Singer is living in
the caste-divided nation of Illéa, which formed after the war that
destroyed the United States. America is chosen to compete in
the Selection—a contest to see which girl can win the heart of
Illéa's prince—but all she really wants is a chance for a future with
her secret love, Aspen, who is a caste below her"— Provided by
publisher.
. ISBN 978-0-06-205994-9
[1. Marriage—Fiction.   2. Contests—Fiction.   3. Social
classes—Fiction.   4. Princes—Fiction.   5. Love—Fiction.
6. Revolutionaries—Fiction.]   I. Title.
PZ7.C2685133Sel   2012   2011042113
[Fic]—dc23   CIP
                                                                  AC

Typography by Sarah Hoy
13 14 15 16 17   CG/RRDH   10 9 8 7 6 5 4
❖
First paperback edition, 2013

Hi, Dad!
waves

CHAPTER 1

WHEN WE GOT THE LETTER in the post, my mother was ecstatic. She had already decided that all our problems were solved, gone forever. The big hitch in her brilliant plan was me. I didn't think I was a particularly disobedient daughter, but this was where I drew the line.

I didn't want to be royalty. And I didn't want to be a One. I didn't even want to *try*.

I hid in my room, the only place to avoid the chattering of our full house, trying to come up with an argument that would sway her. So far, I had a solid collection of my honest opinions . . . I didn't think there was a single one she would listen to.

I couldn't avoid her much longer. It was approaching dinnertime, and as the oldest child left in the house, cooking duties fell on me. I pulled myself out of bed and walked into the snake pit.

I got a glare from Mom but no words.

We did a silent dance through the kitchen and dining room as we prepared chicken, pasta, and apple slices, and set the table for five. If I glanced up from a task, she'd fix me with a fierce look as if she could shame me into wanting the same things she did. She tried that every so often. Like if I didn't want to take on a particular job because I knew the family hosting us was unnecessarily rude. Or if she wanted me to do a massive cleaning when we couldn't afford to have a Six come and help.

Sometimes it worked. Sometimes it didn't. And this was one area where I was unswayable.

She couldn't stand it when I was stubborn. But I got that from her, so she shouldn't have been surprised. This wasn't just about me, though. Mom had been tense lately. The summer was ending, and soon we'd be faced with cold. And worry.

Mom set down the pitcher of tea in the center of the table with an angry thud. My mouth watered at the thought of tea with lemon. But I would have to wait; it would be such a waste to have my glass now and then have to drink water with my meal.

"Would it kill you to fill out the form?" she said, no longer able to contain herself. "The Selection could be a wonderful opportunity for you, for all of us."

I sighed aloud, thinking that filling out that form might actually be something close to death.

It was no secret that the rebels—the underground colonies

that hated Illéa, our large and comparatively young country—made their attacks on the palace both violent and frequent. We'd seen them in action in Carolina before. One of the magistrates' houses was burned to the ground, and a handful of Twos had their cars vandalized. There was even a magnificent jailbreak once, but considering they only released a teenage girl who'd managed to get herself pregnant and a Seven who was a father to nine, I couldn't help thinking they were in the right that time.

But beyond the potential danger, I felt like it would hurt my heart to even consider the Selection. I couldn't help smiling as I thought about all the reasons I had to stay exactly where I was.

"These last few years have been very hard on your father," she hissed. "If you have any compassion at all, you might think of him."

Dad. Yeah. I really did want to help Dad. And May and Gerad. And, I supposed, even my mother. When she talked about it that way, there was nothing to smile about. Things had been strained around here for far too long. I wondered if Dad would see this as a way back to normal, if any amount of money could make things better.

It wasn't that our situation was so precarious that we were living in fear of survival or anything. We weren't destitute. But I guess we weren't that far off either.

Our caste was just three away from the bottom. We were artists. And artists and classical musicians were only three steps up from dirt. Literally. Our money was stretched as tight as a high wire, and our income was highly dependent on the changing seasons.

I remembered reading in a timeworn history book that all the major holidays used to be cramped into the winter months. Something called Halloween followed by Thanksgiving, then Christmas and New Year's. All back to back.

Christmas was still the same. It's not like you could change the birth date of a deity. But when Illéa made the massive peace treaty with China, the New Year came in January or February, depending on the moon. All the individual celebrations of thankfulness and independence from our part of the world were now simply the Grateful Feast. That came in the summer. It was a time to celebrate the forming of Illéa, to rejoice in the fact that we were still here.

I didn't know what Halloween was. It never resurfaced.

So at least three times a year, the whole family would be fully employed. Dad and May would make their art, and patrons would purchase them as gifts. Mom and I would perform at parties—me singing and her on piano—not turning down a single job if we could manage it. When I was younger, performing in front of an audience terrified me. But now I just tried to equate myself to background music. That's what we were in the eyes of our employers: meant to be heard and not seen.

Gerad hadn't found his talent yet. But he was only seven. He still had a little time.

Soon the leaves would change, and our tiny world would be unsteady again. Five mouths but only four workers. No guarantees of employment until Christmastime.

When I thought of it that way, the Selection seemed like a rope, something sure I could grab onto. That stupid letter could lift me out of the darkness, and I could pull my family along with me.

I looked over at my mother. For a Five, she was a little on the heavy side, which was odd. She wasn't a glutton, and it's not like we had anything to overeat anyway. Perhaps that's just the way a body looks after five children. Her hair was red, like mine, but full of brilliant white streaks. Those had appeared suddenly and in abundance about two years ago. Lines creased the corners of her eyes, though she was still pretty young, and I could see as she moved around the kitchen that she was hunched over as if an invisible weight rested on her shoulders.

I knew she had a lot to carry. And I knew that was why she had taken to being particularly manipulative with me. We fought enough without the extra strain, but as the empty fall quietly approached, she became much more irritable. I knew she thought I was being unreasonable now, to not even want to fill out a silly little form.

But there were things—important things—in this world that I loved. And that piece of paper seemed like a brick wall keeping me away from what I wanted. Maybe what I wanted was stupid. Maybe it wasn't even something I could have. But still, it was mine. I didn't think I could sacrifice my dreams, no matter how much my family meant to me. Besides, I had given them so much already.

I was the oldest one left now that Kenna was married and Kota was gone, and I did my best to contribute. We scheduled my homeschooling around my rehearsals, which took up most of the day since I was trying to master several instruments as well as singing.

But with the letter here, none of my work mattered anymore. In my mom's mind, I was already queen.

If I was smart, I would have hidden that stupid notice before Dad, May, and Gerad came in. But I didn't know Mom had it tucked away in her clothes, and mid-meal she pulled it out.

"'To the House of Singer,'" she sang out.

I tried to swipe it away, but she was too quick for me. They would find out sooner or later anyway, but if she did it like this, they'd all be on her side.

"Mom, please!" I pleaded.

"I want to hear!" May squealed. That was no surprise. My little sister looked just like me, only on a three-year delay. But where our looks were practically identical, our personalities were anything but. Unlike me, she was outgoing and hopeful. And currently very boy crazy. This whole thing would seem incredibly romantic to her.

I felt myself blush. Dad listened intently, and May was practically bouncing with joy. Gerad, sweet little thing, he just kept eating. Mother cleared her throat and went on.

"'The recent census has confirmed that a single woman between the ages of sixteen and twenty currently resides in your home. We would like to make you aware of an upcoming opportunity to honor the great nation of Illéa.'"

May squealed again and grabbed my wrist. "That's you!"

"I know, you little monkey. Stop before you break my arm." But she just held my hand and bounced some more.

"'Our beloved prince, Maxon Schreave,'" Mom continued, "'is coming of age this month. As he ventures into this new part of his life, he hopes to move forward with a partner, to marry a true Daughter of Illéa. If your eligible daughter, sister, or charge is interested in possibly becoming the bride of Prince Maxon and the adored princess of Illéa, please fill out the enclosed form and return it to your local Province Services Office. One woman from each province will be drawn at random to meet the prince.

"'Participants will be housed at the lovely Illéa Palace in Angeles for the duration of their stay. The families of each participant will be *generously compensated*'"—she drew out the words for effect—"'for their service to the royal family.'"

I rolled my eyes as she went on. This was the way they did it with sons. Princesses born into the royal family were sold off into marriage in an attempt to solidify our young relations with other countries. I understood why it was done—we needed allies. But I didn't like it. I hadn't had to see such a thing, and I hoped I never would. The royal family hadn't produced a princess in three generations. Princes, however, married women of the people to keep up the morale of our sometimes volatile nation. I think the Selection was meant to draw us together and remind everyone that Illéa itself was born out of next to nothing.

The idea of being entered into a contest for the whole country to watch as this stuck-up little wimp picked the most gorgeous and shallow one of the bunch to be the silent, pretty face that stood beside him on TV . . . it was enough to make me scream. Could anything be more humiliating?

Besides, I'd been in the homes of enough Twos and Threes to be sure I never wanted to live among them, let alone be a One. Except for the times when we were hungry, I was quite content to be a Five. Mom was the caste climber, not me.

"And of course he would love America! She's so beautiful," Mom swooned.

"Please, Mom. If anything, I'm average."

"You are not!" May said. "Because I look just like you, and *I'm* pretty!" Her smile was so wide, I couldn't contain my laughter. And it was a good point. Because May really was beautiful.

It was more than her face, though, more than her winning smile and bright eyes. May radiated an energy, an enthusiasm that made you want to be wherever she was. May was magnetic, and I, honestly, wasn't.

"Gerad, what do you think? Do you think I'm pretty?" I asked.

All eyes fell on the youngest member of our family.

"No! Girls are gross!"

"Gerad, please." Mom gave an exasperated sigh, but her heart wasn't in it. He was hard to get upset with. "America, you must know you're a very lovely girl."

"If I'm so lovely, how come no one ever comes by to ask me out?"

"Oh, they come by, but I shoo them away. My girls are too pretty to marry Fives. Kenna got a Four, and I'm sure you can do even better." Mom took a sip of her tea.

"His name is James. Stop calling him a number. And since when do boys come by?" I heard my voice getting higher and higher.

"A while," Dad said, making his first comment on all of this. His voice had a hint of sorrow to it, and he was staring decidedly at his cup. I was trying to figure out what upset him so much. Boys coming by? Mom and me arguing again? The idea of me not entering the contest? How far away I'd be if I did?

His eyes came up for the briefest of moments, and I suddenly understood. He didn't want to ask this of me. He wouldn't want me to go. But he couldn't deny the benefits if I managed to make it in, even for a day.

"America, be reasonable," Mom said. "We have to be the only parents in the country trying to talk our daughter into this. Think of the opportunity! You could be queen one day!"

"Mom. Even if I wanted to be queen, which I thoroughly don't, there are thousands of other girls in the province entering this thing. Thousands. And if I somehow was drawn, there would still be thirty-four other girls there, no doubt much better at seduction than I could ever pretend to be."

Gerad's ears perked up. "What's seduction?"

"Nothing," we all chorused back.

"It's ridiculous to think that, with all of that, I'd somehow manage to win," I finished.

My mother pushed her chair out as she stood and leaned across the table toward me. "Someone is going to, America. You have as good a chance as anyone else." She threw her napkin down and went to leave. "Gerad, when you finish, it's time for your bath."

He groaned.

May ate in silence. Gerad asked for seconds, but there weren't any. When they got up, I started clearing the table while Dad sat there sipping his tea. He had paint in his hair again, a smattering of yellow that made me smile. He stood, brushing crumbs off his shirt.

"Sorry, Dad," I murmured as I picked up plates.

"Don't be silly, kitten. I'm not mad." He smiled easily and put an arm around me.

"I just . . ."

"You don't have to explain it to me, honey. I know." He kissed me on my forehead. "I'm going back to work."

And with that I moved to the kitchen to start cleaning. I wrapped my mostly untouched plate under a napkin and hid it in the fridge. No one else left more than crumbs.

I sighed, heading to my room to get ready for bed. The whole thing was infuriating.

Why did Mom have to push me so much? Wasn't she happy? Didn't she love Dad? Why wasn't this good enough for her?

I lay on my lumpy mattress, trying to wrap my head

around the Selection. I guess it had its advantages. It would be nice to eat well for a while at least. But there was no reason to bother. I wasn't going to fall in love with Prince Maxon. From what I'd seen on the *Illéa Capital Report*, I wouldn't even like the guy.

It seemed like forever until midnight rolled around. There was a mirror by my door, and I stopped to make sure my hair looked as good as it had this morning and put on a little lip gloss so there'd be some color on my face. Mom was pretty strict about saving makeup for when we had to perform or go out in public, but I usually snuck some on nights like tonight.

As quietly as I could, I crept into the kitchen. I grabbed my leftovers, some bread that was expiring, and an apple and bundled it all up. It was painful to walk back to my room so slowly, now that it was late. But if I'd done it earlier, I would have just been antsy.

I opened my window and looked out into our little patch of backyard. There wasn't much of a moon out, so I had to let my eyes adjust before I moved. Across the lawn, the tree house stood barely silhouetted in the night. When we were younger, Kota would tie up sheets to the branches so it looked like a ship. He was the captain, and I was always his first mate. My duties mainly consisted of sweeping the floor and making food, which was dirt and twigs stuffed into Mom's baking pans. He'd take a spoonful of dirt and "eat" it by throwing it over his shoulder. This meant that I'd have to sweep again, but I didn't mind. I was just happy to be on the ship with Kota.

I looked around. All the neighboring houses were dark. No one was watching. I crawled out of the window carefully. I used to get bruises across my stomach from doing it the wrong way, but now it was easy, a talent I'd mastered over the years. And I didn't want to mess up any of the food.

I scurried across the lawn in my cutest pajamas. I could have left my day clothes on, but this felt better. I supposed it didn't matter what I wore, but I felt pretty in my little brown shorts and fitted white shirt.

It wasn't hard anymore to scale the slats nailed into the tree with only one hand. I'd developed that skill as well. Each step up was a relief. It wasn't much of a distance, but from here it felt like all the commotion from my house was miles away. Here I didn't have to be anyone's princess.

As I climbed into the tiny box that was my escape, I knew I wasn't alone. In the far corner, someone was hiding in the night. My breath sped; I couldn't help it. I set my food down and squinted. The person shifted, lighting an all but unusable candle. It wasn't much light—no one in the house would see it—but it was enough. Finally the intruder spoke, a sly grin spreading across his face.

"Hey there, gorgeous."

CHAPTER 2

I CRAWLED DEEPER INTO THE tree house. It wasn't much more than a five-by-five-foot cube; even Gerad couldn't stand up straight in here. But I loved it. There was the one opening to crawl into and then a tiny window on the opposite wall. I'd placed an old step stool in the corner to act as a desk for the candle, and a little rug that was so old it was barely better than sitting on the slats. It wasn't much, but it was my haven. *Our* haven.

"Please don't call me gorgeous. First my mom, then May, now you. It's getting on my nerves." By the way Aspen was looking at me, I could tell I wasn't helping my "I'm not pretty" case. He smiled.

"I can't help it. You're the most beautiful thing I've ever seen. You can't hold it against me for saying it the only time I'm allowed to." He reached up and cupped my face, and I looked deep into his eyes.

That was all it took. His lips were on mine, and I couldn't think about anything anymore. There was no Selection, no miserable family, no Illéa itself. There were only Aspen's hands on my back pulling me closer, Aspen's breath on my cheeks. My fingers went to his black hair, still wet from his shower—he always took showers at night—and tangled themselves into a perfect little knot. He smelled like his mother's homemade soap. I dreamed about that smell. We broke apart, and I couldn't help but smile.

His legs were propped open wide, so I sat sideways between them, like a kid who needed cradling. "Sorry I'm not in a better mood. It's just that . . . we got this stupid notice in the post today."

"Ah, yes, the letter." Aspen sighed. "We got two."

Of course. The twins had just turned sixteen.

Aspen studied my face as he spoke. He did that when we were together, like he was recommitting my face to memory. It had been over a week, and we both got anxious when it was more than a few days.

And I looked him over, too. No caste excluded, Aspen was, by far, the most attractive guy in town. He had dark hair and green eyes, and this smile that made you think he had a secret. He was tall, but not too tall. Thin, but not too thin. I noticed in the dim light that there were tiny bags under his eyes; no doubt he'd been working late all week. His black T-shirt was worn to threads in several places, just like the shabby pair of jeans he wore almost every day.

If only I could sit and patch them up for him. That was my great ambition. Not to be Illéa's princess. To be Aspen's.

It hurt me to be away from him. Some days I went crazy wondering what he was doing. And when I couldn't handle it, I practiced music. I really had Aspen to thank for me being the musician that I was. He drove me to distraction.

And that was bad.

Aspen was a Six. Sixes were servants and only a step up from Sevens in that they were better educated and trained for indoor work. Aspen was smarter than anyone knew and devastatingly handsome, but it was atypical for a woman to marry down. A man from a lower caste could ask for your hand, but it was rare to get a yes. And when anyone married into a different caste, they had to fill out paperwork and wait for something like ninety days before any of the other legal things you needed could be done. I'd heard more than one person say it was to give people a chance to change their minds. So us being this personal and out well past Illéa's curfew . . . we could both get in serious trouble. Not to mention the hell I'd get from my mother.

But I loved Aspen. I'd loved Aspen for nearly two years. And he loved me. As he sat there stroking my hair, I couldn't imagine entering the Selection.

"How do you feel about it? The Selection, I mean?" I asked.

"Okay, I guess. He's got to find a girl *somehow*, poor guy." I could hear the sarcasm. But I really wanted to know his opinion.

"Aspen."

"Okay, okay. Well, part of me thinks it's kind of sad. Doesn't the prince date? I mean, can he seriously not get *anyone*? If they try to wed the princesses to other princes, why don't they do the same for him? There's got to be some royal out there good enough for him. I don't get it. So there's that.

"But then . . ." He sighed. "Part of me thinks it's a good idea. It's exciting. He's going to fall in love in front of everyone. And I like that someone gets a happily ever after and all that. Anybody could be our next queen. It's kind of hopeful. Makes me think that I could have a happily ever after, too."

His fingers were tracing my lips. Those green eyes searched deep into my soul, and I felt that spark of connection that I'd only ever had with him. I wanted our happily ever after, too.

"So you're encouraging the twins to enter, then?" I asked.

"Yes. I mean, we've all seen the prince from time to time; he looks like a nice enough guy. A snot, no doubt, but friendly. And the girls are so eager; it's funny to watch. They were dancing in the house when I came home today. And no one can deny that it'd be good for the family. Mom's hopeful because we have two entries from the house instead of one."

That was the first good news about this horrible competition. I couldn't believe I'd been so self-absorbed that I hadn't thought about Aspen's sisters. If one of them went, if one of them won . . .

"Aspen, do you realize what that would mean? If Kamber or Celia won?"

He closed his hold tighter around me, his lips brushing my forehead. One hand moved up and down my back.

"It's all I've thought about today," he said. The gritty sound of his voice pushed out every other thought. All I wanted was for Aspen to touch me, kiss me. And that's exactly where the night would have gone, but his stomach growled and snapped me out of it.

"Oh, hey, I brought us a snack," I said lightly.

"Oh, yeah?" I could tell he was trying not to sound excited, but some of his eagerness came through.

"You'll love this chicken; I made it."

I found my little bundle and brought it to Aspen, who, to his merit, nibbled it all slowly. I took one bite of the apple so he would feel like it was for *us*, but then I set it down and let him have the rest.

Where meals were a worry at my house, they were a disaster at Aspen's. He had much steadier work than we did but got paid significantly less. There was never enough food for his family. He was the oldest of seven, and in the same way I'd stepped up to help as soon as I could, Aspen had stepped aside. He passed his share of the little food they had down to his siblings and to his mom, who was always tired from working. His dad had died three years ago, and Aspen's family depended on him for almost everything.

I watched with satisfaction as he licked the spices from the chicken off his fingers and tore into the bread. I couldn't imagine when he'd eaten last.

"You're such a good cook. You're going to make someone

very fat and happy one day," he said, his mouth half full with a bite of apple.

"I'm going to make *you* fat and happy. You know that."

"Ah, to be fat!"

We laughed, and he told me about life since the last time I'd seen him. He'd done some clerical work for one of the factories, and it was going to carry him through next week, too. His mom had finally gotten into a routine of house-cleaning for a few of the Twos in our area. The twins were both sad because their mom had made them drop their after-school drama club so they could work more.

"I'm going to see if I can pick up some work on Sundays, make a little more money. I hate for them to give up something they love so much." He said this with hope, like he really could do it.

"Aspen Leger, don't you dare! You work too hard as it is."

"Aw, Mer," he whispered into my ear. It gave me chill bumps. "You know how Kamber and Celia are. They need to be around people. They can't be cooped up cleaning and writing all the time. It's just not in their nature."

"But it's not fair for them to expect you to do it all, Aspen. I know exactly how you feel about your sisters, but you need to watch out for yourself. If you really love them, you'll take better care of their caregiver."

"Don't you worry about a thing, Mer. I think there are some good things on the horizon. I wouldn't be doing it forever."

But he would. Because his family would always need

money. "Aspen, I know you could do it. But you're not a superhero. You can't expect to be able to provide everything for everyone you love. You just . . . you can't do everything."

We were quiet for a moment. I hoped he was taking my words to heart, realizing that if he didn't slow down, he'd wear himself out. It wasn't anything new for a Six, Seven, or Eight to just die of exhaustion. I couldn't bear that. I pressed myself even closer to his chest, trying to get the image of it out of my head.

"America?"

"Yes?" I whispered.

"Are you going to enter the Selection?"

"No! Of course not! I don't want anyone to think I'd even *consider* marrying some stranger. I love *you*," I said earnestly.

"You want to be a Six? Always hungry? Always worried?" he asked. I could hear the pain in his voice, but also the genuine question: If I had to choose between sleeping in a palace with people waiting on me or the three-room apartment with Aspen's family, which one did I really want?

"Aspen, we'll make it. We're smart. We'll be fine." I willed it to be true.

"You know that's not how it'll be, Mer. I'd still have to support my family; I'm not the abandoning type." I squirmed a little in his arms. "And if we had kids—"

"*When* we have kids. And we'll just be careful about it. Who says we have to have more than two?"

"You know that's not something we can control!" I could hear the anger building in his voice.

I couldn't blame him. If you were wealthy enough, you could regulate having a family. If you were a Four or worse, they left you to fend for yourselves. This had been the subject of many an argument for us over the last six months, when we seriously started trying to find a way to be together. Children were the wild card. The more you had, the more there were to work. But then again, so many hungry mouths . . .

We fell quiet again, both unsure of what to say. Aspen was a passionate person; he tended to get a little carried away in an argument. He had gotten better about catching himself before he got too angry, and I knew that's what he was doing now.

I didn't want him to worry or be upset; I really thought we could handle it. If we just planned for everything we could, we'd make it through everything we couldn't. Maybe I was too optimistic, maybe I was just too far in love, but I really believed that anything Aspen and I wanted badly enough, we could make happen.

"I think you should do it," he said suddenly.

"Do what?"

"Enter the Selection. I think you should do it."

I glared at him. "Are you out of your mind?"

"Mer, listen to me." His mouth was right to my ear. It wasn't fair; he knew this distracted me. When his voice came, it was breathy and slow, like he was saying something romantic, though what he was suggesting was anything but. "If you had a chance for something better than this, and you didn't take it because of me, I'd never forgive myself. I couldn't stand it."

I let out my breath in a quick huff. "It's so ridiculous. Think of the thousands of girls entering. I won't even get picked."

"If you won't get picked, then why does it matter?" His hands were rubbing up and down my arms now. I couldn't argue when he did that. "All I want is for you to enter. I just want you to try. And if you go, then you go. And if you don't, then at least I won't have to beat myself up for holding you back."

"But I don't love him, Aspen. I don't even like him. I don't even *know* him."

"No one knows him. That's the thing, though, maybe you would like him."

"Aspen, stop. I love *you*."

"And I love you." He kissed me slowly to make his point. "And if you love me, you'll do this so I won't go crazy wondering what if."

When he made it about him, I didn't stand a chance. Because I couldn't hurt him. I was doing everything I could to make his life easier. And I was right. There was absolutely no way I'd get chosen. So I should just go through the motions, appease everyone, and when I didn't get picked, everyone would drop it.

"Please?" he breathed into my ear. The feeling sent chills down my body.

"Fine," I whispered. "I'll do it. But know now that I don't

want to be some princess. All I want is to be your wife."

He stroked my hair.

"You will be."

It must have been the light. Or the lack thereof. Because I swore his eyes welled up when he said that. Aspen had been through a lot, but I had seen him cry only once, when they whipped his brother in the square. Little Jemmy had stolen some fruit off a cart in the market. An adult would have had a brief trial and then, depending on the value of what was stolen, either been thrown in jail or sentenced to death. Jemmy was only nine, so he was beaten. Aspen's mom didn't have the money to take him to a proper doctor, so Jemmy had scars all up and down his back from the incident.

That night I waited by my window to see if Aspen would climb up into the tree house. When he did, I snuck out to him. He cried in my arms for an hour about how if he'd only worked harder, if he'd only done better, Jemmy wouldn't have had to steal. How it was so unfair that Jemmy had to hurt because Aspen had failed.

It was agonizing, because it wasn't true. But I couldn't tell him that; he wouldn't hear me. Aspen carried the needs of everyone he loved on his back. Somehow, miraculously, I became one of those people. So I made my load as light as I could.

"Would you sing for me? Give me something good to fall asleep to?"

I smiled. I loved giving him songs. So I settled in close and sang a quiet lullaby.

He let me sing for a few minutes before his fingers started moving absently below my ear. He pulled the neck of my shirt open wide and kissed along my neck and ears. Then he pulled up my short sleeve and kissed as far down my arm as he could reach. It made my breath hitch. Almost every time I sang, he did this. I think he enjoyed the sound of my raspy breathing more than the singing itself.

Before long we were tangled together on the dirty, thin rug. Aspen pulled me on top of him, and I brushed his scraggly hair with my fingers, hypnotized by the feel. He kissed me feverishly and hard. I felt his fingers dig into my waist, my back, my hips, my thighs. I was always surprised that he didn't leave little finger-shaped bruises all over me.

We were cautious, always stopping shy of the things we really wanted. As if breaking curfew wasn't bad enough. Still, whatever our limitations were, I couldn't imagine anyone in Illéa had more passion than we did.

"I love you, America Singer. As long as I live, I'll love you." There was some deep emotion in his voice, and it caught me off guard.

"I love you, Aspen. You'll always be my prince."

And he kissed me until the candle burned itself out.

It had to have been hours, and my eyes were heavy. Aspen never worried about his sleep, but he was always concerned about mine. So I wearily climbed down the ladder, taking my plate and my penny.

When I sang, Aspen ate it up, loved it. From time to time, when he had anything at all, he'd give me a penny to pay for my song. If he managed to scrounge up a penny, I wanted him to give it to his family. There was no doubt they needed every last one. But then, having these pennies—since I couldn't bear to spend them—was like having a reminder of everything Aspen was willing to do for me, of everything I meant to him.

Back in my room, I pulled my tiny jar of pennies out from its hiding spot and listened to the happy sound of the newest one hitting its neighbors. I waited for ten minutes, watching out the window, until I saw Aspen's shadow climb down and run down the back road.

I stayed awake a little while longer, thinking of Aspen and how much I loved him, and how it felt to be loved by him. I felt special, priceless, irreplaceable. No queen on any throne could possibly feel more important than I did.

I fell asleep with that thought securely etched in my heart.

CHAPTER 3

Aspen was dressed in white. He looked angelic. We were in Carolina still, but there was no one else around. We were alone, but we didn't miss anyone. Aspen wove twigs to make me a crown, and we were together.

"America," Mom crowed, jarring me from my dreams.

She flicked on the lights, burning my eyes, and I rubbed my hands into them, trying to adjust.

"Wake up, America, I have a proposal for you." I looked over at the alarm clock. Just past seven in the morning. So that was . . . five hours in bed.

"Is it more sleep?" I mumbled.

"No, honey, sit up. I have something serious to discuss."

I worked myself into a sitting position, clothes rumpled and hair sticking out in strange directions. Mom clapped her hands over and over, as if it would speed up the process.

"Come on, America, I need you to wake up."

I yawned. Twice.

"What do you want?" I said.

"For you to submit your name for the Selection. I think you'd make an excellent princess."

It was way too early for this.

"Mom, really, I just . . ." I sighed as I remembered what I'd promised Aspen last night: that I would at least try. But now, in the light of day, I wasn't sure if I could make myself do it.

"I know you're opposed, but I figured I'd make a deal with you to see if you would change your mind."

My ears perked up. What could she possibly offer me?

"Your father and I spoke last night, and we decided that you're old enough to go on your jobs alone. You play the piano as well as I do, and if you'd try a little more, you'd be nearly flawless on the violin. And your voice, well, there's no one better in the province, if you ask me."

I smiled groggily. "Thanks, Mom. Really." I didn't particularly care to work alone, though. I didn't see how that was supposed to entice me.

"Well, that's not all. You can accept your own work now and go alone and . . . and you can keep half of whatever you make." She sort of grimaced as she said it.

My eyes popped open.

"*But* only if you sign up for the Selection." She was starting to smile now. She knew this would win me over, though I think she was expecting more of a fight. But how could I fight? I was already going to sign up, and now I could earn some money of my own!

"You know I can only agree to sign up, right? I can't make them pick me."

"Yes, I know. But it's worth a shot."

"Wow, Mom." I shook my head, still in shock. "Okay, I'll fill out the form today. Are you serious about the money?"

"Of course. Sooner or later you'd go out on your own anyway. And being responsible for your own money will be good for you. Only, don't forget your family, please. We still need you."

"I won't forget you, Mom. How could I, with all the nagging?" I winked, she laughed, and with that, the deal was done.

I took a shower as I processed everything that had happened in less than twenty-four hours. By simply filling out a form, I was winning the approval of my family, making Aspen happy, and earning the money that would help Aspen and me get married!

I wasn't so concerned about the money, but Aspen insisted we needed to have some savings of our own first. It cost a bit to do the legal stuff, and we wanted to have a very small party with our family after our wedding. I figured it wouldn't take very long for us to save for that once we decided we were ready, but Aspen wanted more. Maybe, finally, he'd trust that we wouldn't always be strapped if I did some serious work.

After my shower, I did my hair and put on the tiniest

bit of makeup to celebrate, then went to my closet and got dressed. There weren't a whole lot of options. Most everything was beige, brown, or green. I had a few nicer dresses for when we worked, but they were hopelessly behind in the fashion department. It was like that, though. Sixes and Sevens were almost always in denim or something sturdy. Fives mostly wore bland clothes, as the artists covered everything with smocks and the singers and dancers only really needed to look special for performances. The upper castes would wear khaki and denim from time to time to change up their looks, but it was always in a way that took the material to a whole new level. As if it wasn't enough that they could have pretty much whatever they wanted, they turned our necessities into luxuries.

I put on my khaki shorts and the green tunic top—by far the most exciting day clothes I owned—and looked myself over before going into the living room. I felt kind of pretty today. Maybe it was just the excitement behind my eyes.

Mom was sitting at the kitchen table with Dad, humming. They both looked up at me a couple of times, but even their stares couldn't bother me.

When I picked up the letter, I was a little surprised. Such high-quality paper. I'd never felt anything like it. Thick and slightly textured. For a moment the weight of the paper hit me, reminding me of the magnitude of what I was doing. Two words jumped into my head: *What if?*

But I shook the thought away and put pen to paper.

It was straightforward enough. I filled in my name, age,

caste, and contact information. I had to put my height and weight, hair, eye, and skin color, too. I was pleased to write that I could speak three languages. Most could speak at least two, but my mother insisted we learn French and Spanish, since those languages were still used in parts of the country. It also helped with the singing. There were so many pretty songs in French. We had to list the highest grade level we'd completed, which could vary immensely, since only Sixes and Sevens went to the public schools and had actual grade levels. I was nearly done with my education. Under special skills, I listed singing and all my instruments.

"Do you think the ability to sleep in counts as a special skill?" I asked Dad, trying to sound torn over the decision.

"Yes, list that. And don't forget to write that you can eat an entire meal in under five minutes," he replied. I laughed. It was true; I did tend to inhale my food.

"Oh, the both of you! Why don't you just write down that you're an absolute heathen!" My mother went storming from the room. I couldn't believe she was so frustrated— after all, she was getting exactly what she wanted.

I gave Dad a questioning look.

"She just wants the best for you, that's all." He leaned back in his chair, relaxing a bit before he started on the commissioned piece that was due by the end of the month.

"So do you, but you're never so angry," I noted.

"Yes. But your mother and I have different ideas of what's best for you." He flashed me a smile. I got my mouth from him—both the look and the tendency to say innocent things that got me into trouble. The temper was Mom's doing, but she was better at holding her tongue if it really mattered. Not me. Like right now . . .

"Dad, if I wanted to marry a Six or even a Seven, and he was someone I really loved, would you let me?"

Dad set his mug down, and his eyes focused on me. I tried not to give anything away with my expression. His sigh was heavy, full of grief.

"America, if you loved an Eight, I'd want you to marry him. But you should know that love can wear away under the stress of being married. Someone you think you love now, you might start to hate when he couldn't provide for you. And if you couldn't take care of your children, it'd be even worse. Love doesn't always survive under those types of circumstances."

Dad rested his hand on top of mine, drawing my eyes up to his. I tried to hide my worry.

"But no matter what, I want you to be loved. You deserve to be loved. And I hope you get to marry for love and not a number."

He couldn't say what I wanted to know—that I *would* get to marry for love and not a number—but it was the best I could hope for.

"Thanks, Dad."

"Go easy on your mother. She's trying to do the right thing." He kissed my head and went off to work.

I sighed and went back to filling out the application. The whole thing made me feel like my family didn't think I had any right to want something of my own. It bothered me, but I knew I couldn't hold it against them in the long run. We couldn't afford the luxury of wants. We had needs.

I took my finished application and went to find Mom in the backyard. She sat there, stitching up a hem as May did her schoolwork in the shade of the tree house. Aspen used to complain about the strict teachers in the public schools. I seriously doubted any of them could keep up with Mom. It was summer, for goodness' sake.

"Did you really do it?" May asked, bouncing on her knees.

"I sure did."

"What made you change your mind?"

"Mom can be very compelling," I said pointedly, though Mom was obviously not ashamed at all of her bribery. "We can go to the Services Office as soon as you're ready, Mom."

She smiled a little. "That's my girl. Go get your things, and we'll head out. I want to get yours in as soon as possible."

I went to grab my shoes and bag as I'd been instructed, but I stopped short at Gerad's room. He was staring at a blank canvas, looking frustrated. We kept rotating through options with Gerad, but none of them were sticking. One look at the battered soccer ball in the corner or the second-hand microscope we'd inherited as payment one Christmas, and it was obvious his heart just wasn't in the arts.

"Not feeling inspired today, huh?" I asked, stepping into his room.

He looked up at me and shook his head.

"Maybe you could try sculpting, like Kota. You have great

hands. I bet you'd be good at it."

"I don't want to sculpt things. Or paint or sing or play the piano. I want to play ball." He kicked his foot into the aging carpet.

"I know. And you can for fun, but you need to find a craft you're good at to make a living. You can do both."

"But why?" he whined.

"You know why. It's the law."

"But that's not fair!" Gerad pushed the canvas to the floor, where it stirred up dust in the light from his window. "It's not our fault our great-grandfather or whoever was poor."

"I know." It really seemed unreasonable to limit everyone's life choices based on your ancestors' ability to help the government, but that was how it all worked out. And I suppose I should just be grateful we were safe. "I guess it was the only way to make things work at the time."

He didn't speak. I breathed a sigh and picked up the canvas, setting it back into place. This was his life, and he couldn't just wipe it away.

"You don't have to give up your hobbies, buddy. But you want to be able to help Mom and Dad and grow up and get married, right?" I poked his side.

He stuck his tongue out in playful disgust, and we both giggled.

"America!" Mom called down the hall. "What's taking you so long?"

"Coming," I yelled back, and then turned to Gerad. "I know it's hard. It's just the way it is, okay?"

But I knew it wasn't okay. It wasn't okay at all.

Mom and I walked all the way to the local office. Sometimes we took the public buses if we were going too far or if we were working. It looked bad to show up sweaty at the house of a Two. They already looked at us funny anyway. But it was a nice day out, and the trip was just shy of being too long.

We obviously weren't the only ones trying to get our submission in right away. By the time we got there, the street in front of the Province of Carolina Services Office was packed with women.

Standing in line, I could see a number of girls from my neighborhood in front of me, waiting to go inside. The trail was nearly four people wide and wrapped halfway around the block. Every girl in the province was signing up. I didn't know whether to feel terrified or relieved.

"Magda!" someone called. My mother and I both turned at the sound of her name.

Celia and Kamber were walking up behind us with Aspen's mother. She must have taken the day off to do this. Her daughters were dressed up as neatly as they could afford, looking very tidy. It wasn't much, but they looked good no matter what they wore, just like Aspen. Kamber and Celia had his same dark hair and beautiful smiles.

Aspen's mother smiled at me, and I returned her grin. I adored her. I only got to talk to her every once in a while, but she was always nice to me. And I knew it wasn't because I was a step up from her; I'd seen her give clothes that didn't fit her kids anymore to families who had next to nothing. She was just kind.

"Hello, Lena. Kamber, Celia, how are you?" Mother greeted them.

"Good!" they sang in unison.

"You guys look beautiful," I said, placing one of Celia's curls behind her shoulder.

"We wanted to look pretty for our picture," Kamber announced.

"Picture?" I asked.

"Yes." Aspen's mom spoke in a hushed voice. "I was cleaning at one of the magistrates' houses yesterday. This lottery isn't much of a lottery at all. That's why they're taking pictures and getting lots of information. Why would it matter how many languages you spoke if it were random?"

That *had* struck me as funny, but I thought that was all information for after the fact.

"It appears to have leaked a little; look around. Lots of girls are way overdone."

I scanned the line. Aspen's mother was right, and there was a clear line between those who knew and those who didn't. Just behind us was a girl, obviously a Seven, still in her work clothes. Her muddy boots might not make the picture, but the dust on her overalls probably would. A few yards back another Seven was sporting a tool belt. The best I could say about her was that her face was clean.

On the other end of the spectrum, a girl in front of me had her hair up in a twist with little tendrils framing her face. The girl beside her, clearly a Two based on her clothes, looked like she was trying to drown the world in her cleavage. Several had on so much makeup, they looked kind of like clowns to me. But at least they were trying.

I looked decent, but I hadn't gone to any such lengths. Like the Sevens, I hadn't known to bother. I felt a sudden flutter of worry.

But why? I stopped myself and rearranged my thoughts.

I didn't want this. If I wasn't pretty enough, surely that was a good thing. I would at least be a notch below Aspen's sisters. They were naturally beautiful, and looked even lovelier with the little hints of makeup. If Kamber or Celia won, Aspen's whole family would be elevated. Surely my mother couldn't disapprove of me marrying a One just because he wasn't the prince himself. My lack of information was a blessing.

"I think you're right," Mom said. "That girl looks like she's getting ready for a Christmas party." She laughed, but I could tell she hated that I was at a disadvantage.

"I don't know why some girls go so over the top. Look at America. She's so pretty. I'm so glad you didn't go that route," Mrs. Leger said.

"I'm nothing special. Who could pick me next to Kamber or Celia?" I winked at them, and they smiled. Mom did, too, but it was forced. She must have been debating staying in the line or forcing me to run home and change.

"Don't be silly! Every time Aspen comes home from helping your brother, he always says the Singers inherited more than their fair share of talent and beauty," Aspen's mother said.

"Does he really? What a nice boy!" my mother cooed.

"Yes. A mother couldn't ask for a better son. He's supportive, and he works so hard."

"He's going to make some girl very happy one day," my mother said. She was only half into the conversation as she continued to size up the competition.

Mrs. Leger took a quick look around. "Between you and me, I think he might already have someone in mind."

I froze. I didn't know if I should comment or not, unsure if either response would give me away.

"What's she like?" my mother asked. Even when she was planning my marriage to a complete stranger, she still had time for gossip.

"I'm not sure! I haven't actually met her. And I'm only guessing that he's seeing someone, but he seems happier lately," she replied, beaming.

Lately? We'd been meeting for nearly two years. Why only lately?

"He hums," Celia offered.

"Yeah, he sings, too," Kamber agreed.

"He sings?" I exclaimed.

"Oh, yeah," they chorused.

"Then he's definitely seeing someone!" my mother chimed in. "I wonder who she is."

"You've got me. But I'm guessing she must be a wonderful girl. These last few months he's been working hard—harder than usual. And he's been putting money away. I think he must be trying to save up to get married."

I couldn't help the little gasp that escaped. Lucky me, they all attributed it to the general excitement of the news.

"And I couldn't be more pleased," she continued. "Even if he's not ready to tell us who she is, I love her already. He's smiling, and he just seems satisfied. It's been hard since we lost Herrick, and Aspen's taken so much on himself. Any girl who makes him this happy is already a daughter to me."

"She'd be a lucky girl! Your Aspen is a wonderful boy," Mom replied.

I couldn't believe it. Here his family was, trying to make ends meet, and he was putting away money for me! I didn't know whether to scold him or kiss him. I just . . . I had no words.

He really *was* going to ask me to marry him!

It was all I could think about. *Aspen, Aspen, Aspen.* I went through the line, signed at the window to confirm that everything on my form was true, and took my picture. I sat in the chair, flipped my hair once or twice to give it some life, and turned to face the photographer.

I don't think any girl in all of Illéa could have been smiling more than me.

CHAPTER 4

IT WAS FRIDAY, SO THE *Illéa Capital Report* would be on at eight. We weren't exactly obligated to watch, but it was unwise to miss it. Even Eights—the homeless, the wandering—would find a store or a church where they could see the *Report*. And with the Selection coming up, the *Report* was more than a semi-requirement. Everyone wanted to know what was happening in that department.

"Do you think they'll announce the winners tonight?" May asked, stuffing mashed potatoes into her mouth.

"No, dear. Everyone who's eligible still has nine days to submit their applications. It'll probably be two more weeks until we know." Mom's voice was the calmest it had been in years. She was completely at ease, pleased to have gotten something she really wanted.

"Aw! I can't stand the wait," May complained.

She couldn't stand the wait? It was *my* name in the pot!

"Your mother tells me you had quite a long wait in line." I was surprised Dad wanted in on this conversation.

"Yeah," I said. "I wasn't expecting that many girls. I don't know why they're giving people nine more days; I swear everyone in the province has already gone in."

Dad chuckled. "Did you have fun gauging the competition?"

"Didn't bother," I said honestly. "I left that to Mom."

She nodded in agreement. "I did, I did. I couldn't help it. But I think America looked good. Polished but natural. You are *so* beautiful, honey. If they really are looking through instead of picking at random, you have an even better chance than I thought."

"I don't know," I hedged. "There was that girl who had on so much red lipstick she looked like she was bleeding. Maybe the prince likes that kind of thing."

Everyone laughed, and Mom and I continued to regale them with commentary on the outfits we'd noticed. May drank it all in, and Gerad just sat smiling between bites of dinner. Sometimes it was easy to forget that as long as Gerad had been able to really understand the world around him, things had been stressful in our house.

At eight we all piled into the living room—Dad in his chair, May next to Mom on the couch with Gerad on her lap, and me on the floor all stretched out—and turned the TV to the public access channel. It was the one channel you didn't have to pay to have, so even the Eights could get it if they had a TV.

The anthem played. Maybe it's silly, but I always loved our national anthem. It was one of my favorite songs to sing.

The picture of the royal family came into view. Standing at a podium was King Clarkson. His advisers, who had updates on infrastructure and some environmental concerns, were seated to one side, and the camera cut to show them. It looked like there would be several announcements tonight. On the left of the screen, the queen and Prince Maxon sat in their typical cluster of thronelike seats and elegant clothes, looking regal and important.

"There's your boyfriend, Ames," May announced, and everyone laughed.

I looked closely at Maxon. I guess he was handsome in his own way. Not at all like Aspen, though. His hair was a honey color, and his eyes were brown. He kind of looked like summertime, which I guess was attractive to some people. His hair was cropped short and neatly done, and his gray suit was perfectly fitted to him.

But he sat way too rigidly in his chair. He looked so uptight. His clean hair was too perfect, his tailored suit too crisp. He seemed more like a painting than a person. I almost felt bad for the girl who ended up with him. That would probably be the most boring life imaginable.

I focused on his mother. She looked serene. She sat up in her chair, too, but not in an icy way. I realized that, unlike the king and Prince Maxon, she hadn't grown up in the palace. She was a celebrated Daughter of Illéa. She might have been someone like me.

The king was already talking, but I had to know.

"Mom?" I whispered, trying not to distract Dad.

"Yes?"

"The queen . . . what was she? Her caste, I mean."

Mom smiled at my interest. "A Four."

A Four. She'd spent her formative years working in a factory or a shop, or maybe on a farm. I wondered about her life. Did she have a large family? She probably hadn't had to worry about food growing up. Were her friends jealous of her when she was chosen? If I had any really close friends, would they be jealous of me?

That was stupid. I wasn't going to be picked.

Instead I focused on the king's words.

"Just this morning, another attack in New Asia rocked our bases. It has left our troops slightly outnumbered, but we are confident that with the fresh draft next month will come lifted morale, not to mention a swelling of fresh forces."

I hated war. Unfortunately, we were a young country that had to protect itself against everyone. It wasn't likely this land would survive another invasion.

After the king gave us an update on a recent raid on a rebel camp, the Financial Team updated us on the status of the debt, and the head of the Infrastructure Committee announced that in two years they were planning to start work on rebuilding several highways, some of which hadn't been touched since the Fourth World War. Finally the last person, the Master of Events, came to the podium.

"Good evening, ladies and gentlemen of Illéa. As you all

know, notices to participate in the Selection were recently distributed in the mail. We have received the first count of submitted applications, and I am pleased to say that thousands of the beautiful women in Illéa have already placed their names in the lottery for the Selection!"

In the back corner Maxon shifted a little in his seat. Was he sweating?

"On behalf of the royal family, I would like to thank you for your enthusiasm and patriotism. With any luck, by the New Year we will be celebrating the engagement of our beloved Prince Maxon to an enchanting, talented, and intelligent Daughter of Illéa!"

The few advisers sitting there applauded. Maxon smiled but looked uncomfortable. When the applause died down, the Master of Events started up again.

"Of course, we will be having lots of programming dedicated to meeting the young women of the Selection, not to mention specials on their lives at the palace. We could not think of anyone more qualified to guide us through this exciting time than our very own Mr. Gavril Fadaye!"

There was another smattering of applause, but it came from my mom and May this time. Gavril Fadaye was a legend. For something like twenty years he'd done running commentary on Grateful Feast parades and Christmas shows and anything they celebrated at the palace. I'd never seen an interview with members of the royal family or their closest friends and family done by anyone but him.

"Oh, America, you could meet Gavril!" Mom crooned.

"He's coming!" May said, flailing her little arms.

Sure enough, there was Gavril, sauntering onto the set in his crisp blue suit. He was maybe in his late forties, and he always looked sharp. As he walked across the stage, the light caught on the pin on his lapel, a flash of gold that was similar to the forte signs in my piano music.

"Goooood evening, Illéa!" he sang. "I have to say that I am so honored to be a part of the Selection. Lucky me, I get to meet thirty-five beautiful women! What idiot wouldn't want my job?" He winked at us through the camera. "But before I get to meet these lovely ladies, one of which will be our new princess, I have the pleasure of speaking with the man of the hour, our Prince Maxon."

With that Maxon walked across the carpeted stage to a pair of chairs set up for him and Gavril. He straightened his tie and adjusted his suit, as if he needed to look *more* polished. He shook Gavril's hand and sat across from him, picking up a microphone. The chair was high enough that Maxon propped his feet on a bar in the middle of the legs. He looked much more casual that way.

"Nice to see you again, Your Highness."

"Thank you, Gavril. The pleasure is all mine." Maxon's voice was as poised as the rest of him. He radiated waves of formality. I wrinkled my nose at the idea of just being in the same room with him.

"In less than a month, thirty-five women will be moving into your house. How do you feel about that?"

Maxon laughed. "Honestly, it *is* a bit nerve-racking. I'm imagining there will be much more noise with so many guests. I'm looking forward to it all the same."

"Have you asked dear old dad for any advice on how he managed to get ahold of such a beautiful wife when it was his turn?"

Both Maxon and Gavril looked over to the king and queen, and the camera panned over to show them looking at each other, smiling and holding hands. It seemed genuine, but how would we know any better?

"I haven't actually. As you know, the situation in New Asia has been escalating, and I've been working with him more on the military side of things. Not much time to discuss girls in there."

Mom and May laughed. I suppose it was kind of funny.

"We don't have much time left, so I'd like to have one more question. What do you imagine your perfect girl would be like?"

Maxon looked taken aback. It was hard to tell, but he may have been blushing.

"Honestly, I don't know. I think that's the beauty of the Selection. No two women who enter will be exactly the same—not in looks or preferences or disposition. And through the process of meeting them and talking to them, I'm hoping to discover what I want, to find it along the way." Maxon smiled.

"Thank you, Your Highness. That was very well said. And I think I speak for all of Illéa when I wish you the best of luck." Gavril held out his hand for another shake.

"Thank you, sir," Maxon said. The camera didn't cut away quick enough, and you could see him looking over to his parents, wondering if he'd said the right thing. The next shot zoomed in on Gavril's face, so there was no way to see what their response was.

"I'm afraid that's all the time we have for this evening. Thank you for watching the *Illéa Capital Report*, and we'll see you next week."

With that, the music played and credits rolled.

"America and Maxon sitting in a tree," sang May. I grabbed a pillow and chucked it at her, but I couldn't help laughing at the thought. Maxon was so stiff and quiet. It was hard to imagine anyone being happy with such a wimp.

I spent the rest of the night trying to ignore May's teasing, and finally went to my room to be alone. Even the thought of being near Maxon Schreave made me uncomfortable. May's little jabs stayed in my head all night and made it difficult for me to sleep.

It was hard to pinpoint the sound that woke me, but once I was aware of it, I tried to survey my room in absolute stillness, just in case someone was there.

Tap, tap, tap.

I turned over slowly to face my window, and there was Aspen, grinning at me. I got out of bed and tiptoed to the door, shutting it all the way and locking it. I went back to the bed, unlocking and slowly opening my window.

A rush of heat that had nothing to do with summer swept

over me as Aspen climbed through the window and onto my bed.

"What are you doing here?" I whispered, smiling in the dark.

"I had to see you," he breathed into my cheek as he wrapped his arms around me, pulling me down until we were lying side by side on the bed.

"I have so much to tell you, Aspen."

"Shhh, don't say a word. If anyone hears, there'll be hell to pay. Just let me look at you."

And so I obeyed. I stayed there, quiet and still, while Aspen stared into my eyes. When he had his fill of that, he went to nuzzling his nose into my neck and hair. And then his hands were moving up and down the curve of my waist to my hip over and over and over. I heard his breathing get heavy, and something about that drew me in.

His lips, hidden in my neck, started kissing me. I drew in sharp breaths. I couldn't help it. Aspen's lips traveled up my chin and covered my mouth, effectively silencing my gasps. I wrapped myself around him, our rushed grabbing and the humidity of the night covering us both in sweat.

It was a stolen moment.

Aspen's lips finally slowed, though I was nowhere near ready to stop. But we had to be smart. If we went any further, and there was ever evidence of it, we'd both be thrown in jail.

Another reason everyone married young: Waiting is torture.

"I should go," he whispered.

"But I want you to stay." My lips were by his ears. I could smell his soap again.

"America Singer, one day you will fall asleep in my arms every night. And you'll wake up to my kisses every morning. And then some." I bit my lip at the thought. "But now I have to go. We're pushing our luck."

I sighed and loosened my grip. He was right.

"I love you, America."

"I love you, Aspen."

These secret moments would be enough to get me through everything coming: Mom's disappointment when I wasn't chosen, the work I'd have to do to help Aspen save, the eruption that was coming when he asked Dad for my hand, and whatever struggles we'd go through once we were married. None of it mattered. Not if I had Aspen.

CHAPTER 5

A WEEK LATER, I BEAT Aspen to the tree house.

It took a bit of work to get the things I wanted up there in silence, but I managed. I rearranged the plates one last time as I heard someone climbing the tree.

"Boo."

Aspen started and laughed. I lit the new candle I'd purchased just for us. He crossed the tree house to kiss me, and after a moment, I started talking about all that had happened during the week.

"I never got to tell you about the sign-ups," I said, excited about the news.

"How'd it go? Mom said it was packed."

"It was crazy, Aspen. You should have seen what people were wearing! And I'm sure you know that it's less of a lottery than they're claiming. So I was right all along. There are far more interesting people to choose in Carolina than me, so this was all a big nothing."

"All the same, thank you for doing it. It means a lot to me." His eyes were still focused on me. He hadn't even bothered looking around the tree house. Drinking me in, like always.

"Well, the best part is that since my mother had no idea I'd already promised you, she bribed me to sign up." I couldn't contain my smile. This week families had already started throwing parties for their daughters, sure that they would be the one chosen for the Selection. I'd sung at no less than seven celebrations, packing two into a night for the sake of getting my own paychecks. And Mom was true to her word. It felt liberating to have money that was mine.

"Bribed you? With what?" His face was lit with excitement.

"Money, of course. Look, I made you a feast!" I pulled away from him and started grabbing plates. I'd made too much dinner on purpose to save him some, and I'd been baking pastries for days. May and I both had a terrible addiction to sweets anyway, and she was jubilant that this was how I was choosing to spend my money.

"What's all this?"

"Food. I made it myself." I was beaming with pride at my efforts. Finally, tonight, Aspen could be full. But his smile faded as he took in plate after plate.

"Aspen, is something wrong?"

"This isn't right." He shook his head and looked away from the treats.

"What do you mean?"

"America, I'm supposed to be providing for you. It's humiliating for me to come here and have you do all this for me."

"But I give you food all the time."

"Your little leftovers. You think I don't know better? I don't feel bad about taking something you don't want. But to have you—*I'm* supposed to—"

"Aspen, you give me things all the time. You provide for me. I have all my pen—"

"Pennies? You think bringing that up *now* is a good idea? Don't you know how much I hate that? That I love to hear you sing but can't really pay you when everyone else does?"

"You shouldn't pay me at all! It's a gift. Anything of mine you want you can have!" I knew we needed to be careful to keep our voices down. But at the moment I didn't care.

"I'm not some charity case, America. I'm a man. I'm supposed to be a provider."

Aspen put his hands in his hair. I could see his breaths coming fast. Just like always, he was thinking his way through the argument. But this time, there was something different in his eyes. Instead of his face growing focused, it fell into confusion one millimeter at a time. My anger faded quickly as I saw him there, looking so lost. I felt guilty instead. I had meant to spoil him, not humiliate him.

"I love you," I whispered.

He shook his head.

"I love you, too, America." But he still wouldn't look at

me. I picked up some of the bread I'd made and put it in his hand. He was too hungry not to take a bite.

"I didn't mean to hurt you. I thought it would make you happy."

"No, Mer, I love it. I can't believe you did all this for me. It's just . . . you don't know how much it bothers me that I can't do this for you. You deserve better." Mercifully, he kept eating as he spoke.

"You've got to stop thinking of me that way. When it's just you and me, I'm not a Five and you're not a Six. We're just Aspen and America. And I don't want anything in the world but you."

"But I can't stop thinking that way." He looked at me. "That's how I was raised. Since I was little, it was 'Sixes are born to serve' and 'Sixes aren't meant to be seen.' My whole life, I've been taught to be invisible." He grabbed my hand in a viselike grip. "If we're together, Mer, you're going to be invisible, too. And I don't want that for you."

"Aspen, we've talked about this. I know that things will be different, and I'm prepared. I don't know how to make it any clearer." I put my hand on his heart. "The moment you're ready to ask, I'm ready to say yes."

It was terrifying to put myself out there like that, to make it absolutely clear how deep my affections ran. He knew what I was saying. But if making myself vulnerable meant he'd be brave, I'd endure it. His eyes searched mine. If he was looking for doubt, he was wasting his time. Aspen was the one thing I was sure of.

"No."

"What?"

"No." The word felt like a slap across the face.

"Aspen?"

"I don't know how I fooled myself into ever thinking this would work." He ran his fingers through his hair again, like he was trying to get all the thoughts he'd ever had about me out of his head.

"But you just said you loved me."

"I do, Mer. That's the point. I can't make you like me. I can't stand the thought of you hungry or cold or scared. I can't make you a Six."

I felt the tears coming. He didn't mean that. He couldn't. But before I could tell him to take it back, Aspen was already moving to crawl out of the tree house.

"Where . . . where are you going?"

"I'm leaving. I'm going home. I'm sorry I did this to you, America. It's over now."

"What?"

"It's over. I won't come around anymore. Not like this."

I started crying. "Aspen, please. Let's talk about this. You're just upset."

"I'm more upset than you know. But not at you. I just can't do this, Mer. I can't."

"Aspen, please . . ."

He pulled me in tight and kissed me—really kissed me—one last time. Then he disappeared into the night. And because this country is the way it is, because of all the rules that had kept us in hiding, I couldn't even call out after him. I couldn't tell him I loved him one more time.

As the next few days passed, I knew my family could tell that something was wrong, but they must have assumed I was nervous about the Selection. I wanted to cry a thousand times, but held it back. I just pushed on to Friday, hoping that everything would go back to normal after the *Capital Report* broadcast the names.

I dreamed it up in my head. How they would announce Celia or Kamber, and my mother would be disappointed, but not as disappointed as she would have been if it was a stranger. Dad and May would be excited for them; our families were close. I knew Aspen had to be thinking about me like I'd been thinking about him. I bet he'd be over here before the program was over, begging me for forgiveness and asking for my hand. It would be a little premature, since there was nothing guaranteed for the girls, but he could capitalize on the general excitement of the day. It would probably smooth a lot of things over.

In my head, it worked out perfectly. In my head, everyone was happy . . .

It was ten minutes until the *Report* came on, and we were all in place early. I couldn't imagine we were alone in not wanting to miss a second of this announcement.

"I remember when Queen Amberly was chosen! Oh, I knew from the beginning she would make it." Mom was making popcorn, as if this were a movie.

"Did you go in the lottery, Mama?" Gerad asked.

"No, sweetie, Mama was two years too young for the cut-off. But lucky me, I got your father instead." She smiled and winked.

Whoa. She must have been in a good mood. I couldn't remember the last time she was that affectionate toward Dad.

"Queen Amberly is the best queen ever. She's so beautiful and smart. Every time I see her on TV, I want to be just like her," May said with a sigh.

"She is a good queen," I added quietly.

Finally eight o'clock rolled around, and the national emblem rose on the screen along with the instrumental version of our anthem. Was I actually trembling? I was so ready for this to be over.

The king appeared and gave a brief update on the war. The other announcements were also short. It seemed like everyone there was in a good mood. I guessed this must be exciting for them, too.

Finally the Master of Events came up and introduced Gavril, who walked straight over to the royal family.

"Good evening, Your Majesty," he said to the king.

"Gavril, always good to see you." The king was border-line giddy.

"Looking forward to the announcement?"

"Ah, yes. I was in the room yesterday as a few were drawn; all very lovely girls."

"So you know who they are already?" Gavril exclaimed.

"Just a few, just a few."

"Did he happen to share any of this information with you, sir?" Gavril turned to Maxon.

"Not at all. I'll see them when everyone else does," Maxon replied. You could see he was trying to hide his nerves.

I realized my palms were sweating.

"Your Majesty," Gavril went over to the queen. "Any advice for the Selected?"

She smiled her serene smile. I didn't know what the other women looked like when she went through the Selection, but I couldn't imagine anyone being as graceful and lovely as her.

"Enjoy your last night as an average girl. Tomorrow, no matter what, your life will be different forever. And it's old advice, but it's good: Be yourself."

"Wise words, my queen, wise words. And with that, let us reveal the thirty-five young ladies chosen for the Selection. Ladies and gentlemen, please join me in congratulating the following Daughters of Illéa!"

The screen changed to the national emblem. In the upper right-hand corner, there was a small box with Maxon's face, to see his reactions as the pictures went across the monitor. He would already be making decisions about them, the way we all would.

Gavril had a set of cards in his hands, ready to read out the names of the girls whose worlds, according to the queen, were about to change forever.

"Miss Elayna Stoles of Hansport, Three." A photo of a

tiny girl with porcelain skin popped up. She looked like a lady. Maxon beamed.

"Miss Tuesday Keeper of Waverly, Four." A girl with freckles appeared. She looked older, more mature. Maxon whispered something to the king.

"Miss Fiona Castley of Paloma, Three." A brunette with smoldering eyes this time. Maybe my age, but she seemed more . . . experienced.

I turned to Mom and May on the couch. "Doesn't she seem awfully—"

"Miss America Singer of Carolina, Five."

I whipped my head back around, and there it was. The picture of me just after I'd found out Aspen was saving up to marry me. I looked radiant, hopeful, beautiful. I looked like I was in love. And some idiot thought that love was for Prince Maxon.

Mom screamed by my ear, and May jumped up, sending popcorn everywhere. Gerad got excited too and started dancing. Dad . . . it's hard to say, but I think he was secretly smiling behind his book.

I missed what Maxon's expression was.

The phone rang.

And it didn't stop for days.

CHAPTER 6

THE NEXT WEEK WAS FULL of officials swarming into our house to prepare me for the Selection. There was an obnoxious woman who seemed to think I'd lied about half my application, followed by an actual palace guard who came to go over security measures with the local soldiers and give our home a once-over. Apparently I didn't have to wait until getting to the palace to worry about potential rebel attacks. Wonderful.

We got two phone calls from a woman named Silvia— who sounded very perky and businesslike at the same time—wanting to know if we needed anything. My favorite visitor was a lean, goateed man who came to measure me for my new wardrobe. I wasn't sure how I felt about wearing dresses that were as formal as the queen's all the time, but I was looking forward to a change.

The last of these visitors came on Wednesday afternoon, two days before I was to leave. He was in charge of going over all the official rules with me. He was incredibly skinny with greasy black hair that was smoothed back, and he kept sweating. Upon entering the house, he asked if there was someplace private we could talk. That was my first clue that something was going on.

"Well, we can sit in the kitchen, if that's all right," Mom suggested.

He dabbed his head with a handkerchief and looked over at May. "Actually, anyplace is fine. I just think you might want to ask your younger daughter to leave the room."

What could he possibly say that May couldn't hear?

"Mama?" she asked, sad to be missing out.

"May, darling, go and work on your painting. You've been neglecting your work a bit this last week."

"But—"

"Let me walk you out, May," I offered, looking at the tears welling up in her eyes.

When we were down the hall and no one could hear, I pulled her in for a hug.

"Don't worry," I whispered. "I'll tell you everything tonight. Promise."

To her credit, she didn't blow our cover by jumping up and down as usual. She merely nodded somberly and went away to her little corner in Dad's studio.

Mom made tea for Skinny, and we sat at the kitchen table to talk. He had a stack of papers and a pen laid out next to another folder with my name on it. He arranged his information neatly and spoke.

"I'm sorry to be so secretive, but there are certain things I need to address that are unfit for young ears."

Mom and I exchanged a quick glance.

"Miss Singer, this is going to sound harsh, but as of last Friday, you are now considered property of Illéa. You must take care of your body from here on out. I have several forms for you to sign as we go through this information. Any failure to comply on your part will result in your immediate removal from the Selection. Do you understand?"

"Yes," I said warily.

"Very good. Let's start with the easy stuff. These are vitamins. Since you are a Five, I'll assume that you may not always have access to necessary nutrition. You must take one of these every day. You're on your own now, but at the palace, you'll have someone to help you." He passed a large bottle across the table to me, along with a form I had to sign to say that I had received it.

I had to stop myself from laughing. Who needs help taking a pill?

"I have with me the physical from your doctor. Not much of a worry there. You seem to be in excellent health, although he said you haven't been sleeping well?"

"Umm, I mean . . . just with the excitement, it's been a little hard to sleep." It was almost the truth. The days were whirlwinds of palace preparation, but at night, when I was still, I thought of Aspen. It was the one time I couldn't avoid him coming into my mind, and it appeared he wasn't eager to leave.

"I see. Well, I can have some sleep aids here tonight if you need them. We want you well rested."

"No, I don't—"

"Yes," Mom interrupted. "Sorry, honey, but you look exhausted. Please, get her the sleep aids."

"Yes, ma'am." Skinny made another note in my file. "Moving on. Now, I know this is personal, but I've had to discuss it with every contestant, so please don't be shy." He paused. "I need confirmation that you are, in fact, a virgin."

Mom's eyes nearly popped out. So this was why May had to leave.

"Are you serious?" I couldn't believe they'd send someone out to do this. At least send a woman . . .

"I'm afraid so. If you're not, we need to know that immediately."

Eww. And with my mother in the room. "I know the law, sir. I'm not stupid. Of course I am."

"Consider, please. If you are found to be lying . . ."

"For goodness' sake, America's never even had a boyfriend!" Mom said.

"That's right." I grabbed that rope, hoping it would end this discussion.

"Very good. I'll just need you to sign this form to confirm your statement."

I rolled my eyes but obeyed. I was glad Illéa existed, considering that this very land had nearly been turned to rubble, but these regulations were starting to make me feel like I was suffocating, like there were invisible chains keeping me down. Laws about who you could love, forms about your virginity being intact; it was infuriating.

"I need to go over the rules with you. They are very straightforward, and you shouldn't have a hard time complying. If you have any questions, just speak up."

He looked up from his stack of forms and made eye contact with me.

"I will," I mumbled.

"You cannot leave the palace of your own accord. You have to be dismissed by the prince himself. Even the king and queen cannot force you out. They can tell the prince they do not approve of you, but he makes every decision on who stays and who leaves.

"There is no set timeline for the Selection. It can be over in a matter of days or stretch into years."

"Years?" I asked in horror. The thought of being gone that long set me on edge.

"Not to worry. The prince is unlikely to let it go for very long. This is a moment for him to show his decisiveness, and allowing the Selection to drag on doesn't look good. But should he choose to take it that way, you will be required to stay for as long as the prince needs to make his choice."

My fear must have shown on my face because Mom reached over and patted my hand. Skinny, however, was unfazed.

"You do not arrange your times with the prince. He will

seek you out for one-on-one company if he wants it. If you are in a larger social setting and he is present, that is different. But you do not go to him without invitation.

"While no one expects you to get along with the other thirty-four contestants, you are not to fight with them or sabotage them. If you are found laying hands on another contestant, causing her stress, stealing from her, or doing anything that might diminish her personal relationship with the prince, it is in his hands whether or not to dismiss you on the spot.

"Your only romantic relationship will be with Prince Maxon. If you are found writing love notes to someone here or are caught in a relationship with another person in the palace, that is considered treason and is punishable by death."

Mom rolled her eyes at that one, though that might be the only rule that worried me.

"If you are found breaking any of Illéa's written laws, you will receive the punishment tied to that offense. Your status as one of the Selected does not put you above the law.

"You must not wear any clothes or eat any food that is not specifically provided for you by the palace. This is a security issue and will be strictly enforced.

"On Fridays you will be present for all *Capital Report* broadcasts. On occasion, but always with warning, there will be cameras or photographers in the palace, and you will be courteous and allow them to see your lifestyle with the prince.

"For each week you stay at the palace, your family will be

compensated. I will give you your first check before I leave. Also, should you not stay at the palace, an aide will help you adjust to your life after the Selection. Your aide will assist you with final preparations before you leave for the palace, as well as help you seek new housing and employment afterward.

"Should you make it to the top ten, you will be considered an Elite. Once you reach that status, you will be required to learn about the particular inner workings of the life and obligations you would have as a princess. You are not permitted to seek out such details before that time.

"From this moment on, your status is a Three."

"A Three?" Mom and I both exclaimed.

"Yes. After the Selection, it's hard for girls to go back to their old lives. Twos and Threes do fine, but Fours and below tend to struggle. You are a Three now, but the rest of your family remain Fives. Should you win, you and your entire family become Ones as members of the royal family."

"Ones." The word was faint on Mom's lips.

"And should you go to the end, you will marry Prince Maxon and become the crowned princess of Illéa and take on all the rights and responsibilities of that title. Do you understand?"

"Yes." That part, as big as it sounded, was the easiest to bear.

"Very good. If you could just sign this form saying you've heard all the official rules, and Mrs. Singer, if you could just sign this form saying you received your check, please."

I didn't see the sum, but it made her eyes well. I was miserable at the idea of leaving, but I was sure if I went there only to be sent back the next day, this check alone would provide us with enough money for a very comfortable year. And when I got back, everyone would want me to sing. I'd have plenty of work. But would I be allowed to sing as a Three? If I had to pick one of the career paths of a Three, I think I'd teach. Maybe I could at least help others learn music.

Skinny collected his forms and stood to leave, thanking us for our time and for the tea. I would have to interact with only one more official before I left, and that would be my aide: the person who would guide me through getting from my house to the send-off to the airport. And then . . . then I'd be on my own.

Our guest asked if I would show him to the door, and Mom consented, as she wanted to start dinner. I didn't like being alone with him, but it was a short walk.

"One more thing," Skinny said with his hand on the door. "This isn't exactly a rule, but it would be unwise of you to ignore it. When you are invited to do something with Prince Maxon, you do not refuse. No matter what it is. Dinner, outings, kisses—more than kisses—anything. Do not turn him down."

"Excuse me?" Was the same man who made me sign a form affirming my purity suggesting that I let Maxon have it if he wanted it?

"I know it sounds . . . unbecoming. But it would not

behoove you to reject the prince under any circumstances. Good evening, Miss Singer."

I was disgusted, revolted. The law, Illéan law, was that you were to wait until marriage. It was an effective way of keeping diseases at bay, and it helped keep the castes intact. Illegitimates were thrown into the street to become Eights, and the penalty for being discovered, either by a person or through pregnancy, was jail time. If someone was even suspicious, you could spend a few nights in a cell. True, it restricted me from being intimate with the one person I loved, and that had bothered me. But now that Aspen and I were over, I was glad I'd been forced to save myself.

I was infuriated. Hadn't I just signed a form saying I'd be punished if I broke Illéan law? I wasn't above the rules; that was what he'd said. But apparently the prince was. And I felt dirty, lower than an Eight.

"America, honey, it's for you," Mom sang. I'd heard the doorbell myself but was in no rush to answer it. If this was another person asking for an autograph, I didn't think I'd be able to handle it.

I walked down the hall and turned the corner. There, with a handful of wildflowers, was Aspen.

"Hello, America." His voice was restrained, almost professional.

"Hello, Aspen." Mine was weak.

"These are from Kamber and Celia. They wanted to wish you luck." He closed the distance between us and gave me the flowers. Flowers from his sisters, not from him.

"That's awfully sweet!" Mom exclaimed. I had almost forgotten she was in the room.

"Aspen, I'm glad you're here." I tried to sound as removed as he had. "I've made a mess trying to pack. Could you help me clean?"

With my mom there, he had to accept. As a general rule, Sixes didn't turn down work. We were the same in that way.

He exhaled through his nose and nodded once.

Aspen followed me down the hall. I thought about how many times I'd wanted just this: for Aspen to walk in my house and come to my room. Could the circumstances have been any worse?

I pushed open the door to my room and Aspen laughed out loud.

"Did you let a dog do your packing?"

"Shut up! I had a little trouble finding what I was looking for." In spite of myself, I smiled.

He went to work, setting things upright and folding shirts. I helped, of course.

"Aren't you taking any of these clothes?" he whispered.

"No. They dress me from tomorrow on out."

"Oh. Wow."

"Were your sisters disappointed?"

"No, actually." He shook his head in disbelief. "The moment they saw your face, the whole house erupted. They're crazy about you. My mom in particular."

"I love your mom. She's always really nice to me."

A few minutes passed in silence as my room went slowly back to normal.

"Your picture . . . ," he began, "was absolutely beautiful."

It hurt to have him tell me I was beautiful. It wasn't fair. Not after everything he'd done.

"It was for you," I whispered.

"What?"

"It's just . . . I thought you were going to be proposing soon." My voice was thick.

Aspen was quiet for a moment, choosing his words.

"I'd been thinking about it, but it doesn't matter anymore."

"It does. Why didn't you tell me?"

He rubbed his neck, deciding.

"I was waiting."

"For what?" What could possibly be worth waiting for?

"For the draft."

That *was* an issue. It was hard to know whether to wish to be drafted or not. In Illéa, every nineteen-year-old male was eligible for it. Soldiers were chosen at random twice a year, to catch everyone within six months of their birthday. You served from the time you were nineteen until you were twenty-three. And it was coming soon.

We'd talked about it, of course, but not in a realistic way. I guess we both hoped that if we ignored the draft, it would ignore us, too.

It was a blessing in that being a soldier meant you were an automatic Two. The government trained you and paid you for the rest of your life. The drawback was you never knew where you would go. They sent you away from your province, for sure. They assumed you were more likely to be lenient with people you knew. You might end up at the palace or in some other province's local police force. Or you might end up in the army, shipped off to war. Not very many men sent into battle made it home.

If a man wasn't married before the draft, he'd almost always wait. You'd be separated from your wife for four years, at the very best. At the worst, she'd be a young widow.

"I just . . . I didn't want to do that to you," he whispered.

"I understand."

He straightened up, trying to change the subject. "So what are you taking to the palace?"

"A change of clothes to wear whenever they finally kick me out. Some pictures and books. I've been told I won't need my instruments. Anything I want will be there already. So that little bag there, that's it."

The room was tidy now, and that backpack seemed huge for some reason. The flowers he'd brought looked so bright on my desk compared to the drab things I owned. Or maybe it was just that everything seemed paler now . . . now that it was over.

"That's not much," he noted.

"I've never needed very much to be happy. I thought you knew that."

He closed his eyes. "Stop it, America. I did the right thing."

"The right thing? Aspen, you made me believe we could do it. You made me love you. And then you talked me into this damn contest. Do you know they're practically shipping me off to be one of Maxon's playthings?"

He whipped his head around to face me. "What?"

"I'm not allowed to turn him down. Not for *anything*."

Aspen looked sick, angry. His hands clenched up into fists. "Even . . . even if he doesn't want to marry you . . . he could . . . ?"

"Yes."

"I'm sorry. I didn't know." He took a few deep breaths. "But if he does pick you . . . that'll be good. You deserve to be happy."

That was it. I slapped him. "You idiot!" I whisper-yelled at him. "I hate him! I loved you! I wanted you; all I ever wanted was you!"

His eyes welled up, but I couldn't care. He'd hurt me enough, and now it was his turn.

"I should go," he said, and started heading to the door.

"Wait. I didn't pay you."

"America, you don't have to pay me." He went to leave again.

"Aspen Leger, don't you dare move!" My voice was fierce. And he stopped, finally paying attention to me.

"That'll be good practice for when you're a One." If it hadn't been for his eyes, I would have thought it was a joke, not an insult.

I just shook my head and went to my desk, pulling out all

the money I'd earned by myself. I put every last bit of it in his hands.

"America, I'm not taking this."

"The hell you aren't. I don't need it and you do. If you ever loved me at all, you'll take it. Hasn't your pride done enough for us?" I could feel a part of him shut down. He stopped fighting.

"Fine."

"And here." I dug behind my bed, pulled out my tiny jar of pennies, and poured them into his hand. One rebellious penny that must have been sticky stayed glued to the bottom. "Those were always yours. You should use them."

Now I didn't have anything of his. And once he spent those pennies out of desperation, he wouldn't have anything of mine. I felt the hurt coming up. My eyes got wet, and I breathed hard to keep the sobs back.

"I'm sorry, Mer. Good luck." He shoved the money and the pennies into his pockets and ran out.

This wasn't how I thought I'd cry. I was expecting huge, jarring sobs, not slow, tiny tears.

I started to put the jar on a shelf, but I noticed that little penny again. I put my finger in the jar and got it unstuck. It rattled around in the glass all by itself. It was a hollow sound, and I could feel it echo in my chest. I knew, for better or for worse, I wasn't really free of Aspen, not yet. Maybe not ever. I opened the backpack, put in my jar, and sealed it all away.

May snuck into my room, and I took one of those stupid pills. I fell asleep holding her, finally feeling numb.

CHAPTER 7

THE NEXT MORNING, I DRESSED myself in the uniform of the Selected: black pants, white shirt, and my province flower— a lily—in my hair. My shoes I got to pick. I chose worn-out red flats. I figured I should make it clear from the start that I wasn't princess material.

We were set to leave for the square shortly. Each of the Selected was getting a send-off in her home province today, and I wasn't looking forward to mine. All those people staring while I did nothing more than stand there. The whole thing already felt ridiculous, as I had to be driven the two short miles for security reasons.

The day began uncomfortably. Kenna came with James to send me off, which was kind of her, considering she was pregnant and tired. Kota came by, too, though his presence added more tension than ease. As we walked from our house to the car we'd been provided, Kota was by far the slowest, letting the few photographers and well-wishers who were there get a good look at him. Dad just shook his head.

May was my only solace. She held my hand and tried to inject some of her enthusiasm into me. We were still linked when I stepped into the crowded square. It seemed like everyone in the province of Carolina came out to see me off. Or just see what the big deal was.

Standing on the raised stage, I could see the boundaries between the castes. Margareta Stines was a Three, and she and her parents were staring daggers at me. Tenile Digger was a Seven, and she was blowing kisses. The upper castes looked at me like I'd stolen something that was theirs. The Fours on down were cheering for me—an average girl who'd been elevated. I became aware of what I meant to everyone here, as if I represented something for all of them.

I tried to focus in on those faces, holding my head high. I was determined to do this well. I would be the best of us, the Highest of the Lows. It gave me a sense of purpose. America Singer: the champion of the lower castes.

The mayor spoke with a flourish.

"And Carolina will be cheering on the beautiful daughter of Magda and Shalom Singer, the new Lady America Singer!"

The crowd clapped and cheered. Some threw flowers.

I took in the sound for a moment, smiling and waving, and then went back to surveying the crowd, but this time for a different purpose.

I wanted to see his face one more time if I could. I didn't know if he would come. He told me I looked beautiful yesterday but was even more distant and guarded than he had been in the tree house. It was over, and I knew that. But you don't love someone for almost two years and then turn it off overnight.

It took a few passes of the crowd before I found him. I immediately wished I hadn't. Aspen was standing there with Brenna Butler in front of him, casually holding her around the waist and smiling.

Maybe some people could turn it off overnight.

Brenna was a Six and about my age. Pretty enough, I supposed, though she didn't look a bit like me. I guessed she'd get the wedding and life he'd been saving for with me. And apparently the draft didn't bother him so much anymore. She smiled at him and walked away to her family.

Had he liked her all along? Was she the girl he saw every day and was I the girl who fed him and showered him with kisses once a week? It occurred to me that maybe all the time he omitted in our stolen conversations wasn't simply long, boring hours of inventory.

I was too angry to cry.

Besides, I had admirers here who wanted my attention. So, without Aspen even knowing that I'd seen him, I went back to those adoring faces. I put my smile back on, bigger than ever, and started waving. Aspen would not have the satisfaction of breaking my heart anymore. He'd put me here, and I would just have to take advantage of it.

"Ladies and gentlemen, please join me in sending off America Singer, our favorite Daughter of Illéa!" the mayor called. Behind me, a small band played the national anthem.

More cheers, more flowers. Suddenly the mayor was at my ear.

"Would you like to say something, dear?"

I didn't know how to say no without being rude. "Thank you, but I'm so overwhelmed, I don't think I could."

He cupped my hands in his. "Of course, dear girl. Don't you worry, I'll take care of everything. They'll train you for this kind of thing at the palace. You'll need it."

The mayor then told the gathered crowd of my attributes, slyly mentioning that I was very intelligent and attractive for a Five. He didn't seem too bad a guy, but sometimes even the nicer members of the upper castes were condescending.

I caught Aspen's face once more as my eyes swept the crowd. He looked pained. It was the polar opposite of the face he'd worn with Brenna a few minutes ago. Another game? I broke my gaze.

The mayor finished speaking, and I smiled and everyone cheered, as if he'd just given the most inspiring speech known to man.

And suddenly it was time to say good-bye. Mitsy, my aide, told me to say my farewells quietly and briefly, and then she'd escort me back to the car that would take me to the airport.

Kota hugged me, telling me he was proud of me. Then, not so subtly, he told me to mention his art to Prince Maxon.

I wiggled out of that embrace as gracefully as I could.

Kenna was crying.

"I barely see you as it is. What will I do when you're gone?" she cried.

"Don't worry. I'll be home soon enough."

"Yeah, right! You're the most beautiful girl in Illéa. He'll love you!"

Why did everyone think it all came down to beauty? Maybe it did. Maybe Prince Maxon didn't need a wife to speak to, just someone to look pretty. I actually shivered, considering that as my future. But there were many girls much more attractive than me going.

Kenna was hard to hug over her pregnant belly, but we managed. James, who I really didn't know that well, hugged me, too. Then it was Gerad.

"Be a good boy, okay? Try the piano. I'll bet you're amazing. I expect to hear it all when I come home."

Gerad just nodded, abruptly sad. He threw his tiny arms around me.

"I love you, America."

"I love you, too. Don't be sad. I'll be home soon."

He nodded again, but crossed his arms to pout. I'd had no idea he'd take my leaving this way. It was the exact opposite of May. She was bouncing on her toes, absolutely giddy.

"Oh, America, you're going to be the princess! I know it!"

"Oh, hush! I'd rather be an Eight and stay with you any day. Just be good for me, and work hard."

She nodded and bounced some more, and then it was time for Dad, who was close to tears.

"Daddy! Don't cry." I fell into his arms.

"Listen to me, kitten. Win or lose, you'll always be a princess to me."

"Oh, Daddy." I finally started to cry. That was all it took to unleash the fear, the sadness, the worry, the nerves—the one sentence that meant none of it mattered.

If I came back used and unwanted, he'd still be proud of me.

It was too much to bear, to be loved that much. I'd be surrounded by scores of guards at the palace, but I couldn't imagine a place safer than my father's arms. I pulled away and turned to hug Mom.

"Do whatever they tell you. Try to stop sulking and be happy. Behave. Smile. Keep us posted. Oh! I just knew you'd turn out to be special."

It was meant to be sweet, but it wasn't what I needed to hear. I wished she could have said that I was already something special to her, like I was to my father. But I guessed she would never stop wanting more for me, more from me. Maybe that's what mothers did.

"Lady America, are you ready?" Mitsy asked. My face was away from the crowd, and I quickly wiped away my tears.

"Yes. All ready."

My bag was waiting in the shiny white car. This was it. I started to walk to the edge of the stage to the stairs.

"Mer!"

I turned. I'd know that voice anywhere.

"America!"

I searched and found Aspen's flailing arms. He was pushing the crowd aside, people protesting at his not-so-gentle shoves.

Our eyes met.

He stopped and stared. I couldn't read his face. Worry? Regret? Whatever it was, it was too late. I shook my head. I was done with Aspen's games.

"This way, Lady America," Mitsy instructed from the bottom of the stairs. I gave myself a quick second to absorb my new name.

"Good-bye, sweetheart," my mother called.

And I was led away.

CHAPTER 8

I WAS THE FIRST ONE to the airport, and I was beyond terrified. The giddy excitement of the crowd had faded, and now I was faced with the horrific experience of flying. I would be traveling with three other Selected girls, and I tried to get control of my nerves. I really didn't want to have a panic attack in front of them.

I'd already memorized the names, faces, and castes of all the Selected. It started as a therapeutic exercise, something to calm me down. I did the same thing with memorizing scales and bits of trivia. Originally, I had been looking for friendly faces, girls I might want to spend time with while I was there. I'd never really had a friend. I'd spent most of my childhood playing with Kenna and Kota. Mom did all my schooling, and she was the only person I worked with. When the older siblings moved on, I dedicated myself to

May and Gerad. And Aspen . . .

But Aspen and I were never just friends. From the moment I became truly aware of him, I was in love with him.

Now he was holding some other girl's hand.

Thank goodness I was alone. I couldn't have handled the tears in front of the other girls. It ached. *I* ached. And there was nothing I could do.

How in the hell did I get here? A month ago, I was sure of everything in my life, and now any little piece of familiarity was gone. New home, new caste, new life. All because of a stupid piece of paper and a picture. I wanted to sit and cry, to mourn for everything I'd lost.

I wondered if any of the others girls were *sad* today. I imagined that everyone except for me was celebrating. And I at least needed to look like I was too, because everyone would be watching.

I braced myself for all that was coming, and I made myself be brave. As for everything I was leaving behind, I decided I'd do just that: leave him behind. The palace would be my sanctuary. I'd never think or say his name again. He wasn't allowed to come with me there—my own rule for this little adventure.

No more.

Good-bye, Aspen.

About half an hour later, two girls in white shirts and black pants just like mine walked through the doors with their own aides hauling their bags. They were both smiling, confirming my thought that I was the only one of the Selected who might be depressed today.

It was time to follow through on my promise. I put on a smile and stood to shake their hands.

"Hi," I said brightly. "I'm America."

"I know!" said the girl on the right. She was a blonde with brown eyes. I recognized her immediately as Marlee Tames of Kent. A Four. She didn't bother with my extended hand; she moved in for an immediate hug.

"Oh!" I exhaled. I hadn't expected that. Though Marlee was one of the girls whose faces seemed genuine and friendly, Mom had been telling me for the last week to look at these girls as enemies, and her offensive thinking had leaked into my own. So here I was expecting at the very best a cordial welcome from the girls who were prepared to fight me to the death for someone I didn't want. Instead I was embraced.

"I'm Marlee and this is Ashley." Yes, Ashley Brouillette of Allens, Three. She had blond hair, too, but much lighter than Marlee's. And her eyes were very blue, which looked delicate in her peaceful face. She seemed fragile next to Marlee.

They were both from the North; I guessed that was why they came together. Ashley gave a neat little wave and smiled, but that was it. I wasn't sure if she was shy or if she was already trying to figure us out. Maybe it was that she was a Three by birth and knew to behave better.

"I love your hair!" Marlee gushed. "I wish I'd been born with red hair. It makes you look so alive. I hear that people with red hair have bad tempers. Is that true?"

Despite my rotten day, Marlee's manner was so vivacious that my smile grew wider. "I don't think so. I mean, I can have a bad temper at times, but my sister is a redhead, and she's as sweet as can be."

With that we settled into an easy conversation about what got us mad and what always fixed our moods. Marlee liked movies, and so did I, though I rarely got to see them. We talked about actors who were unbearably attractive, which seemed strange since we were off to be Maxon's pack of girl-friends. Ashley giggled every once in a while but never more than that. If she was asked a direct question, she'd give a brief answer and go back to her guarded smile.

Marlee and I got along easily, and it gave me hope that maybe I'd come out of this with a friend to show for it. Though we talked for probably half an hour, the time flew by. We wouldn't have stopped talking except for the distinct sound of high heels clicking across the floor. Our heads all turned in unison, and I heard Marlee's mouth open with a pop.

There, walking toward us, was a brunette with sunglasses on. She had a daisy in her hair, but it had been dyed red to match her lipstick. Her hips swayed as she walked, and each fall of her three-inch heels accentuated her confident stride. Unlike Marlee and Ashley, she didn't smile.

But it wasn't because she was unhappy. No, she was focused. Her entrance was meant to inspire intimidation. And it worked on ladylike Ashley, who I heard breathe an

" as the new girl walked closer.

...person, who I recognized as Celeste Newsome of Clermont, Two, didn't bother me. She assumed we were fighting for the same thing. But you can't be pushed if it's something you don't want.

Celeste finally reached us, and Marlee squeaked out a hello, trying to be friendly even in the midst of intimidation. Celeste merely looked her over and sighed.

"When do we leave?" she asked.

"We don't know," I answered without a hint of fear. "You've been holding up the show."

She didn't like that at all, and I got a once-over from her. She wasn't impressed.

"Sorry, quite a few people wanted to see me off. I couldn't help it." She smiled wide, as if it was obvious she was meant to be worshipped.

And I was about to surround myself with girls like this. Great.

As if on cue, a man appeared through the door to our left.

"I hear all four of our Selected girls are here?"

"We sure are," Celeste replied sweetly. The man sort of melted a little, you could see it in his eyes. Ah. So this was her game.

The captain paused a moment and then snapped to. "Well. Ladies, if you'll just follow me, we'll get you on the plane and off to your new home."

The flight, which was really only terrifying during the takeoff and landing, lasted a few short hours. We were offered movies and food, but all I wanted to do was look out the window. I watched the country from above, amazed at just how big it all was.

Celeste chose to sleep through the flight, which was a small mercy. Ashley had a foldout desk set up and was already writing letters about her adventure. That was smart of her to pack paper. I bet May would love to hear about this part of the journey, even though it didn't include the prince.

"She's so elegant," Marlee whispered to me, tilting her head toward Ashley. We were sitting across from each other in plush seats in the very front of the small plane. "From the moment we met, she's been nothing but proper. She's going to be tough competition," she said with a sigh.

"You can't think about it that way," I answered. "Yes, you're trying to make it to the end, but not by beating someone else. You've just got to be you. Who knows? Maybe Maxon would prefer someone more relaxed."

Marlee thought that over. "I guess that's a good point. It's hard to not like her. She's awfully kind. And so beautiful." I nodded in agreement. Marlee's voice dropped to a whisper. "Celeste, on the other hand . . ."

I widened my eyes and shook my head. "I know. It's only been an hour, and I'm already looking forward to her going home."

Marlee covered her mouth to hide a laugh. "I don't want to talk badly about anyone, but she's so aggressive. And Maxon's not even around yet. I'm a little nervous about her."

"Don't be," I assured her. "Girls like that? They'll take

themselves out of the competition."

Marlee sighed. "I hope so. Sometimes I wish . . ."

"What?"

"Well, sometimes I wish that the Twos had an idea about what it felt like to be treated the way they treat us."

I nodded. I'd never really thought of myself being on the same level as a Four, but I guess we were in a similar place. If you weren't a Two or Three, it was just varying shades of bad.

"Thanks for talking to me," she said. "I was worried that everyone would just be out for themselves, but you and Ashley have been really nice. Maybe this will be fun." Her voice lifted with hope.

I wasn't so sure, but I smiled back. I had no reason to shun Marlee or be rude to Ashley. The other girls might not be so laid-back.

When we landed, the air was silent as we walked the distance from the plane to the terminal with guards at our side. But once the doors were opened, we were met with ear-shattering screams.

The terminal was full of people jumping and cheering. A path had been cleared for us with a golden carpet lined with coordinating rope barriers. At regular intervals along this channel were guards, looking around anxiously and poised to strike at the first hint of danger. Surely there were more important things they should be doing?

Luckily, Celeste was in front, and she started waving. I knew immediately that that was the right response, not the cowering I had been considering. And since the cameras were there to catch our every move, I was doubly glad I hadn't been leading the pack.

The crowd was wild with joy. These would be the people we lived the closest to, and they were all looking forward to catching the first glimpses of the girls coming to town. One of us would be their queen someday.

I turned my head a dozen times in a matter of seconds as people called my name from all over the packed terminal. There were signs with my name on them, too. I was amazed. Already there were people here—people not in my caste or from my province—who hoped it would be me. I felt a little roll of guilt in my stomach that I would let them all down.

I dropped my head for a moment and saw a little girl pressed up against the railing. She couldn't have been more than twelve years old. In her hands was a sign that said RED-HEADS RULE! with a little crown painted in the corner and tiny stars everywhere. I knew I was the only redhead in the competition, and I noticed that her hair and mine were very nearly the same shade.

The girl wanted an autograph. Beside her, someone wanted a photograph, and beside him someone wanted to shake my hand. So I went practically down the entire line, turning around once or twice to talk to people on the other side of the carpet, too.

I was the last one to leave, making the other girls wait at least twenty minutes for me. Quite honestly, I probably wouldn't have left as soon as I did except the next plane of

Selected girls was coming in, and it seemed rude to overlap their time.

Getting into the car, I saw Celeste roll her eyes, but I didn't care. I was still sort of in awe of how I'd adjusted so quickly to something that had frightened me only moments before. I had made it through my good-byes, meeting the first girls, my flight, and interacting with our mob of fans. All without doing anything embarrassing.

I thought about the cameras following me in the terminal and pictured my family watching my entrance on TV. I hoped they'd be proud.

CHAPTER 9

EVEN AFTER THE SUBSTANTIAL GREETING party at the airport, the roads leading up to the palace were lined with masses of people calling out their well-wishes. The sad thing was that we weren't allowed to roll down the windows to acknowledge them. The guard in the front said to think of ourselves as extensions of the royal family. Many adored us, but there were people out there who wouldn't be above hurting us to hurt the prince. Or the monarchy itself.

I was stuck next to Celeste in the car—a special one that had two rows of seats facing each other in the back and darkened windows—with Ashley and Marlee sitting together in front of us. Marlee beamed as she stared out the windows, and it was obvious why. Her name was on several of the signs. It would be impossible to count how many admirers she had.

Ashley's name was sprinkled in there, too, almost as much as Celeste's, and far more than mine. Ashley, ever the lady, took not being a runaway favorite in stride. Celeste, I could see, was irritated.

"What do you think she did?" Celeste whispered in my ear, as Marlee and Ashley spoke to each other of home.

"What do you mean?" I whispered back.

"To be so popular. You think she bribed someone?" Her cold eyes focused in on Marlee as if she was weighing her worth in her head.

"She's a Four," I said doubtfully. "She wouldn't have the means to bribe someone."

Celeste sucked her teeth. "Please. A girl has more than one way she can pay for what she wants," she said, and pulled away to look out the window.

It took me a moment to understand what she was suggesting, and it didn't sit well with me. Not because it was obvious that someone as innocent as Marlee would never think about sleeping with someone to get ahead—or even consider breaking a law—but because it was becoming clear that life at the palace might be more vicious than I had imagined.

I didn't have a very good view coming up to the palace, but I noticed the walls. They were a pale yellow stucco and very, very high. Guards were placed on top at either side of the wide gate that swung open as we approached. Inside we were greeted with a long gravel drive that circled a fountain and led to the front doors, where officials waited to welcome us.

With barely more than a hello, two women took me by the arms and ushered me inside.

"So sorry to rush, miss, but your group is running late," one said.

"Oh, I'm afraid that's my fault. I got a little too chatty at the airport."

"Talking to the crowds?" the other asked in surprise.

They exchanged a look I didn't understand before they started calling out locations as we passed.

The dining room was to the right, they told me, and the Great Room was to the left. I caught a glimpse of sprawling gardens out the glass doors and wished I could stop. Before I could even process where we were going, they pulled me into a huge room full of bustling people.

A swarm parted, and I saw rows of mirrors with people working on girls' hair and painting their nails. Clothes hung on racks, and people were shouting things like "I found the dye!" and "That makes her look pudgy."

"Here they are!" I saw a woman coming up to us, clearly the person in charge. "I'm Silvia. We spoke on the phone," she said as a means of introduction, then immediately went to work. "First things first. We need 'before' pictures. Come over here," she commanded, pointing us to a chair in the corner in front of a backdrop. "Don't mind the cameras, ladies. We'll be doing a special on your makeovers, since every girl in Illéa's going to want to look like you by the time we're done today."

Sure enough, teams of people with cameras were

wandering around the room, zooming in on girls' shoes, and interviewing them. Once the pictures were done, Silvia began shouting orders. "Take Lady Celeste to station four, Lady Ashley to five . . . and it looks like they just finished up at ten. Take Lady Marlee there, and Lady America to six."

"So here's the thing," a short, dark-haired man said, pulling me over to a seat with a six on the back. "We need to talk about your image." He was all business.

"My image?" Wasn't I just me? Wasn't that what got me here?

"How do we want to make you look? With that red hair, we can make you quite the temptress, but if you want to play that kind of thing down, we can work that out, too," he said matter-of-factly.

"I'm not changing everything about me to cater to some guy I don't even know." *Or like*, I added in my head.

"Oh, my. Do we have an individual here?" he sang, as if I were a child.

"Aren't we all?"

The man smiled at me. "Fine, then. We won't change your image, we'll just enhance it. I need to polish you up a bit, but your aversion to all things fake might just be your greatest asset here. Hold on to that, honey." He patted me on the back and walked away, sending a group of women swarming my way.

I didn't realize that when he said "polish," he meant it literally. I had women scrub my body because I apparently couldn't be trusted to do a good enough job on my own. Then every exposed bit of skin was covered with lotions and oils that left me smelling like vanilla, which according to the girl who applied them was one of Maxon's favorite smells.

After they were done making me smooth and supple, attention was turned to my nails. They were trimmed and buffed and the tough little pieces of skin around them were miraculously smoothed away. I told them I'd prefer not to have my nails painted, but they looked so disappointed that I told them they could do my toes. The one girl picked a nice neutral shade, so it wasn't too bad.

The team of people who worked on my nails left me for another girl, and I sat quietly in my chair, waiting for the next round of beautification. A camera crew came past, zooming in on my hands.

"Don't move," a woman ordered. She squinted at my hand. "Do you even have anything on your nails?"

"No."

She sighed, got her shot, and moved on.

I heaved a heavy sigh myself. Out of the corner of my eye, I saw a jerking motion just to my right. I looked and saw a girl staring into nowhere while her leg bounced up and down under a large cape they'd draped over her.

"You okay?" I asked.

My voice shocked her out of her trance. She sighed. "They want to dye my hair blond. They said it would look better with my skin tone. I'm just nervous, I guess."

She gave me a tight smile, and I returned it. "You're Sosie, right?"

"Yeah." She smiled in earnest then. "And you're America?" I nodded. "I heard you came in with that Celeste girl. She's terrible!"

I rolled my eyes. Since we'd arrived, every few minutes the entire room could hear Celeste yelling at some poor maid to bring her something or to get out of her way.

"You have no idea," I muttered, and we both giggled. "Listen, I think your hair's very pretty." It was, too. Not too dark, not too light, and very full.

"Thanks."

"If you don't want to change it, you shouldn't have to."

Sosie smiled, but I could tell she wasn't completely sure if I was trying to be friendly or hold her back. Before she could say anything, teams of people came to work on us, directing one another so loudly there was no way for us to finish talking.

My hair was washed, conditioned, hydrated, and smoothed. It was long and all one length when I came in—my mom usually cut it, and that was the best she could do—but by the time they were done, it was several inches shorter and had layers. I liked those; they made my hair catch the light in interesting ways. Some girls got things called highlights, and others, like Sosie, had the color changed completely. But my attendants and I all agreed that mine should go untouched in that department.

A very pretty-looking girl did my makeup. I instructed

her to go light, and it was nice. Lots of the other girls looked a little older or younger or just nicer after the makeup. I still looked like me when I was done. Of course, so did Celeste, since she insisted upon piling it on.

I'd gone through most of this process in a robe, and once they were done fixing me up, I was led over to the racks of clothes. My name was hanging above a bar holding a week's worth of dresses. I guessed princesses-in-training didn't wear pants.

The one I ended up in was a cream color. It fell off my shoulders, fit snugly at my waist, and hit just at my knees. The girl helping me into it called it a day dress. She told me that my evening dresses were already in my room, and the rest of these would go up there as well. Then she placed a silver pin near the top of my dress. My name glittered across it. Finally she put me into shoes she called kitten heels and sent me back to the corner so I could take my "after" shot. From there I was ordered to one of four little stations lined up against the wall. Each had a chair with a backdrop and a camera sitting in front of it.

I sat down as instructed and waited. A woman came up with a clipboard of information in her hand and asked me to be patient while she found my papers.

"What's this for?" I asked.

"The makeover special. We'll be airing one about your arrivals tonight, the makeovers are on Wednesday, and then Friday you'll do your first *Report*. People have seen your pictures and know a little bit about what was on your applications," she said as she located her papers and placed them on the top of her clipboard. Then she laced her fingers together and continued. "But we want to make them really pull for you. And that won't happen unless they can get to know you. So we'll just do a little interview here, and you do your best on the *Reports*, and then don't be shy when you see us around the palace. We aren't here every day, but we'll be around."

"Okay," I said meekly. I really didn't want to talk to camera crews. It all felt so intrusive.

"So, America Singer, yes?" she asked just seconds after a red light lit up on the top of the camera.

"Yes." I tried to push the nerves out of my voice.

"I have to be honest, you don't look like you changed too much to me. Can you tell us what happened in your makeover today?"

I thought. "They put layers in my hair. I like that." I ran my fingers through the red strands, feeling how soft my hair was after professional care. "And they covered me in vanilla lotion. I kind of smell like dessert," I said, sniffing my arm.

She laughed. "It is lovely. And that dress really suits you."

"Thanks," I said, looking down at my new clothes. "I don't typically wear a lot of dresses, so this is going to take a little getting used to."

"That's right," my interviewer said. "You're one of only three Fives in the Selection. How has this experience been so far?"

I searched my head for something that would describe how

everything had felt today. From my disappointment in the square to the sensation of flying to the comfort of Marlee.

"Surprising," I said.

"I imagine there will be more surprising days to come," she commented.

"I hope they're at least a little calmer than today," I said with a sigh.

"How do you feel about your competition so far?"

I swallowed. "The girls are all really nice." With one glaring exception.

"Mm-hmm," she said, seeing through my answer. "So how do you feel about the way your makeover turned out? Worried about anyone else's look?"

I considered that. To say no sounded snotty, to say yes sounded needy. "I think the staff has done a great job bringing out each girl's individual beauty."

She smiled and said, "All right, I think that'll be enough."

"That's all?"

"We have to fit thirty-five of you into an hour and a half, so that will be plenty."

"Okay." That wasn't so bad.

"Thank you for your time. You can head over to that couch over there, and you'll be taken care of."

I stood and went to sit on the large circular couch in the corner. Two girls I had yet to meet were sitting there, talking quietly. I looked around the room and saw someone announcing that the last batch was heading in. A new flurry began around the stations. I was focused on it and almost didn't notice Marlee sit down beside me.

"Marlee! Look at your hair!"

"I know. They put extensions in it. Do you think Maxon will like it?" She looked genuinely worried.

"Of course! What guy doesn't like a gorgeous blonde?" I said with a playful smile.

"America, you're so nice. All those people at the airport loved you."

"Oh, I was just being friendly. You met people, too," I countered.

"Yeah, but not half as many as you."

I lowered my head, a little embarrassed for being complimented over something that seemed so obvious. When I looked up, I turned to the other two girls sitting with us. Emmica Brass and Samantha Lowell and I hadn't been introduced, but I knew who they were. I did a double take. They were looking at me funny. Before I had time to guess why, Silvia, the woman from earlier, approached us.

"All right, girls, are we all ready?" She checked her watch and looked at us expectantly. "I'm going to give you a quick tour and take you to your assigned rooms."

Marlee clapped her hands, and the four of us rose to leave. Silvia told us the space we were currently using to get pampered was the Women's Room. Usually the queen, her maids, and the handful of other female family members entertained themselves there.

"Get used to that room—you'll be spending a lot of time there. Now, on your way in you passed the Great Room, which is generally used for parties and banquets. If there were too many more of you ladies here, that's where you'd be taking your meals. But the regular dining room is large enough to meet your needs. Let's take a quick step in there."

We were shown where the royal family ate, at a table alone. We would be seated at long tables to either side, so the setup looked like a very stiff U. Our places were currently assigned, set with elegant place markers. I would be sitting next to Ashley and Tiny Lee, who I'd seen go through the Women's Room earlier, and across from Kriss Ambers.

We left the dining hall and continued on down a set of stairs and saw the room used to broadcast the *Illéa Capital Report*. Back upstairs our guide pointed down a hall where the king and Maxon spent most of their time working. That area was off-limits to us.

"Another thing that is off-limits: the third floor. The royal family has their private rooms up there, and any sort of intrusion will not be tolerated. Your rooms are all located on the second floor. You will inhabit a large portion of the guest rooms. Not to worry, though; we still have room for any visitors coming through.

"These doors here go out to the back garden. Hello, Hector, Markson." The two guards at the doors gave her a quick nod. It took me a moment to recognize that the large archway to our right was the side door to the Great Room, meaning the Women's Room was just around the corner. I was proud of myself for figuring that out. The palace was kind of like an opulent maze.

"You are not to go outside under any circumstances," Silvia continued. "During the day, there will be times when you can go into the garden, but not without permission. This is merely a safety restriction. Try as we may, rebels have gotten within the grounds before."

A chill went down my body.

We rounded a corner and walked up the massive stairs to the second floor. The carpets felt so lush under my shoes, like I was sinking an inch every time I took a step. High windows let in light, and it smelled like flowers and sunshine. Large paintings hung on the walls, depicting the kings of the past and a few renderings of old American and Canadian leaders. At least, that's what I guessed they were. They didn't wear any crowns.

"Your things are already in your rooms. If the decor is unsuitable, just tell your maids. You each have three, and they are already in your rooms, too. They will help with any unpacking you might have and will help you get dressed for dinner.

"Before dinner tonight, you will meet in the Women's Room for a special screening of the *Illéa Capital Report*. Next week, you'll all be on the show yourselves! Tonight you'll get to see some of the footage they've taken of you leaving your homes and arriving here. It promises to be very special. You should know that Prince Maxon hasn't seen anything yet today. He'll see what all of Illéa will see tonight, and then you will officially meet him tomorrow.

"You girls will all be having dinner as a group, so you will be able to meet one another, and then, tomorrow, the games begin!"

I gulped. Too many rules, too much structure, too many people. I just wanted to be alone with a violin.

We moved across the second floor, dropping off Selected girls at their rooms. Mine was tucked around a corner in a little hallway with Bariel, Tiny, and Jenna. I was glad it wasn't quite in the middle of things, like Marlee's room was. Maybe I'd have a little privacy like this.

Once Silvia left, I opened my door to the excited gasps of three women. One was sewing in a corner, and the others were cleaning an already perfect room. They scurried over and introduced themselves as Lucy, Anne, and Mary, but I forgot which was which almost immediately. It took quite a bit of convincing to get them to leave. I didn't want to be rude since they were so eager to serve, but I needed time alone.

"I just need a little nap. I'm sure you've had a long day, too, getting ready and all. The best thing you could do is let me rest, get some rest yourselves, and please come wake me up when it's time to go downstairs."

There was a flurry of thanks and bows, which I tried to discourage, and then I was alone. It didn't help. I tried to stretch out on my bed, but every part of my body pulled tight, refusing to let me get comfortable in a place that was so obviously not meant for me.

There was a violin in the corner, as well as a guitar and a gorgeous piano, but I couldn't bring myself to bother with them. My backpack was securely fastened, waiting at the foot of my bed, but that felt like too much work, too. I knew they'd set special things for me in my closet and drawers and bathroom, but I didn't feel like exploring.

I just lay there, still. It felt like only a few moments before my maids quietly tapped on my door. I let them in and, as strange as it was, let them dress me. They were just so excited to be helpful, I couldn't ask them to leave again.

They pulled parts of my hair back with delicate pins and freshened my makeup. The dress—which, along with the rest of my wardrobe, had been created by their hands—was deep green and floor length. Without those tiny heels again I'd stumble all over it. Silvia knocked on my door promptly at six to take me and my three neighbors down the hall. We waited in the foyer by the stairway for everyone to come and then marched down to the Women's Room. Marlee spotted me, and we walked together.

The sound of thirty-five pairs of heels on the marble stairs was the music of some elegant stampede. There were a few murmurs, but most girls were silent. I noticed as we passed the dining room that the doors were closed. Was the royal family in there now? Perhaps taking in one last meal as the three of them?

It seemed strange that we were their guests but hadn't met a single one of them yet.

The Women's Room had changed since we left. The mirrors and racks were all gone, and tables and chairs dotted the floor along with some very comfortable-looking couches.

Marlee looked at me and inclined her head toward one of the couches, and we sat there together.

Once we were all settled the TV was turned on, and we watched the *Report*. There were the same announcements as ever—budget updates for projects, progress of the war, and another rebel attack in the East—and then the last half hour was Gavril making commentary over footage of our day.

"Here Miss Celeste Newsome says good-bye to her many admirers in Clermont. It took this lovely young lady more than an hour to break away from her fans."

I saw Celeste smile smugly as she watched herself on-screen. She was sitting next to Bariel Pratt, who had hair straight as a bone and so pale blond it looked white as it fell to her waist. There was no mild way to put it: Her breasts were huge. They crept out of her strapless dress, tempting anyone to try and ignore them.

Bariel was beautiful, but in a typical way. It was similar to Celeste's style. I wasn't sure exactly how, but the image of them side by side prompted the thought, *Keep your enemies closer.* I think they'd singled each other out right away as the other's strongest competition.

"The others from the Mideast were just as popular. Ashley Brouillette's quiet, refined demeanor sets her apart immediately as a lady. As she carries herself through the crowd, she wears a humble, beautiful expression not too different from the face of the queen herself."

"And Marlee Tames of Kent was all bubbles as she departed today, singing the national anthem with her send-off band."

Pictures of Marlee smiling and embracing people from her home province flashed across the screen. "She's an immediate favorite of several people we interviewed today."

Marlee reached over and squeezed my hand. That settled it; I was pulling for Marlee.

"Also traveling with Miss Tames was America Singer, one of only three Fives who made it into the Selection." They made me look better than I felt in the moment. All I remembered was searching the crowds, sad. But the footage they chose of me searching made me appear mature and caring. The image of me hugging my father was touching, beautiful.

Still, it was nothing compared to the images of me in the airport. "But we know castes mean nothing in the Selection, and it seems Lady America is not to be overlooked. Upon landing in Angeles, Lady Singer was the crowd darling at the airport, stopping to take pictures, sign autographs, and simply speak to anyone there. Miss America Singer is not afraid to get her hands dirty, a quality that many believe our next princess needs."

Nearly everyone turned to look at me. I could see it in their eyes, the same look I'd gotten from Emmica and Samantha. Suddenly those stares made sense. My intentions didn't matter. They didn't know I didn't want this. In their eyes, I was a threat. And I could see they wanted me gone.

CHAPTER 10

I KEPT MY HEAD DOWN at dinner. In the Women's Room I could be brave because Marlee was beside me, and she just thought I was nice. But here, sandwiched between people whose hate I could feel radiating off in waves, I was a coward. I looked up from my plate once to see Kriss Ambers twirling her fork menacingly. And Ashley, who was so ladylike, had her lips pouted and didn't speak to me. I just wanted to escape to my room.

I didn't understand why it was all so important. So the people seemed to like me, so what? They were outranked in here; their little signs and cheers didn't matter.

After everything was said and done, I didn't know whether to feel honored or annoyed.

I focused my energies on the food. The last time I'd had steak was for Christmas a few years ago. I knew Mom did her best, but it was nothing like this. So juicy, so tender, so flavorful. I wanted to ask someone else if this wasn't the best steak they'd ever had. If Marlee had been nearby, I would have. I took a tentative peek around the room. Marlee was chattering quietly with the people around her.

How did she manage to do that? Hadn't that same clip declared her one of the immediate favorites? How did she get people to talk to her?

Dessert was an assortment of fruits in vanilla ice cream. It was like I'd never eaten before. If this was food, what had I been putting in my mouth up to this point? I thought of May and her equal love for all things sweet. She would have loved this. I bet she would have excelled here.

We weren't allowed to leave dinner until everyone had finished, and after that we were under strict orders to go straight to bed.

"You'll be meeting Prince Maxon in the morning, and you'll want to look your best," Silvia instructed. "He is someone in this room's future husband, after all."

A few girls sighed at the thought.

The click and clack of shoes up the stairs was quieter this time around. I couldn't wait to get out of mine. Out of the dress, too. I had one set of clothes from home in my backpack and was debating putting them on just to feel like myself for a moment.

We dispersed at the top of the stairs, each girl heading off to her own room. Marlee pulled me aside.

"Are you okay?" she asked.

"Yes. It's just that some of the girls were looking at me funny during dinner." I tried not to come across as whiny.

"They're just a little nervous because everyone liked you so much," she said, waving off their behavior.

"But the people liked you, too. I saw the signs. Why weren't the girls being mean to you?"

"You haven't spent a whole lot of time with groups of girls, have you?" She was smiling slyly, like I should know what was happening.

"No. Just my sisters mostly," I confessed.

"Homeschooled?"

"Yes."

"Well, I get tutored with a bunch of other Fours back home, all girls, and they each have their ways of getting under other people's skin. See, it's all about knowing the person, figuring out what will bug them the most. Lots of girls give me backhanded compliments, or little remarks, things like that. I know I come across as bubbly, but I'm shy underneath that, and they think they can wear me down with words."

I scrunched my forehead. They did that on purpose?

"For you, someone kind of quiet and mysterious—"

"I'm not mysterious," I interrupted.

"You are a little. And sometimes people don't know whether to interpret silence as confidence or fear. They're looking at you like you're a bug so maybe you'll feel like you are one."

"Huh." That kind of made sense. I wondered what I was

doing, if I was picking away at others' insecurities somehow. "What do you do? When you want to get the best of them, I mean?"

She smiled. "I ignore it. I know one girl at home who gets so irritated when she can't bother you, she just ends up sulking. So don't worry," she said. "All you have to do is not let them know they're getting to you."

"They're not."

"I almost believe you . . . but not quite." She laughed a little, a warm sound that evaporated in the quiet hallway. "Can you believe we meet him in the morning?" she asked, moving on to more important things in her eyes.

"No, actually, I can't." Maxon seemed like a ghost haunting the palace—implied but never really there.

"Well, good luck tomorrow." And I could tell she meant it.

"Better luck to you, Marlee. I'm sure Prince Maxon will be more than pleased to meet you." I squeezed her hand one time.

She smiled in a way that was both excited and timid and walked off to her room.

When I got to mine, Bariel's door was still open, and I heard her muttering something to a maid. She caught sight of me and slammed the door in my face.

Thanks for that.

My maids were there, of course, waiting to help me wash and undress. My nightgown, a flimsy little green thing, had been laid out for me on the bed. Kindly, none of them had touched my bag.

They were efficient but purposeful. They obviously had this end-of-the-day routine down, but they didn't rush through it. I suppose the effect was meant to be soothing, but I was ready to have them gone. I couldn't speed them up as they washed my hands and unlaced my dress and pinned my silver name tag to my silken nightgown. And as they did all these things that made me incredibly self-conscious, they asked questions. I tried to answer them without being rude.

Yes, I'd finally seen all the other girls. No, they weren't very talkative. Yes, dinner was fantastic. No, I wouldn't meet the prince until tomorrow. Yes, I was very tired.

"And it would really help me wind down if I could have some time alone," I added to the end of that last answer, hoping they would take the hint.

They looked disappointed. I tried to recover.

"You're all very helpful. I'm just used to spending time alone. And I've been swarmed with people today."

"But Lady Singer, we're supposed to help you. It's our job," the head girl said. I'd figured out that she was Anne. Anne seemed to be on top of things, Mary was easygoing, and Lucy I guessed was just shy.

"I really do appreciate you all, and I'll definitely want your help getting started tomorrow. But tonight, I just need to unwind. If you want to be helpful, some time to myself would be good for me. And if you're all rested, I'm sure it will make things better in the morning, right?"

They looked at one another. "Well, I suppose so," Anne acquiesced.

"One of us is supposed to stay here while you sleep. In case you need something." Lucy looked nervous, like she was afraid of whatever decision I would make. She seemed to have little tremors now and then, which I guessed was her shyness coming to the surface.

"If I need anything, I'll ring the bell. It'll be fine. Besides, I won't be able to rest knowing someone's watching me."

They looked at one another again, still a little skeptical. I knew one way to stop this, but I hated using it.

"You're supposed to obey my every command, right?"

They nodded hopefully.

"Then I command you all to go to bed. And come help me in the morning. Please."

Anne smiled. I could tell she was starting to get me.

"Yes, Lady Singer. We'll see you in the morning." They curtsied and quietly left the room. Anne gave me one last look. I supposed I wasn't quite what she had been expecting. She didn't seem too upset about it, though.

Once they were gone, I stepped out of my fancy slippers and stretched my toes on the floor. It felt good, natural, to be barefoot. I went to unpack my things, which was quick. I kept my change of clothes tucked in the bag and stored it in my massive closet. I surveyed the dresses as I did so. There were only a few. Enough to get me through a week or so. I assumed this was the same for everyone. Why make a dozen dresses for a girl who might leave the next day?

I took the few photos I had of my family and stuck them in the edge of my mirror. It stretched so high and wide, I could look at the pictures without having anything interrupt my view of myself. I had a small box of personal trinkets—earrings and ribbons and headbands I loved. They'd probably look incredibly plain here, but they were all so personal that I'd had to have them with me. The few books I'd brought found their way to the helpful shelf near the doors that opened to my balcony.

I peeked out the entry to the balcony and saw the garden. There was a maze of paths with fountains and benches. Flowers blossomed everywhere, and each hedge was perfectly trimmed. Past this obviously manicured piece of land was a short, open field and then a massive forest. It stretched back so far that I couldn't tell if it was entirely closed in by palace walls. I wondered for a moment why it existed and then debated the last article from home that I held in my hand.

My tiny jar with its rattling penny. I rolled it in my hands a few times, listening to the penny skate around the edges of the glass. Why had I even brought this? To remind myself of something I couldn't have?

That tiny thought—that this love I had been building in a quiet, secret place for years was really beyond my reach now—made my eyes well up. On top of all the tension and excitement of the day, it was just too much. I didn't know where the jar's permanent place here would be, but for the moment I set it on the table by my bed.

I dimmed the lights, crawled up on top of the luxurious blankets, and stared at my jar. I let myself be sad. I let myself think of *him*.

How had I lost so much in such a short period of time? It would seem like leaving your family, living in some foreign place, and being separated from the person you love should be events that take years to roll into place, not just a day.

I wondered what exactly he had wanted to tell me before I left. The only thing I could deduce was that he didn't feel comfortable saying it out loud. Was it about *her*?

I stared at the jar.

Maybe he was trying to say he was sorry? I had given him a sound scolding last night. So perhaps that was it.

That he'd moved on? Well, I could see that pretty clearly myself, thank you very much.

That he *hadn't* moved on? That he still loved me?

I shut the thought down. I couldn't let that hope build in me. I needed to hate him right now. That anger would keep me going. Staying as far away from him as I could for as long as possible was half my reason for being here.

But the hope ached. And with the hope came home-sickness, wishing May was sneaking into my bed like she sometimes did. And then fear that the other girls wanted me gone, that they might keep trying to make me feel small. And then nervousness at being presented to the nation on television for as long as I was here. And terror that people might try to kill me just to make a political statement. It all came at me too fast for my dizzy head to compute after such a long day.

My vision got blurry. I didn't even register that I'd started crying. I couldn't breathe. I was shaking. I jumped up and ran to the balcony. I was so panicked, it took me a moment to open the latch, but I did. I thought the fresh air would be enough, but it wasn't. My breaths were still shallow and cold.

There was no freedom in this. The bars of my balcony caged me in. And I could still see the walls around the palace, high with guards atop the points. I needed to be outside the palace, and no one was going to let that happen. Desperation made me feel even weaker. I looked at the forest. I'd bet I couldn't see anything but greenery from there.

I turned and bolted. I was a little unsteady with the tears in my eyes, but I managed to get out the door. I ran down the one hallway I knew, not seeing the art or the drapery or golden trim. I barely noticed the guards. I didn't know my way around the palace, but I knew if I got down the stairs and turned the right way, I'd see the massive glass doors that led to the garden. I just needed the doors.

I ran down the grand stairwell, my bare feet making slapping sounds on the marble. There were a few more guards along the way, but no one stopped me. That is, until I actually found the place I was looking for.

Just like earlier, two men were stationed at either side of the doors, and when I tried to run for them, one of them stepped in my way, the spearlike staff in his hand barring me from the exit.

"Excuse me, miss, you need to go back to your room," he said with authority. Even though he wasn't speaking loudly, his voice seemed thunderous in the still of the elegant hallway.

"No . . . no. I need . . . outside." The words were tangled; I couldn't breathe right.

"Miss, you need to get back to your room now." The second guard was taking steps toward me.

"Please." I started gasping. I thought I might faint.

"I'm sorry . . . Lady America, is it?" He found my pin. "You need to go back to your room."

"I . . . I can't breathe," I stammered, falling into the guard's arms as he moved close enough to push me away. His staff fell to the ground. I feebly clawed at him, feeling woozy with the effort.

"Let her go!" This was a new voice, young but full of authority. My head half turned, half fell in its direction. There was Prince Maxon. He looked a little odd, thanks to the angle my head was hanging at, but I recognized the hair and the stiff way he stood.

"She collapsed, Your Majesty. She wanted to go outside." The first guard looked nervous as he explained. He would be in terrible danger if he damaged me. I was the property of Illéa now.

"Open the doors."

"But—Your Majesty—"

"Open the doors and let her go. Now!"

"Right away, Your Highness." The first guard went to work, pulling out a key. My head stayed in its strange position as I heard the sound of keys clanking against one another and then one sliding into the lock. The prince looked at me warily as I tried to stand. And then the sweet smell of fresh air pulsed through me, giving me all the motivation I needed. I pulled myself out of the guard's arms and ran like a drunk into the garden.

I was staggering quite a bit, but I didn't care if I looked less than graceful. I just needed to be outside. I let myself feel the warm air on my skin, the grass beneath my toes. Somehow even things in nature seemed to be bred into something extravagant here. I meant to go all the way into the trees, but my legs only carried me so far. I collapsed in front of a small stone bench and sat there, my fine green nightgown in the dirt, and my head resting in my arms on the seat.

My body didn't have the energy to sob, so the tears that came were quiet. Still, they took all my focus. How did I get here? How had I let this happen? What would become of me here? Would I ever get back any piece of the life I'd had before this? I just didn't know. And there wasn't a damn thing I could do about any of it.

I was so consumed with my thoughts that I didn't realize I wasn't alone until Prince Maxon spoke.

"Are you all right, my dear?" he asked me.

"I am *not* your dear." I looked up to glare at him. There would be no mistaking the disgust in my tone or eyes.

"What have I done to offend you? Did I not just give you the very thing you asked for?" He was genuinely confused by my response. I suppose he expected us to adore him and thank our lucky stars for his existence.

I stared him down without fear, though the effect was probably weakened by my tearstained cheeks.

"Excuse me, dear, are you going to keep crying?" he asked, sounding very put out by the thought.

"Don't call me that! I am no more dear to you than the thirty-four other strangers you have here in your cage."

He walked closer, not seeming at all offended by my loose speech. He just looked . . . thoughtful. It was an interesting expression on his face.

His walk was graceful for a boy, and he looked incredibly comfortable as he paced around me. My bravery melted a little in the face of how awkward this was. He was fully dressed in his sharp suit, and I was cowering and half-naked. As if his rank didn't threaten me enough, his demeanor did. He must have had plenty of experience dealing with unhappy people; he was exceptionally calm as he answered.

"That is an unfair statement. You are all dear to me. It is simply a matter of discovering who shall be the dearest."

"Did you really just use the word 'shall'?"

He chuckled. "I'm afraid I did. Forgive me, it's a product of my education."

"Education," I muttered, rolling my eyes. "Ridiculous."

"I'm sorry?" he asked.

"It's ridiculous!" I yelled, regaining some of my courage.

"What is?"

"This contest! The whole thing! Haven't you ever loved anyone at all? Is this how you want to pick a wife? Are you really so shallow?" I shifted on the ground a little. To make things easier for me, he sat on the bench so I wouldn't have to twist. I was too upset to be thankful.

"I can see how I would appear that way, how this whole thing could seem like it's nothing more than cheap entertainment. But in my world, I am very guarded. I don't meet very many women. The ones I do are daughters of diplomats, and we usually have very little to discuss. And that's when we manage to speak the same language."

Maxon seemed to think that was a joke, and he laughed lightly. I wasn't amused. He cleared his throat.

"Circumstances being what they are, I haven't had the opportunity to fall in love. Have you?"

"Yes," I said matter-of-factly. As soon as the word came out, I wished I could steal it back. That was a private thing, none of his business.

"Then you have been quite lucky." He sounded jealous.

Imagine that. The one thing I could hold over the head of the Prince of Illéa, the very thing I was here to forget.

"My mother and father were married this way and are quite happy. I hope to find happiness, too. To find a woman that all of Illéa can love, someone to be my companion and to help entertain the leaders of other nations. Someone who will befriend my friends and be my confidante. I'm ready to find my wife."

Something in his voice struck me. There wasn't a trace of sarcasm. This thing that seemed like little more than a game show to me was his only chance for happiness. He couldn't try with a second round of girls. Well, maybe he could, but how embarrassing. He was so desperate, so hopeful. I felt my distaste for him lessen. Marginally.

"Do you really feel like this is a cage?" His eyes were full of compassion.

"Yes, I do." My voice came out quiet. I quickly added, "Your Majesty."

"I've felt that way more than once myself. But you must admit, it is a very beautiful cage."

"For you. Fill your beautiful cage with thirty-four other men all fighting over the same thing. See how nice it is then."

He raised his eyebrows. "Have there really been arguments over me? Don't you all realize I'm the one doing the choosing?"

"Actually, that was unfair. They're fighting over two things. Some fight for you, others fight for the crown. And they all think they've already figured out what to say and do so your choice will be obvious."

"Ah, yes. The man or the crown. I'm afraid some cannot tell the difference." He shook his head.

"Good luck there," I said dryly.

It was quiet for a moment in the wake of my sarcasm. I looked up at him out of the corner of my eye, waiting for him to speak. He gazed at an unfixed point in the grass, concern marking his face. It seemed this thought had been plaguing him. He took a breath and turned back to me.

"Which do you fight for?"

"Actually, I'm here by mistake."

"Mistake?"

"Yes. Sort of. Well, it's a long story. And now . . . I'm here.

And I'm not fighting. My plan is to enjoy the food until you kick me out."

He laughed out loud at that, actually doubling over and slapping his knee. It was a bizarre mix of rigidity and calm.

"What are you?" he asked.

"I'm sorry?"

"A Two? Three?"

Wasn't he paying attention at all? "Five."

"Ah, yes, then food would probably be good motivation to stay." He laughed again. "I'm sorry, I can't read your pin in the dark."

"I'm America."

"Well, that's perfect." Maxon looked off into the night and smiled at nothing in particular. Something in all this was amusing to him. "America, my dear, I do hope you find something in this cage worth fighting for. After all this, I can only imagine what it would be like to see you actually try."

He came down from the bench to crouch beside me. He was too close. I couldn't think right. Maybe I was a little starstruck or still feeling shaky from my crying episode. Either way I was too shocked to protest when he took my hand.

"If it would make you happy, I could let the staff know you prefer the garden. Then you can come out here at night without being manhandled by the guard. I would prefer if you had one nearby, though."

I wanted that. Freedom of any kind sounded heavenly, but he needed to be absolutely sure of my feelings.

"I don't . . . I don't think I want anything from you." I pulled my fingers from his loose grip.

He was a little taken aback, hurt. "As you wish." I felt more regret. Just because I didn't like the guy didn't mean I wanted to hurt him. "Will you be heading inside soon?"

"Yes," I breathed, looking at the ground.

"Then I'll leave you with your thoughts. There will be a guard near the door waiting for you."

"Thank you, um, Your Majesty." I shook my head. How many times had I addressed him wrongly in this conversation?

"Dear America, will you do me a favor?" He took my hand again. He was persistent.

I squinted at him, not sure of what to say. "Maybe."

His smile returned. "Don't mention this to the others. Technically, I'm not supposed to meet you until tomorrow, and I don't want anyone getting upset. Though I wouldn't call you yelling at me anything close to a romantic tryst, would you?"

It was my turn to smile. "Not at all!" I took a deep breath. "I won't tell."

"Thank you." He took the hand he was holding and lowered his lips to it. When he pulled away, he gently placed my hand in my lap. "Good night."

I looked at the warm spot on my hand, stunned for a moment. Then I turned to watch Maxon as he walked away, giving me the privacy I'd wanted all day.

CHAPTER 11

IN THE MORNING I WOKE not to the sound of the maids coming in—though they had—or my bath being drawn—though it was. I woke to the light coming through my window as Anne gently pulled back the rich, heavy curtains. She hummed a quiet song to herself, absolutely happy with her task.

I wasn't ready to move. It had taken me a long time to come down from getting so worked up, and even more time to relax after I'd realized exactly what that conversation in the garden would mean for me. If I got a chance, I would apologize to Maxon. It would be a miracle if he let me get that far.

"Miss? Are you awake?"

"Noooo," I moaned into the pillow. I hadn't had nearly enough sleep, and the bed was far too comfortable. But Anne,

Mary, and Lucy laughed at my groan, which was enough to make me smile and decide to start moving.

These girls would probably be the easiest for me to get along with in the palace. I wondered if they could become confidantes of some kind, or if training and protocol would render them completely unable to even share a cup of tea with me. Though I was a born Five, I was covered with Threeness now. And if they were maids, that made them all Sixes. But that was fine with me. I did enjoy the company of Sixes.

I moved slowly into the monstrous bathroom, every step echoing against the vastness of tile and glass. In the long mirrors I saw Lucy eyeing the dirt stains on my nightgown. Then Anne's careful eyes caught them. Then Mary's. Thankfully, none of them asked any questions. Yesterday I thought they had been prying with all their inquiries, but I was wrong. They were obviously overly concerned with my comfort. Questions about what I was doing outside my room—let alone the palace—would only be awkward.

All they did was remove the gown with care and usher me toward the bath.

I wasn't used to being naked around other people—not even Mom or May—but there seemed to be no way around it. These three would be dressing me for as long as I was here, so I would have to bear it until I left. I wondered what would happen to them when I was gone. Would they get assigned to other girls who would need more attention as the competition drew on? Did they already have other jobs in the palace they were temporarily excused from? It seemed rude to ask what they used to do or imply that I was leaving soon, so I didn't.

After my bath, Anne dried my hair, pulling half up with ribbons I'd brought from home. They were blue and just so happened to accent the flowers in one of the day dresses my maids had created for me, so that was what I wore. Mary did my makeup, which was just as light as the day before, and Lucy rubbed lotion into my arms and legs.

There was an array of jewelry to choose from, but I asked for my box instead. There was a tiny necklace with a songbird on it that my dad had given me, and it was silver so it matched my name pin. I did take a pair of earrings from the royal store, but they were probably the smallest ones in the collection.

Anne, Mary, and Lucy looked me over and smiled at the results. I took that as a sign I was decent enough to leave for breakfast. With bows and smiles, they wished me well as I went to leave. Lucy's hands were trembling again.

I went into the upstairs foyer where we had all met yesterday. I was the first one there, so I took to a small sofa to wait for the rest. Slowly, others started to trickle in. I quickly noticed a theme. Every one of the girls looked phenomenal. They had their hair pulled up in intricate braids or curls, away from their faces. The makeup was meticulously done, dresses pressed to perfection.

I had probably chosen my plainest dress for the first day, and everyone else's had something sparkly on it. I saw two girls walk into the foyer and realize they were wearing almost the exact same dress. They both turned back around to change. Everyone wanted to stand out, and they all did in their own ways. Even me.

Everyone here looked like a One. I looked like a Five in a nice dress.

I thought it had taken me a long time to get ready, but it took the other girls much, much longer. Even when Silvia came to escort us downstairs, we still had to wait for Celeste and Tiny, who, true to her name, had to have her dress taken in.

Once we were all assembled, everyone started to move toward the stairs. There was a gilded mirror on the wall, and we all turned to take one last peek as we descended. I caught a glimpse of myself next to Marlee and Tiny. I looked positively plain.

But at least I looked like me, and that was a minor consolation.

We went downstairs expecting to be taken into the dining room, where we had been told we would be eating. But instead we were taken into the Great Room, where individual tables and chairs had been set up in rows, all with plates, glasses, and silverware. There wasn't any food, though. Not even a hopeful smell. In the front corner, tucked away in a small nook, I noticed a small set of couches. A few cameramen, stationed around the room, filmed our arrival.

We filed in, sitting wherever we wanted as there were no place cards here. Marlee was in the row in front of me, and Ashley sat to my right. I didn't bother to take in anyone else. It seemed like several people had made at least one ally, just as I had in Marlee. Ashley had chosen her seat beside me, so I assumed she wanted my company. Still, she didn't speak. Maybe she was upset over the news reports last night. Then again, she was quiet when we met. Maybe it was just her nature. I figured the worst she could do was not answer back, so I decided to at least acknowledge her.

"Ashley, you look lovely."

"Oh, thank you," she said quietly. We both checked to make sure the camera crews were far away. Not that this was private, but who wanted them around for everything? "Isn't it fun to wear all this jewelry? Where's yours?"

"Umm, it was too heavy for me. I decided to go light instead."

"It is heavy! I feel like I have twenty pounds on my head. Still, I couldn't pass it up. Who knows how long any of us will stay?"

That was funny. Ashley had seemed quietly confident from the very beginning. With the way she looked and carried herself, she was prime princess material. It seemed strange that she would doubt herself.

"But don't you think you'll win?" I asked.

"Of course," she whispered. "But it's rude to say so!" She winked at me, which made me giggle.

Yet another mistake on my part. That giggle caught the attention of Silvia, who was walking in the door.

"Tsk–tsk. A lady never raises her voice above a gentle whisper."

Every murmur hushed. I wondered if the cameras had caught my mistake, and my cheeks filled with warmth.

"Hello again, ladies. I hope you all had a restful first night in the palace, because now our work begins. Today I will begin to instruct you on conduct and protocol, a process that will continue for the duration of your stay. Please know that I will be reporting any missteps on your part to the royal family.

"I know it sounds harsh, but this isn't a game to be taken lightly. Someone in this room will be the next princess of Illéa. It is no small task. You must endeavor to elevate yourselves, no matter your previous station. You will become ladies from the ground up. And this very morning, you will receive your first lesson.

"Table manners are very important, and before you can eat in front of the royal family, you must be aware of certain etiquette. The faster we get through this little lesson, the sooner you get to have your breakfasts, so faces forward, please."

She began explaining how we would be served from the right, which glass was for what beverage, and to never, ever reach for a pastry with our hands. Always use the tongs. Hands were to rest in our lap when not in use, napkin draped underneath. We weren't to speak unless spoken to. Of course, we could talk quietly to our neighbors, but always at a level befitting the palace. She eyed me seriously as she gave that last note.

Silvia went on and on in her elegant tone, taunting my

stomach. Even if they were small, I was used to getting my three meals at home. I needed food. I was getting a bit grumpy when we heard a knock at the door. Two guards stepped away, and in came Prince Maxon.

"Good morning, ladies," he called.

The lift in the room was tangible. Backs straightened, locks of hair were tossed over shoulders, and hems were rearranged. I looked not at Maxon, but Ashley, whose chest was moving fast. She stared in such a way that I felt embarrassed for noticing.

"Your Majesty," Silvia said with a low curtsy.

"Hello, Silvia. If you don't mind, I would like to introduce myself to these young women."

"Of course." She bowed again.

Prince Maxon surveyed the room and found me. Our eyes met for a moment, and he smiled. I wasn't expecting that. I was thinking that he'd probably changed his opinion of how to act toward me in the night, and I'd be called out in front of everyone for my behavior. But maybe he wasn't mad at all. Maybe he found me entertaining. He had to get incredibly bored around here. Whatever the reason, that brief smile led me to believe that maybe this wasn't going to be such a terrible experience after all. I settled into the decision I couldn't make last night and hoped Prince Maxon would hear out my apology.

"Ladies, if you don't mind, one at a time I'll be calling you over to meet with me. I'm sure you're all eager to eat, as am I. So I won't take up too much of your time. Do forgive me if I'm slow with names; there are quite a few of you."

There was a low rumble of giggles. Quickly, he went over to the girl in the front row on the far right and escorted her over to the couches. They spoke for a few minutes, then both rose. He bowed to her, she curtsied back. She went back to her table, spoke to the girl beside her, and it happened all over again. These conversations lasted only a few minutes and were spoken in hushed voices. He was trying to get a feel for each girl in less than five minutes.

"I wonder what he wants to know," Marlee turned and asked.

"Maybe he wants to know which actors you think are the most handsome. Keep your mental list ready," I whispered back. Marlee and Ashley both chuckled at that.

We weren't the only ones talking. Around the room voices lifted like gentle hums, as we tried to distract ourselves until it was our turn. Not to mention the cameramen were hopping around, asking girls about their first day in the palace, how they liked their maids, and things like that. When they stopped by Ashley and me, I let her do all the talking.

I kept looking over to the couches as each of the Selected were interviewed. Some were calm and ladylike, others fidgeted in excitement. Marlee blushed wildly as she walked over to Prince Maxon, and beamed when she walked back. Ashley straightened her dress several times, like a nervous little tic of her hands.

I was near sweating when she came back, meaning it was my turn to go. I took a deep breath and steadied myself. I was about to ask for a monumental favor.

He stood and went to read my pin as I approached. "America, is it?" he said, a smile playing on his lips.

"Yes, it is. And I know I've heard your name before, but could you remind me?" I wondered if opening with a joke was a bad idea, but Maxon laughed and motioned for me to sit.

He leaned in and whispered, "Did you sleep well, my dear?"

I didn't know what my face looked like in response to that name, but Maxon's eyes glittered with amusement.

"I am still not your dear," I replied, but with a smile. "But yes. Once I calmed down, I slept very well. My maids had to pull me out of bed, I was so cozy."

"I am glad you were comfortable, my . . . America," he corrected himself.

"Thank you," I said. I fidgeted with a piece of my dress for a moment, trying to think of how to say this right. "I'm very sorry I was mean to you. I realized as I was trying to fall asleep that even though this is a strange situation for me, I shouldn't blame you. You're not the reason I got swept up in all this, and the whole Selection thing isn't even your idea. And then, when I was feeling miserable, you were nothing but nice to me, and I was, well, awful. You could have thrown me out last night, and you didn't. Thank you."

Maxon's eyes were tender. I bet every girl before me had already melted because he'd given them a look like this. I would have been bothered that he looked at me that way, but it was obviously just part of his nature. He ducked his head for a moment. When he looked at me again, he leaned forward, resting his elbows on his knees as if he wanted me to understand the importance of what was coming next.

"America, you have been very up front with me so far. That is a quality that I deeply admire, and I'm going to ask you to be kind enough to answer one question for me."

I nodded, a little afraid of what he wanted to know. He leaned in even closer to whisper. "You say you're here by mistake, so I'm assuming you don't want to be here. Is there any possibility of you having any sort of . . . of loving feelings toward me?"

I couldn't help but fidget a little. I genuinely didn't want to hurt his feelings, but I couldn't beat around the bush on this.

"You are very kind, Your Majesty, and attractive, and thoughtful." He smiled at that. In a low voice I added, "But for very valid reasons, I don't think I could."

"Would you explain?" His face hid it well, but I could hear the disappointment caused by my immediate rejection. I guessed he wasn't used to that.

It wasn't something I wanted to share, but I didn't think anything else would make him understand. In an even lower whisper than I'd used before, I told him the truth.

"I . . . I'm afraid my heart is elsewhere." I could feel my eyes getting wet.

"Oh, please don't cry!" Maxon's whisper was marked with a genuine worry. "I never know what to do when women cry!"

That made me laugh, and any threat of tears retreated for the moment. The relief on his face was unmistakable.

"Would you like me to let you go home to your love today?" he asked. It was obvious that my preference for someone else bothered him, but instead of choosing to be angry, he showed compassion. The gesture made me trust him.

"That's the thing. . . . I don't want to go home."

"Really?" He ran his fingers through his hair, and I had to laugh again at how lost he seemed.

"Could I be perfectly honest with you?"

He nodded.

"I need to be here. My family needs me to be here. Even if you could let me stay for a week, that would be a blessing for them."

"You mean you need the money?"

"Yes." I felt bad admitting it. It must have seemed like I was using him. In truth, I guess I was. But there was more to it. "And there are . . . certain people"—I looked up at him— "at home who I can't bear to see right now."

Maxon nodded his head in understanding but did not speak.

I hesitated. I guessed the worst that could happen now was being sent home anyway, so I continued. "If you would be willing to let me stay, even for a little while, I'd be willing to make a trade," I offered.

His eyebrows shot up. "A trade?"

I bit my lip. "If you let me stay . . ." This was going to sound so stupid. "All right, well, look at you. You're the prince. You're busy all day, what with helping run a country and all, and you're supposed to find time to narrow thirty-five, well, thirty-four girls, down to one? That's a lot to ask, don't you think?"

He nodded. I could see his genuine exhaustion at the thought.

"Wouldn't it be much better for you if you had someone on the inside? Someone to help? Like, you know, a friend?"

"A friend?" he asked.

"Yes. Let me stay, and I'll help you. I'll be your friend." He smiled at the words. "You don't have to worry about pursuing me. You already know that I don't have feelings for you. But you can talk to me anytime you like, and I'll try and help. You said last night that you were looking for a confidante. Well, until you find one for good, I could be that person. If you want."

His expression was affectionate but guarded. "I've met nearly every woman in this room, and I can't think of one who would make a better friend. I'd be glad to have you stay."

My relief was inexpressible.

"Do you think," Maxon asked, "that I could still call you 'my dear'?"

"Not a chance," I whispered.

"I'll keep trying. I don't have it in me to give up." And I believed him. It was annoying to think he'd press that issue.

"Did you call all of them that?" I nodded my head toward the rest of the room.

"Yes, and they all seemed to like it."

"That is the exact reason why I don't." And I stood.

Maxon was chuckling as he rose with me. I would have scowled, but it actually was kind of funny. He bowed, I curtsied, and I went back to my seat.

I was so hungry that it felt like an eternity until he'd gone through the last rows. But finally the last girl was back in her seat, and I was eagerly anticipating my first breakfast at the palace.

Maxon walked to the center of the room. "If I have asked you to remain behind, please stay in your seats. If not, please proceed with Silvia here into the dining hall. I will join you shortly."

Asked to stay? Was that a good thing?

I stood, as did most of the girls, and started walking. He must just want some special time with those girls. I saw that Ashley was one of them. No doubt she was special, a born princess by the looks of her. The rest were girls I hadn't managed to meet. Not that they had wanted to meet me. The cameras lingered behind to capture whatever special moment was about to occur, and the rest of us moved on.

We walked into the banquet room and there, looking more majestic than even I could imagine, were King Clarkson and Queen Amberly. Also in the room, more camera crews swarmed to catch our first meeting. I hesitated, wondering if we should all go back to the door and be invited in. But most everyone else—if somewhat hesitantly—kept walking. I walked quickly to my chair, hoping I hadn't drawn attention to myself.

Silvia walked in not two seconds later and took in the scene.

"Ladies," she said, "I'm afraid we didn't get this far. Whenever you enter a room where the king or queen is present, or if they should enter a room you are in, the proper thing to do is curtsy. Then when you are addressed, you may rise and take your seat. All together, shall we?" And we all curtsied in the direction of the head table.

"Welcome, girls," the queen said. "Please take your seats, and welcome to the palace. We're pleased to have you." There was something pleasant about her voice. It was calm in the same way her expression was, but not lifeless by any means.

As Silvia had said, the servers came to our right to pour orange juice into our glasses. Our plates came covered on large trays, and the butlers lifted the covers off right in front of us. I was hit in the face with a fragrant blast of steam from my pancakes. Mercifully, the murmurs of awe across the room covered my growling stomach.

King Clarkson blessed our food, and we all began to eat. A few minutes later, Maxon walked in to take his seat, but before we could move, he called out.

"Please don't rise, ladies. Enjoy your breakfasts." He walked up to the head table, kissed his mother on the cheek, gave his father a firm pat on the back, and settled into his own chair just to the king's left. He made a few comments to the closest butler, who laughed quietly, and then dug into his own plate.

Ashley didn't come. Or any of the other girls. I looked around, confused, counting to see how many were missing. Eight. Eight girls were not here.

It was Kriss, sitting across from me, who answered the question in my eyes.

"They're gone," she said.

Gone? Oh. Gone . . .

I couldn't imagine what they had done in less than five minutes to displease Maxon, but I was suddenly grateful I'd chosen to be honest.

Just like that, we were down to twenty-seven.

CHAPTER 12

THE CAMERAS DID A LAP around the room and left to let us enjoy our breakfast in peace, getting one last shot of the prince before they departed.

I was a little thrown off by the sudden elimination, but Maxon didn't seem too distressed. He ate his food without a care, and as I watched I realized I should eat my own breakfast before it got cold. Again, it was almost too delicious. The orange juice was so pure that I had to take smaller sips just to absorb it. The eggs and bacon were heaven, and the pancakes were perfectly done, not too thin like the ones I made at home.

I heard lots of little sighs all around me and knew I wasn't the only one enjoying the food. Remembering to use the tongs, I picked up a strawberry tart from the basket in the center of the table. As I did so, I looked around the room to see how the other Fives were enjoying their meals. That was when I noticed that I was the only Five left.

I didn't know if Maxon was aware of that information—he barely seemed to know our names—but it was strange they were both gone. If I had been another stranger to Maxon when I walked into that room, would I have been kicked out, too? I mulled this over as I bit into the strawberry tart. It was so sweet and the dough was so flaky, every millimeter of my mouth was engaged, taking over the rest of my senses entirely. I didn't mean to make the little moan, but it was by far the best thing I had ever tasted. I took another bite before I even swallowed the first.

"Lady America?" a voice called.

The other heads in the room turned to the voice, which belonged to Prince Maxon. I was shocked that he'd address me, or any of us, so casually and in front of the others.

What was worse than being called out so unexpectedly was that my mouth was full of food. I covered my mouth with my hand and chewed as quickly as I could manage. It couldn't have been more than a few seconds, but with so many eyes on me, it felt like an eternity. I noted Celeste's smug face as she watched me. I must have looked like an easy kill in her eyes.

"Yes, Your Majesty?" I replied as soon as I had most of it swallowed.

"How are you enjoying the food?" Maxon seemed on the verge of laughter, either from my bewildered expression or because he'd brought up a detail from our very first and highly unauthorized conversation.

I tried to stay calm myself. "It's excellent, Your Majesty. This strawberry tart . . . well, I have a sister who loves sweets more than I do. I think she'd cry if she tasted this. It's perfect."

Maxon swallowed a bite of his own breakfast and leaned back in his chair. "Do you really think she would cry?" He seemed exceedingly amused at the idea. He did have strange feelings toward women and crying.

I thought about it. "Yes, actually, I do. She doesn't have much of a filter when it comes to her emotions."

"Would you wager money on it?" he asked quickly. I noticed the heads of every girl turning back and forth between us like they were watching a game of tennis.

"If I had any to bet, I certainly would." I smiled at the idea of betting over someone else's tears of joy.

"What would you be willing to barter instead? You seem to be very good at striking deals." He was enjoying this little game. Fine. I'd play.

"Well, what do you want?" I posed. Then I wondered what in the world I could offer someone who had everything.

"What do *you* want?" he countered.

Now that was a fascinating question. Almost as interesting as thinking about what I could offer Maxon was what he could offer me. He had the world at his disposal. So what did I want?

I wasn't a One, but I was living like I was. I had more

food than I could finish and the most comfortable bed I could imagine. People were waiting on me hand and foot, whether I liked it or not. And if I needed anything, all I had to do was ask.

The only thing I really wanted was something that made this place feel like less of a palace. If my family were running around somewhere, or if I wasn't so done up. I couldn't ask for my family to visit. I'd only been here a day.

"If she cries, I want to wear pants for a week," I offered.

Everyone laughed, but in a quiet, polite way. Even the king and queen seemed to find my request amusing. I liked the way the queen looked at me, like I was less of a foreigner to her now.

"Done," Maxon said. "And if she doesn't, you owe me a walk around the grounds tomorrow afternoon."

A walk on the grounds? That was it? It didn't seem like anything special to me. I remembered what Maxon had said last night, that he was guarded. Maybe he didn't know how to just ask a girl for time alone. Maybe this was his way of navigating something very alien to him.

Someone next to me made a disapproving sound. Oh. I realized that if I lost, I'd be the first person to officially get time one-on-one with the prince. Part of me wanted to renegotiate, but if I was going to be helpful—as I'd promised him—I couldn't brush off his first attempts at trying to date.

"You drive a hard bargain, sir, but I accept."

"Justin?" The butler he had spoken to earlier stepped forward. "Go make a parcel of strawberry tarts and send it to the lady's family. Have someone wait while her sister tastes it, and let us know if she does, in fact, cry. I'm most curious about this."

Justin nodded and was off.

"You should write a note to send with it, and tell your family you're safe. In fact, you all should. After breakfast, write a letter to your families, and we'll make sure they receive them today."

Everyone smiled and sighed, happy to finally be included in the goings-on. We finished the rest of our breakfast and went to write our letters. Anne found me some stationery, and I wrote a quick letter to my family. Even though things had gotten off to a very awkward start, the last thing I wanted was for them to worry. I tried to sound breezy.

Dear Mom, Dad, May, and Gerad,

I miss you all so much already! The prince wanted us to write home and let our families know we were safe and well. I am both. The plane ride was a little scary, but it was fun in a way, too. The world looks so small from up so high!

They've given me lots of wonderful clothes and things, and I have three sweet maids who help me get dressed and clean for me and tell me where to go. So even if I get totally confused, they always know just where I'm supposed to be and help me get there on time.

The other girls are mostly shy, but I think I might have a friend. You remember Marlee from Kent? I met

her on the way over to Angeles. She's very bright and
friendly. If I have to come home anytime soon, I'm
hoping she makes it to the end.

I have met the prince. The king and queen, too. They're
even more regal in person. I haven't spoken to them
yet, but I did talk to Prince Maxon. He's a surprisingly
generous person . . . I think.

I have to go, but I love you and miss you, and I'll write
again as soon as I can.

Love,
America

I didn't think there was anything shocking in there, but I could have been wrong. I was imagining May reading it over and over again, finding hidden details about my life in the words. I wondered if she'd read this before she ate the pastries.

P.S. May, don't these strawberry tarts just make you
want to cry?

There. That was the best I could do.

Apparently, it wasn't good enough. A butler knocked on my door that evening with an envelope from my family and an update.

"She didn't cry, miss. She said they were so good she could have—as you suggested—but she did not actually cry. His Majesty will come and get you from your room around five tomorrow. Please be ready."

I wasn't so upset about losing, but I seriously would have enjoyed the pants. At least, if I couldn't have that, I had letters. I realized that this was the first time I'd been parted from my family for more than a few hours. We weren't wealthy enough to go on trips, and since I didn't really have friends growing up, I'd never even spent the night away. If only there was a way I could get letters every day. I supposed it could be done, but it would have to be so expensive.

I read Dad's first. He went on and on about how beautiful I looked on TV and how proud he was of me. He said I shouldn't have sent three boxes of tarts, because May was going to get spoiled. Three boxes! For goodness' sake.

He went on to say that Aspen had been at the house helping with paperwork, so he'd taken a box home to his family. I didn't know how to feel about that. On the one hand, I was glad they would have something so decadent to eat. On the other, I just imagined him sharing some with his new girlfriend. Someone he could spoil. I wondered if he was jealous of Maxon's gift, or if he was glad to be rid of my attention.

I lingered on those lines much longer than I meant to.

Dad closed by saying he was pleased I'd made a friend. Said I always was slow in that department. I folded the letter up and ran my finger over his signature on the outside. I'd never noticed how funny he signed his name before.

Gerad's letter was short and to the point. He missed me, he loved me, and please send more food. I laughed out loud at that.

Mom was bossy. Even in print I could hear her tone, smugly congratulating me on already earning the prince's affections—she had been informed that I was the only one to get gifts to send home—and telling me firmly to keep up whatever I was doing.

Yeah, Mom, I'll just keep telling the prince that he has absolutely no shot with me and offend him as often as I can. Great plan.

I was glad I'd saved May's for last.

Her letter was absolutely giddy. She admitted how jealous she was that I was eating like that all the time. She also complained that Mom was bossing her around more. I knew how that felt. The rest was a barrage of questions. Was Maxon as cute in person as he was on TV? What was I wearing now? Could she come and visit the palace? Did Maxon have a secret brother who would be willing to marry her one day?

I giggled and embraced my collection of letters. I'd have to make the effort to write back soon. There had to be a telephone around here somewhere, but so far no one had made us aware of it. Even if I had one in my room, it would probably be overkill to call home daily. Besides, these letters would be fun to hold on to. Proof I'd really been here when this whole place would be a memory.

I went to bed with the comforting knowledge that my family was doing well, and that warmth lulled me into a sound sleep that was only hitched by a twinge of nerves at being alone with Maxon again. I couldn't quite pin down the reason, but I hoped it was all for nothing.

"For the sake of appearances, would you please take my arm?" Maxon asked as he escorted me from my room the next day. I was a little hesitant, but I did.

My maids had already put me in my evening dress: a little blue thing with an empire waist and capped sleeves. My arms were bare, and I could feel the starched fabric of Maxon's suit against my skin. Something about it all made me uncomfortable. He must have noticed, because he tried to distract me.

"I'm sorry she didn't cry," he said.

"No you're not." My joking tone made it clear I wasn't too upset about losing.

"I've never gambled before. It was nice to win." His tone was slightly apologetic.

"Beginner's luck."

He smiled. "Perhaps. Next time we'll try to make her laugh."

I instantly started running scenarios through my mind. What from the palace would make May just die with laughter?

Maxon could tell I was thinking about her. "What's your family like?"

"What do you mean?"

"Just that. Your family must be very different from mine."

"I'd say so." I laughed. "For one, no one wears their tiaras to breakfast."

Maxon smiled. "More of a dinner thing at the Singer house?"

"Of course."

He chuckled quietly. I was starting to think maybe Maxon wasn't nearly the snob I'd suspected he was.

"Well, I'm the middle child of five."

"Five!"

"Yeah, five. Most families out there have lots of kids. I'd have lots if I could."

"Oh, really?" Maxon's eyebrows were raised.

"Yes," I answered. My voice was low. I couldn't quite say why, but that seemed like a very intimate detail about my life. Only one other person had really known about it.

I felt a spasm of sadness but shoved it away.

"Anyway, my oldest sister, Kenna, is married to a Four. She works in a factory now. My mom wants me to marry at least a Four, but I don't want to have to stop singing. I love it too much. But I guess I'm a Three now. That's really weird. I think I'm going to try to stay in music if I can.

"Kota is next. He's an artist. We don't see much of him these days. He did come to see me off, but that's about it.

"Then there's me."

Maxon smiled effortlessly. "America Singer," he announced, "my closest friend."

"That's right." I rolled my eyes. There was no way I could actually be his closest friend. At least not yet. But I had to admit, he was the only person I'd ever really confided in who wasn't family or someone I was in love with. Well,

Marlee, too. Could it be the same way for him?

Slowly we moved down the hallway and toward the stairs. He didn't appear to be in any sort of rush.

"After me there's May. She's the one who sold me out and didn't cry. Honestly, I was robbed; I can't believe she didn't cry! But yeah, she's an artist. I . . . I adore her."

Maxon examined my face. Talking about May softened me a bit. I liked Maxon well enough, but I didn't know how far I wanted to let him in.

"And then Gerad. He's the baby; he's seven. He hasn't quite figured out if he's into music or art yet. Mostly he likes to play ball and study bugs, which is fine except that he can't make a living that way. We're trying to get him to experiment more. Anyway, that's everyone."

"What about your parents?" he pressed.

"What about *your* parents?" I replied.

"You know my parents."

"No, I don't. I know the public image of them. What are they really like?" I pulled on his arm, which was quite a feat. Maxon's arms were huge. Even beneath the layers of his suit, I could feel the strong, steady muscles there. Maxon sighed, but I could tell I didn't really exasperate him at all. He seemed to like having someone pester him. It must be sad to grow up in this place without any siblings.

He started thinking about what he was going to say as we stepped into the garden. The guards all wore sly smiles as we passed. Just past them a camera crew waited. Of course they would want to be present for the prince's first date. Maxon

shook his head at them, and they retreated indoors immediately. I heard someone curse. I wasn't particularly looking
forward to being followed around by cameras, but it seemed
strange to dismiss them.

"Are you all right? You seem tense," Maxon noted.

"You get confused by crying women, I get confused by
walks with princes," I said with a shrug.

Maxon laughed quietly at that but said no more. As we
moved west, the sun was blocked by the massive forest on
the grounds, though it was still early in the evening. The
shade crept over us, creating a tent of darkness. When I'd
sought isolation the other night, this was where I wanted to
be. We truly seemed alone now. We walked on, away from
the palace and out of earshot of the guards.

"What about me is so confusing?"

I hesitated but said what I felt. "Your character. Your intentions. I'm not sure what to expect out of this little stroll."

"Ah." He stopped walking and faced me. We were very
close to each other, and in spite of the warm summer air, a
chill ran down my spine. "I think you can tell by now that
I'm not the type of man to beat around the bush. I'll tell you
exactly what I want from you."

Maxon took a step closer.

My breath caught in my throat. I'd just walked into the
very situation I feared. No guards, no cameras, no one to
stop him from doing whatever he wanted.

Knee-jerk reaction. Literally. I kneed His Majesty in the
thigh. Hard.

Maxon let out a yell and reached down, clutching himself as I backed away from him. "What was that for?"

"If you lay a single finger on me, I'll do worse!" I promised.

"What?"

"I said, if you—"

"No, no, you crazy girl, I heard you the first time." Maxon grimaced. "But just what in the world do you mean by it?"

I felt the heat run through my body. I'd jumped to the worst possible conclusion and set myself up to fight something that obviously wasn't coming.

The guards ran up, alerted by our little squabble. Maxon waved them away from an awkward, half-bent position.

We were quiet for a while, and once Maxon was over the worst of his pain, he faced me.

"What did you think I wanted?" he asked.

I ducked my head and blushed.

"America, what did you think I wanted?" He sounded upset. More than upset. Offended. He had obviously guessed what I'd assumed, and he didn't like that one bit. "In public? You thought . . . for heaven's sake. I'm a gentleman!"

He started to walk away but turned back.

"Why did you even offer to help if you think so little of me?"

I couldn't even look him in the eye. I didn't know how to explain I had been prepped to expect a dog, that the darkness and privacy made me feel strange, that I'd only ever been alone with one other boy and that was how we behaved.

"You'll be taking dinner in your room tonight. I'll deal

with this in the morning."

I waited in the garden until I knew all the others would be in the dining hall, and then I paced up and down the hallway before I went into my room. Anne, Mary, and Lucy were beside themselves when I came in. I didn't have the heart to tell them I hadn't spent the whole time with the prince.

My meal had been delivered and was waiting on the table by the balcony. I was hungry now that I wasn't distracted by my own humiliation. But my long absence wasn't the reason my maids were in a tizzy. There was a very large box on the bed, begging to be opened.

"Can we see?" Lucy asked.

"Lucy, that's rude!" Anne chided.

"They dropped it off the moment you left! We've been wondering ever since!" Mary exclaimed.

"Mary! Manners!" Anne scolded.

"No, don't worry, girls. I don't have any secrets." When they came to kick me out tomorrow, I'd tell my maids why.

I gave them a weak smile as I pulled at the big red bow on the box. Inside were three pairs of pants. A linen set, another that was more businesslike but soft to the touch, and a glorious pair made from denim. There was a card resting on top with the Illéa emblem on it.

You ask for such simple things, I can't deny you. But for my sake, only on Saturdays, please. Thank you for your company.
Your friend,
Maxon

CHAPTER 13

I DIDN'T REALLY HAVE THAT much time to feel ashamed or worried, all things considered. When my maids dressed me the next morning without a hint of worry, I assumed my presence downstairs would be welcome. Even allowing me to come down to breakfast showed a hint of kindness in Maxon I hadn't been expecting: I got a last meal, a last moment as one of the beautiful Selected.

We were halfway through breakfast before Kriss worked up the courage to ask me about our date.

"How was it?" she asked quietly, the way we were meant to speak at mealtimes. But those three small words made ears all up and down the table perk up, and everyone within hearing distance was paying attention.

I took a breath. "Indescribable."

The girls looked at one another, clearly hoping for more.

"How did he act?" Tiny asked.

"Umm." I tried to choose my words carefully. "Not at all how I expected he would."

This time, little murmurs went down the table.

"Are you being like that on purpose?" Zoe interjected. "If you are, it's awfully mean."

I shook my head. How could I explain this? "No, it's just that—"

But I was spared trying to form an answer by the confusing noises coming down the hallway.

The shouts were strange. In my very short time at the palace, not a single sound had registered as anything close to loud. Beyond that, there was a kind of music to the click of the guards' shoes on the floor, the massive doors opening and closing, the forks touching the plates. This was complete and absolute mayhem.

The royal family seemed to understand it before the rest of us.

"To the back of the room, ladies!" King Clarkson yelled, and ran over to a window.

Girls, confused but not wanting to disobey, slowly moved toward the head table. The king was pulling down a shade, but it wasn't the typical light-filtering kind. It was metal and squealed into place. Beside him Maxon came and drew down another. And beside Maxon the lovely and delicate queen was racing to pull down the next.

That was when the wave of guards made it into the dining hall. I saw a number of them lining up outside the room just before the monstrous doors were closed, bolted, and secured with bars.

"They're inside the walls, Majesty, but we're holding them back. The ladies should leave, but we're so close to the door—"

"Understood, Markson," the king replied, cutting off the sentence.

It didn't take more than that for me to comprehend. There were rebels inside the grounds.

I'd figured it would come. This many guests in the palace, so many preparations going on. Surely someone would miss something somewhere and let our safety slip. And even if there were no easy way in, this would be an excellent time to mount a protest. At its barest of bones, the Selection was kind of disturbing. I was sure the rebels hated it along with everything else about Illéa.

But whatever their opinion, I wasn't going down quietly.

I pushed my chair back so quickly it fell over, and I ran to the closest window to pull down the metal shade. A few other girls who understood how threatened we were did the same.

It took me only a moment to get the thing down, but locking it into place was a little more difficult. I had just managed to get the latch right when something crashed into the metal plate from outside the palace, sending me screaming backward until I tripped over my fallen chair and tumbled to the ground.

Maxon appeared immediately.

"Are you hurt?"

I did a quick evaluation. I'd probably have a bruise on my hip, and I was scared, but that was the worst of it.

"No, I'm fine."

"To the back of the room. Now!" he ordered as he helped me off the ground. He raced down the hall, snatching up girls who had begun to freeze up in fear and ushering them to the back corner.

I obeyed, running to the back of the room, toward the clusters of girls huddled together. Some of them were weeping; others were staring into space in shock. Tiny had fainted. The most reassuring sight was King Clarkson talking intently to a guard along the back wall, just far away enough that the girls wouldn't hear. He had one arm wrapped protectively around the queen, who stood quietly and proudly beside him.

How many times had she survived attacks now? We got reports that these happened several times a year. That had to be unnerving. The odds were getting slimmer and slimmer for her . . . and her husband . . . and her only child. Surely, eventually, the rebels would figure out the right alignment of circumstances to get what they wanted. Yet she stood there, her chin set, her still face wearing a quiet calm.

I surveyed the girls. Did any of them have the strength it would take to be the queen? Tiny was still unconscious in someone's arms. Celeste and Bariel were making conversation. I knew what Celeste looked like at ease, and this wasn't it. Still, compared to the others, she hid her emotions well.

Others were near hysterics, whimpering on their knees. Some had mentally shut down, blocking out the entire ordeal. Their faces were blank, and they absently wrung their hands, waiting for it to end.

Marlee was crying a little, but not so much that she looked like a wreck. I grabbed her arm and pulled her upright.

"Dry your eyes and stand up straight," I barked into her ear.

"What?" she squeaked.

"Trust me, do it."

Marlee wiped her face on the side of her gown and stood up a little taller. She touched her face in several places, checking for smudged makeup, I guessed. Then she turned and looked at me for approval.

"Good job. Sorry to be so bossy, but trust me on this one, okay?" I felt bad ordering her around in the middle of something so distressing, but she had to look as calm as Queen Amberly. Surely Maxon would want that in his queen, and Marlee had to win.

Marlee nodded her head. "No, you're right. I mean, for the time being, everyone is safe. I shouldn't be so worried."

I nodded back to her, though she was most assuredly wrong. *Everyone* was not safe.

Guards waited on edge by the massive doors as heavy things were thrown against wall and windows again and again. There wasn't a clock in here. I had no idea how long this attack was lasting, and that only made me more anxious. How would we know if they got inside? Would it only be once they started banging on the doors? Were they already inside and we just didn't know it?

I couldn't take the worry. I stared at a vase of ornate flowers—none of which I knew the names of—and bit away at one of my perfectly manicured nails. I pretended that those flowers were all that mattered in the world.

Eventually Maxon came by to check on me, as he had with the others. He stood beside me and stared at the flowers, too. Neither of us really knew what to say.

"Are you doing all right?" he finally asked.

"Yes," I whispered.

He paused a moment. "You seem unwell."

"What will happen to my maids?" I asked, voicing my greatest worry. I knew I was safe. Where were they? What if one of them had been walking down the hall as the rebels made their way in?

"Your maids?" he asked in a tone that implied I was an idiot.

"Yes, my maids." I looked into his eyes, shaming him into acknowledging that only a choice minority of the throngs who lived in the palace were actually being protected. I was on the verge of tears. I didn't want them to come, and I was breathing rapidly trying to keep my emotions at bay.

He looked into my eyes and seemed to understand that I was only one step up from being a maid myself. That wasn't the reason for my worry, but it did seem strange that a lottery was the main difference between someone like Anne and me.

"They should be hiding by now. The help have their

own places to wait. The guards are very good about getting around quickly and alerting everyone. They ought to be fine. We usually have an alarm system, but the last time they came through, the rebels thoroughly dismantled it. They've been working on fixing it, but . . ." Maxon sighed.

I looked at the floor, trying to quiet all the worries in my head.

"America," he begged.

I turned to Maxon.

"They're fine. The rebels were slow, and everyone here knows what to do in an emergency."

I nodded. We stood there quietly for a minute, and I could tell he was about to move on.

"Maxon," I whispered.

He turned back, a little surprised to be addressed so casually.

"About last night. Let me explain. When they came to prep us, to get us ready to come here, there was a man who told me that I was never to turn you down. No matter what you asked for. Not ever."

He was dumbfounded. "What?"

"He made it sound like you might ask for certain things. And you said yourself that you hadn't been around many women. After eighteen years . . . and then you sent the cameras away. I just got scared when you got that close to me."

Maxon shook his head, trying to process all this. Humiliation, rage, and disbelief all played across his typically even-tempered face.

"Was everyone told this?" he asked, sounding appalled at the idea.

"I don't know. I can't imagine many girls would need such a warning. *They're* probably waiting to pounce on you," I noted, nodding my head toward the rest of the room.

He gave a dark chuckle. "But you're not, so you had absolutely no qualms about kneeing me in the groin, right?"

"I hit your thigh!"

"Oh, please. A man doesn't need that long to recover from a knee to the thigh," he replied, his voice full of skepticism.

A laugh escaped me. Thankfully, Maxon joined in. Just then another mass hit the windows, and we stopped in unison. For a moment I had forgotten where I was.

"So how are you handling a roomful of crying women?" I asked.

There was a comical bewilderment in his expression. "Nothing in the world is more confusing!" he whispered urgently. "I haven't the faintest clue how to stop it."

This was the man who was going to lead our country: the guy rendered useless by tears. It was too funny.

"Try patting them on the back or shoulder and telling them everything is going to be fine. Lots of times when girls cry, they don't want you to fix the problem, they just want to be consoled," I advised.

"Really?"

"Pretty much."

"It can't possibly be that simple." Intrigue and doubt played in his voice.

"I said most of the time, not all the time. But it would probably work for a lot of the girls here."

He snorted. "I'm not so sure. Two have already asked if I'll let them leave if this ever ends."

"I thought we weren't allowed to do that." I shouldn't have been surprised, though. If he had agreed to let me stay on as a friend, he couldn't be too concerned with technicalities. "What are you going to do?"

"What else can I do? I won't keep someone here against her will."

"Maybe they'll change their minds," I offered hopefully.

"Maybe." He paused. "What about you? Have you been scared off yet?" he asked almost playfully.

"Honestly? I was convinced you were sending me home after breakfast anyway," I admitted.

"Honestly? I had considered that myself."

There was a quiet smile between us. Our friendship—if I could even call it that—was obviously awkward and flawed, but at least it was honest.

"You didn't answer me. Do you want to leave?"

Another something hit the wall, and the idea sounded appealing. The worst attack I'd gotten at home was Gerad trying to steal my food. The girls here didn't care for me, the clothes were stifling, people were trying to hurt me, and the whole thing felt uncomfortable. But it was good for my family and nice to be full. Maxon did seem a bit lost, and I'd get to stay away from *him* for a little bit longer. And who knew, maybe I could help pick out the next princess.

I looked Maxon in the eye. "If you're not kicking me out, I'm not leaving."

He smiled. "Good. You'll need to tell me more tricks like this shoulder-patting thing."

I smiled back. Yes, it was all wrong, but some good would come out of this.

"America, could you do me a favor?"

I nodded.

"As far as anyone knows, we spent a lot of time together yesterday evening. If anyone asks, could you please tell them that I'm not . . . that I wouldn't . . . ."

"Of course. And I really am sorry about everything."

"I should have known that if any girl was going to disobey an order, it would be you."

A collection of heavy objects hit the wall at once, making a handful of girls scream.

"Who are they? What do they want?" I asked.

"Who? The rebels?"

I nodded.

"Depends on who you ask. And which group you're talking about," he answered.

"You mean there's more than one?" That made the entire experience much worse. If this was one group, what could two or more do together? As far as I knew, a rebel was a rebel was a rebel, but Maxon made it sound like some could be worse than others. "How many are there?"

"Two generally, the Northerners and the Southerners. The Northerners attack much more frequently. They're closer.

They live in the rainy patch of Likely near Bellingham, just north of here. No one really wants to live there—it's practically all ruins—so they've made it a home of sorts, though I guess they travel. The traveling is one theory of mine—one no one listens to. But they're far less likely to break in, and when they do the results are . . . tame almost. I'd guess that this is a Northern job right now," he said over the din.

"Why? What makes them so different from the Southerners?"

Maxon seemed to hesitate, unsure if this information was something I should know. He looked around to see if anyone could hear us. I looked around, too, and saw that several people were watching us. In particular, Celeste looked like she was trying to set me on fire with her eyes. I didn't keep eye contact for long. Still, even with all the onlookers, no one was close enough to hear. When Maxon came to the same conclusion, he leaned in to whisper.

"Their attacks are much more . . . lethal."

I shivered. "Lethal?"

He nodded. "They only come about once or twice a year, as best I can tell from the aftermath. I think that everyone here is trying to protect me from the statistics, but I'm not stupid. People die when they come. The trouble is, both groups look alike to us—dingy, mostly men, lean but strong, no sort of emblem as far as we can tell—so we don't know what we're getting until it's all over."

I looked around the room. A lot of people were in danger if Maxon was wrong and they happened to be Southerners.

I thought of my poor maids again.

"But I still don't understand. What do they want?"

Maxon shrugged. "The Southerners appear to want us demolished. I don't know why, but I'm guessing some dissatisfaction or another, tired of living on the fringes of society. I mean, they're not even Eights technically, since they have no part in the social network. But the Northerners are a bit of a mystery. Father says they just want to bother us, disrupt our governing, but I don't think so." He looked rather proud for a moment. "I have another theory about that as well."

"Do I get to know it?"

Maxon hesitated again. I guessed this time it wasn't so much out of fear of scaring me, but perhaps not being taken seriously.

He came close again and whispered, "I think they're looking for something."

"What?" I wondered.

"That I don't know. But it's always the same around here after the Northerners come. Guards are knocked out, injured, or tied up, but never killed. It's like they just don't want to be followed around. Though some people get taken with them, and that's a bit disturbing. And then the rooms— well, all the ones they can get into—they're a mess. Every drawer pulled out, shelves searched, carpet upturned. Lots of things get broken. You wouldn't believe the number of cameras I've replaced over the years."

"Cameras?"

"Oh," he said bashfully. "I like photography. But despite

all that, they don't end up taking much. Father thinks my idea is rubbish, of course. What could a bunch of illiterate barbarians be looking for? Still, I think there must be something."

It was intriguing. If I was penniless and knew how to break into the palace, I think I'd take every piece of jewelry I could find, anything I could sell. These rebels must have something in mind beyond a mere political statement or their day-to-day survival in mind when they came here.

"Do you think it's silly?" Maxon asked, bringing me out of my wonderings.

"No, not silly. Confusing, but not silly."

We shared a small smile. I realized that if Maxon had simply been Maxon Schreave and not Maxon, future king of Illéa, he would be the kind of person I would have wanted to be my next-door neighbor, someone to talk to.

He cleared his throat. "I suppose I should finish my rounds."

"Yes, I imagine there are quite a few ladies wondering what's taking you so long."

"So, *buddy*, any suggestions as to whom I should speak with next?"

I smiled and looked behind me to make sure my candidate for princess was still holding it together. She was.

"See the blond girl over there in the pink? That's Marlee. Sweetheart, very kind, loves movies. Go."

Maxon chuckled and walked in her direction.

・＜

The time in the dining hall felt like an eternity, but the attack had only lasted a little over an hour. We found out later that no one had actually gotten inside the palace, just inside the grounds. The guards didn't shoot at the rebels until they tried for the main doors, which accounted for the bricks—bricks that had been gouged out of the palace walls—and rotten food being thrown at the windows for so long.

In the end, two men got too close to the doors, shots were fired, and they all fled. If Maxon's labels were correct, I would assume these were Northerners.

They kept us tucked away for a little while longer, searching the perimeter of the palace. When everything was as it should be, we were released to our rooms. I walked arm in arm with Marlee. Despite holding it together downstairs, the strain of the attack had exhausted me, and I was glad to have someone to distract me from it.

"He let you have the pants anyway?" she asked. I had started talking about Maxon as soon as I could, eager to know how their conversation had gone.

"Yeah. He was very generous about it all."

"I think it's charming that he's a good winner."

"He is a good winner. He's even gracious when he's gotten the raw end of things." Like a knee to the royal jewels, for example.

"What do you mean?"

"Nothing." I didn't want to explain that one. "What did you two talk about today?"

"Well, he asked me if I'd like to see him this week." She blushed.

"Marlee! That's great!"

"Hush!" she said, looking around, though the rest of the girls had already ascended the stairs. "I'm trying not to get my hopes up."

We were quiet for a minute before she burst.

"Who am I kidding? I'm so excited I can barely stand it! I hope he won't take too long to call on me."

"If he's already asked, I'm sure he'll follow through soon. I mean, after he finishes running the country for the day, that is."

She laughed. "I can't believe this! I mean, I knew he was handsome, but I wasn't sure how he'd behave. I was worried he'd be . . . I don't know, stuffy or something."

"Me, too. But he's actually . . ." What was Maxon actually? He was sort of stuffy, but not in a way that was as off-putting as I'd imagined. Undeniably a prince, but still so . . . so . . . "Normal."

Marlee wasn't looking at me anymore. She'd lost herself in a daydream as we walked. I hoped that this image of Maxon that she was building was one he could deliver. And that she would be the kind of girl he wanted. I left her at her door with a small wave and went on to my room.

My thoughts of Marlee and Maxon flew out of my head as soon as I opened the door. Anne and Mary were crouched around a very distressed Lucy. Her face was red with tears falling down her cheeks; her usual tiny trembles were full-on shakes, racking her entire body.

"Calm down now, Lucy, everything's fine," Anne was whispering as she stroked Lucy's messy hair.

"Everything is over now. No one was hurt. You're safe, dear," Mary cooed, holding a twitching hand.

I was too shocked to speak. This moment was Lucy's private struggle, not meant for my eyes. I went to back out of my room, but Lucy caught me before I could back away.

"S-s-sorry, Lady, Lady, Lady . . . ," she stammered. The others looked up with anxious expressions.

"Don't trouble yourself. Are you all right?" I asked, closing the door so no one else would see.

Lucy tried to start again, but couldn't form the words. Her tears and the shaking were overwhelming her little body.

"She'll be fine, miss," Anne interceded. "It takes a few hours, but she calms down once everything's quiet. If it stays bad, we can take her to the hospital wing." Anne dropped her voice. "Only Lucy doesn't want that. If they think you're unfit, they hide you down in the laundry rooms or the kitchen. Lucy likes being a maid."

I didn't know who Anne thought she was hiding her voice from. We were all surrounding Lucy, and she could hear those words clearly, even in her state.

"P-p-please, miss. I don't—I don't—I . . . ," she tried.

"Hush. No one's turning you in," I told her. I looked to Anne and Mary. "Help me get her on the bed."

With the three of us it should have been easy, but Lucy was writhing so that her arms and legs would slip from our hands. It took quite a bit of effort to get her settled. Once we tucked her under the covers, the comfort of the bed seemed to do more than our words could. Lucy's shudders became slower, and she stared vacantly at the canopy above the bed.

Mary sat on the edge of the bed and started humming a tune, reminding me all too much of the way I would baby May when she was sick. I pulled Anne into a corner, far away from Lucy's ears.

"What happened? Did someone get through?" I asked. I would expect to be told if that were the case.

"No, no," Anne assured me. "Lucy always gets like this when the rebels come. Just talking about them will send her into a crying fit. She . . ."

Anne looked down to her polished black shoes, trying to decide if she should tell me something. I didn't want to pry into Lucy's life, but I did want to understand. She took a deep breath and started.

"Some of us were born here. Mary was born in the castle, and her parents are still here. I was an orphan, taken in because the palace needed staff." She straightened her dress, as if she could rub off this piece of her history that seemed to bother her. "Lucy was sold to the palace."

"Sold? How can that be? There aren't slaves here."

"Not technically, no, but that doesn't mean it doesn't happen. Lucy's family needed money for an operation for her mother. They gave their services over to a family of Threes in exchange for the money. Her mother never got better, they never made their way out of the debt, so Lucy and her father had been living with this family for ages. From what I understand, it wasn't much better than living in a barn with the way they were kept.

"The son had taken a liking to Lucy, and I know sometimes it doesn't matter what caste you're in, but Six to Three is quite a jump. When his mother discovered his intentions for Lucy, she sold her and her father to the palace. I remember when she came. Cried for days. They must have been terribly in love."

I looked over at Lucy. At least in my case, one of us got to make the decision. She had no choice when it came to losing the man she loved.

"Lucy's dad works in the stables. He's not very fast or strong, but he's incredibly dedicated. And Lucy is a maid. I know it might seem silly to you, but it's an honor to be a maid in the palace. We are the front line. We are the ones deemed fit enough and smart enough and attractive enough to be seen by anyone who comes to call. We take our positions seriously, and with reason. If you screw up, you're put in the kitchen, where your fingers are working all day, and the clothes are baggy. Or you chop firewood or rake the grounds. It's no small thing to be a maid."

I felt stupid. In my mind, they were all Sixes. But there were rankings even within that, statuses that I didn't understand.

"Two years ago, there was an attack on the palace in the middle of the night. They got the guards' uniforms, and everyone was confused. It was such disarray, no one knew who to attack or defend, and people slipped through holes in the lines . . . it was terrifying."

I shuddered just thinking about it. The dark, the confusion, the wide expanse of the palace. Compared to this morning, it sounded like the work of Southerners.

"One of the rebels got ahold of Lucy." Anne ducked her eyes for a minute. She spoke her next lines quietly. "I'm not sure they have very many women with them, if you catch my meaning."

"Oh."

"I didn't see this myself, but Lucy told me that this man was covered in grime. She said he kept licking her face."

Anne cringed away from the thought. My stomach heaved, threatening to bring up my breakfast. It was positively revolting, and I could see how someone who'd already been as scarred as Lucy would break under that kind of attack.

"He was dragging her off somewhere, and she was screaming as loud as she could. In the commotion, it was hard to hear her cries. But another guard came around the corner, a real one. He took aim and fired a bullet right through the man's head. The rebel fell to the ground, pinning Lucy. She was covered in blood."

I covered my mouth. I couldn't imagine delicate little Lucy going through all that. No wonder she reacted this way.

"She was treated for some cuts, but no one ever really saw to her mind. She's a little jittery now but tries to hide it as best she can. And it's not just for her sake, but her father's. He's so proud that his daughter is good enough to be a maid. She doesn't want to let him down. We try to keep her calm, but every time the rebels come, she thinks it's going to be worse. Someone's going to take her this time, hurt her, kill her.

"She's trying, miss, but I'm not sure how much more of this she can stand."

I nodded, looking over to Lucy in the bed. She had closed her eyes and fallen asleep, even though it was still quite early.

I spent the rest of the day reading. Anne and Mary cleaned things that weren't dirty. We all stayed quiet while Lucy recovered.

I promised myself that, if I could help it, Lucy wouldn't have to go through that again.

CHAPTER 14

As I PREDICTED, THE GIRLS who had asked to go home changed their minds once everything had settled down. None of us knew exactly who had wanted out, but there were some—Celeste in particular—who were determined to find out. For the time being we remained at twenty-seven girls.

The attack was so inconsequential, according to the king, that it barely warranted notice. However, since camera crews had been making their way in that morning, some of it was aired live. Apparently the king wasn't pleased about that. It made me wonder just how many attacks the palace suffered through that we never heard about. Was it far less safe here than I'd thought?

Silvia explained that if the attack had been much worse, we would have all been able to call our families and tell them we were safe. As it was, we were instructed to write letters home instead.

I wrote that I was well and that the attack probably seemed worse than it was and that the king had us all kept safely tucked away. I urged them not to worry about me and told them that I missed them and handed the letter off to a helpful maid.

The day after the attack passed without incident. I had planned on going down to the Women's Room to talk up Maxon to the others, but after seeing Lucy so shaken, I chose to keep to my room.

I didn't know what my three maids busied themselves with while I was away, but when I was in the room, they played card games with me and let pieces of gossip slip into the conversation.

I learned that for every dozen people I saw in the palace, there were a hundred or more behind them. The cooks and laundresses I knew about, but there were also people whose sole job was to keep the windows clean. It took a solid week for the team to get them all done, by the end of which the dust would find its way past the palace walls and cling to the clean glass, and they'd have to be washed all over again. There were also jewelers hidden away, making pieces for the family and gifts for visitors, and teams of seamstresses and buyers keeping the royal family—and now us—immaculately clothed.

I learned other things, too. The guards they thought were the cutest and the horrid new design of a dress the head maid was making the staff wear for the holiday parties. How some in the palace were taking bets on which Selected girl might win and that I was in the top ten picks. A baby of one of the cooks was sick beyond hope, which made Anne tear up a bit. This girl happened to be a close friend of hers, and the couple had been waiting so long for a child.

Listening to them and joining in when I had something worth saying, I couldn't imagine anything more entertaining happening downstairs and was glad to have such company. The mood in my room was a quiet and happy one.

The day had been so nice, I stayed up there the day after as well. This time, we kept the doors open to both the hallway and the balcony, and the warm air filtered in and wrapped itself around us. It seemed to do particularly wonderful things for Lucy, and I wondered how often she actually got to step outside.

Anne made a comment about how this was all inappropriate—me sitting with them, playing games with the doors open—but let it drop almost immediately. She was quickly getting over trying to make me the lady it seemed I ought to be.

We were in the middle of a game of cards when I noticed a figure out of the corner of my eye. It was Maxon, standing at the open door, looking amused. As our eyes met, I could see that his expression was clearly asking what in the world I was doing. I stood, smiling, and walked over to him.

"Oh, sweet Lord," Anne muttered as she realized the prince was at the door. She immediately swept the cards into a sewing basket and stood, Mary and Lucy following suit.

"Ladies," Maxon said.

"Your Majesty," she said with a curtsy. "Such an honor, sir."

"For me as well," he answered with a smile.

The maids looked back and forth to one another, flattered. We were all silent for a moment, not quite sure what to do.

Mary suddenly piped up. "We were just leaving."

"Yes! That's right," Lucy added. "We were—uh—just . . ." She looked to Anne for help.

"Going to finish Lady America's dress for Friday," Anne concluded.

"That's right," Mary said. "Only two days left."

They slowly circled us to get out of the room, huge smiles plastered on their faces.

"Wouldn't want to keep you from your work," Maxon said, following them with his eyes, completely fascinated with their behavior.

Once in the hall, they gave awkwardly mistimed curtsies and walked away at a feverish pace. Immediately after they rounded the corner, Lucy's giggles echoed down the corridor, followed by Anne's intense hushing.

"Quite a group you have," Maxon said, walking into my room, surveying the space.

"They keep me on my toes," I answered with a smile.

"It's clear they have affection for you. That's hard to find." He stopped looking at my room and faced me. "This isn't what I imagined your room would look like."

I raised an arm and let it fall. "It's not really my room, is it? It belongs to you, and I just happen to be borrowing it."

He made a face. "Surely they told you that changes could be made? A new bed, different paint."

I shrugged. "A coat of paint wouldn't make this mine. Girls like me don't live in houses with marble floors," I joked.

Maxon smiled. "What does your room at home look like?"

"Um, what did you come for exactly?" I hedged.

"Oh! I had an idea."

"About?"

"Well," he started, continuing to walk around the room, "I thought that since you and I don't have the typical relationship that I have with the other girls, maybe we should have . . . alternative means of communication." He stopped in front of my mirror and looked at the pictures of my family. "Your little sister looks just like you," he said, amused by this observation.

I walked deeper into my room. "We get that a lot. What was that about alternative communication?"

Maxon finished up with the pictures and moved toward the piano in the back. "Since you are supposed to be helping me, being my friend and all," he continued with a pointed look at me, "perhaps we shouldn't be relying on the traditional notes sent through maids and formal invitations for dates. I was thinking something a little less ceremonial."

He picked up the sheet music on top of the piano. "Did you bring these?"

"No, those were here. Anything I really want to play, I can do from memory."

His eyebrows rose. "Impressive." He moved back in my direction without finishing his explanation.

"Could you please stop poking around and complete an entire thought?"

Maxon sighed. "Fine. What I was thinking was that you and I could have a sign or something, some way of communicating that we need to speak to each other that no one else would catch onto. Perhaps rubbing our noses?" Maxon ran a finger back and forth just above his lips.

"That looks like your nose is stopped up. Not attractive."

He gave me a slightly perplexed look and nodded. "Very well. Perhaps we could simply run our fingers through our hair?"

I shook my head almost immediately. "My hair is almost always pulled up with pins. It's nearly impossible to get my fingers through it. Besides, what if you happen to be wearing your crown? You'd knock it off your head."

He shook a thoughtful finger at me. "Excellent point. Hmmm." He passed me, continuing to think, and stopped near the table by my bed. "What about tugging your ear?"

I considered. "I like it. Simple enough to hide, but not so common we could mistake it for something else. Ear tugging it is."

Maxon's attention was fixated on something, but he

turned to smile at me. "I'm glad you approve. The next time you want to see me, simply tug your ear, and I'll come as soon as I'm able. Probably after dinner," he concluded with a shrug.

Before I could ask about me coming to him, Maxon strolled across the room with my jar in his hand. "What in the world is this about?"

I sighed. "That, I'm afraid, is beyond explanation."

Friday arrived, and with that came our debut on the *Illéa Capital Report*. It was something that was required of us, but at least this week all we had to do was sit there. With the time difference, we'd go on at five, sit through the hour, and then go off to dinner.

Anne, Mary, and Lucy took extra care in dressing me. The gown was a deep blue, hovering near purple. It was fitted through my hips, and fanned out in satiny smooth waves behind me. I couldn't believe I was touching something so beautiful. Button after button was fastened up my back, and my maids put pins bedecked with pearls in my hair. They added tiny pearl earrings and a necklace made of wire so thin and pearls so far apart they looked like they floated on my skin, and I was done.

I looked in the mirror. I still looked like me. It was the prettiest version of myself I'd seen so far, but I knew that face. Ever since my name had been drawn, I'd feared I would become something unrecognizable—covered in layers of makeup and so hung down with jewelry that I'd have to dig out of it for weeks to find myself again. So far, I was still America.

And, exactly like myself, I found that I was covered in a sheen of sweat as I walked down to the room where they recorded messages at the palace. They'd told us to be there ten minutes early. Ten minutes meant fifteen to me. It meant more like three to someone like Celeste. So the arrival of the girls was staggered.

Hordes of people were swarming around, putting the last touches on the set—which now held rows of tiered seating for the Selected. The council members who I recognized from years of watching the *Report* were there, reading over their scripts and adjusting their ties. The Selected crowd were checking themselves in mirrors and tugging at their extravagant dresses. It was a flurry of activity.

I turned and caught the briefest of moments in Maxon's life. His mother, the beautiful Queen Amberly, pushed some stray hairs back into place. He straightened his jacket and said something to her. She gave a reassuring nod, and Maxon smiled. I would have watched a little longer, but Silvia, in all her glory, came to escort me into place.

"Just head over to the risers, Lady America," she said. "You may sit anywhere you like. So you know, most of the girls have already claimed the front row." She looked sorry for me, as if she were delivering bad news.

"Oh, thank you," I said, and went happily to take a seat in the back.

I didn't like climbing the little steps with a snug dress and such strappy shoes. (Were the shoes really necessary? No one was even going to see my feet.) But I managed. When I saw Marlee come in, she smiled and waved and came to sit right next to me. It meant a great deal to me that she chose a place beside me as opposed to a spot in the second row. She was faithful. She'd make a great queen.

Her dress was a brilliant yellow. With her blond hair and sun-kissed skin, she looked like she was radiating light into the room.

"Marlee, I love that dress. You look fantastic!"

"Oh, thank you." She blushed. "I thought it might be a bit too much."

"Not at all! Trust me, it's perfect on you."

"I've wanted to speak to you, but you've been missing. Do you think we could talk tomorrow?" she asked in a whisper.

"Of course. In the Women's Room, right? It's Saturday," I said in a matched tone.

"Okay," she answered excitedly.

Just in front of us, Amy turned around. "I feel like my pins are falling out. Can you guys check them?"

Without a word, Marlee put her slim fingers in the curls of Amy's hair and checked for loose pins. "That feel better?"

Amy sighed. "Yes, thank you."

"America, is there lipstick on my teeth?" Zoe asked. I turned to my left and found her smiling maniacally, exposing all her pearly whites.

"No, you're good," I answered, seeing out of the corner of my eye that Marlee was nodding in confirmation.

"Thanks. How is he so calm?" Zoe asked, pointing over at Maxon, who was talking to a member of the crew. She then bent down and put her head between her legs and started doing controlled breathing.

Marlee and I looked at each other, eyes wide with amusement, and tried not to laugh. It was hard if we looked at Zoe, so we surveyed the room and chatted about what others were wearing. There were several girls in seductive reds and lively greens, but no one else in blue. Olivia had gone so far as to wear orange. I'd admit that I didn't know that much about fashion, but Marlee and I both agreed that someone should have intervened on her behalf. The color made her skin look kind of green.

Two minutes before the cameras turned on, we realized it wasn't the dress making her look green. Olivia vomited into the closest trash can very loudly and collapsed on the floor. Silvia swooped in, and a fuss was made to wipe the sweat off her and get her into a seat. She was placed in the back row with a small receptacle at her feet, just in case.

Bariel was in the seat in front of her. I couldn't hear what she muttered to the poor girl from where I was, but it looked like Bariel was prepared to injure Olivia should she have another episode near her.

I guessed that Maxon had seen or heard some of the commotion, and I looked over to see if he was having any sort of reaction to it all. But he wasn't looking toward the disturbance; he was looking at me. Quickly—so quickly it would look like nothing but scratching an itch to anyone

177

else—Maxon reached up and tugged on his ear. I repeated the action back, and we both turned away.

I was excited to know that tonight, after dinner, Maxon would be stopping by my room.

Suddenly the anthem music was playing, and I could see the national emblem on tiny screens around the room. I shifted to sit up straighter. All I could think was that my family was going to see me tonight, and I wanted them to be proud.

King Clarkson was at the podium speaking about the brief and unsuccessful attack on the palace. I wouldn't have called it unsuccessful. It managed to scare the daylights out of most of us. Announcement after announcement came, and I tried to be aware of everything they said, but it was hard. I was used to watching this on a comfy couch with bowls of popcorn and family commentary.

Many of the announcements tied into the rebels, placing blame for certain things on their shoulders. The roads being built in Sumner were behind schedule because of the rebels, and the number of local officers in Atlin was down because they'd been sent to help with a rebel-caused disturbance in St. George. I had no idea either of those things had happened. Between everything I'd heard and seen growing up and what I'd learned since coming to the palace, I began to wonder just how much we knew about the rebels. Maybe I just didn't understand, but I didn't think they could be blamed for everything that was wrong with Illéa.

And then, as if he had appeared out of thin air, Gavril

was walking on set after being introduced by the Master of Events.

"Good evening, everyone. Tonight I have a special announcement. The Selection has been going for a week now and eight ladies have already gone home, leaving twenty-seven beautiful women for Prince Maxon to choose from. Next week, by hook or by crook, the majority of the *Illéa Capital Report* will be dedicated to getting to know these amazing young women."

I felt the little beads of sweat pooling on my temple. Sit here and look nice . . . I could do that. But answer questions? I knew I wasn't going to win this little game; that wasn't the issue. I just really, really didn't want to look like a moron in front of the entire country.

"Before we get to the ladies, tonight let's take a moment with the man of the hour. How are you tonight, Prince Maxon?" Gavril said, walking across the stage. Maxon had been ambushed. He didn't have a microphone or prepared answers.

Just before Gavril's microphone reached Maxon's face, I caught his eye and gave him a wink. That tiny action was enough to make him smile.

"I'm very well, Gavril, thank you."

"Are you enjoying your company so far?"

"Yes! It's been a pleasure getting to know these ladies."

"Are they all the sweet, gentle ladies they appear to be?" Gavril asked. Before Maxon replied, the answer brought a smile to my face. Because I knew that it was yes . . . sort of.

"Umm . . ." Maxon looked past Gavril at me. "Almost."

"Almost?" Gavril asked, surprised. He turned to us. "Is someone over there being naughty?"

Mercifully, all the girls let out light giggles, so I blended in. The little traitor!

"What exactly did these girls do that isn't so sweet?" Gavril asked Maxon.

"Oh, well, let me tell you." Maxon crossed his legs and got very comfortable in his chair. It was probably the most relaxed I'd ever seen him, sitting there poking fun at me. I liked this side of him. I wished it would come out more often. "One of them had the nerve to yell at me rather forcefully the first time we met. I was given a very severe scolding."

Above Maxon's head, the king and queen exchanged a glance. It seemed they were hearing this story for the first time, too. Beside me the girls were looking at one another, confused. I didn't get it until Marlee said something.

"I don't remember anyone yelling at him in the Great Room. Do you?"

Maxon seemed to have forgotten that our first meeting was meant to be a secret. "I think he's talking it up to make it funnier. I did say some serious things to him. I think he might mean me."

"A scolding, you say? Whatever for?" Gavril continued.

"Honestly, I wasn't really sure. I think it was a bout of homesickness. Which is why I forgave her, of course." Maxon was loose and easy now, talking to Gavril as if he were the only person in the room. I'd have to tell him later how wonderful he did.

"So she's still with us, then?" Gavril looked over at the collection of girls, grinning widely, and then returned to face his prince.

"Oh, yes. She's still here," Maxon said, not letting his eyes wander from Gavril's face. "And I plan on keeping her here for quite a while."

CHAPTER 15

DINNER WAS DISAPPOINTING. NEXT WEEK I'd have to tell my maids to leave some room in the dress for me to eat.

In my room, Anne, Mary, and Lucy waited to help me out of my gown, but I explained that I'd need to stay in it a little bit longer. Anne figured it out first—that Maxon was coming to see me—because I was always eager to get out of the binding clothes.

"Would you like us to stay later tonight? It's no problem," Mary said just a little too hopefully. After the calamity of Maxon visiting earlier this week, I decided sending them out as early as possible was the best way to go. Besides, I couldn't bear to have them watching me until he showed up.

"No, no. I'm fine. If I have a problem with the dress later, I'll ring."

They reluctantly backed out the door and left me to wait

for Maxon. I didn't know how long he'd be, and I didn't want to start a book and have to stop, or sit down at the piano only to hop right back up. I ended up just lounging on the bed, waiting. I let my mind wander. I thought of Marlee and her kindness. I realized that, besides a few small details, I knew very little about her. Still, I trusted that her actions toward me were in no way fake. And then I thought of the girls who were all too fake. I wondered if Maxon could tell the difference.

It seemed like Maxon's experience with women was so great and so small at once. He was gentlemanly enough, but when he got too close, he came undone. It was like he knew how to treat a lady, he just didn't know how to treat a date.

It was quite a contrast to Aspen.

Aspen.

His name, his face, his memory hit me so quickly it was hard to process. Aspen. What was he doing now? It was getting close to curfew in Carolina. He'd still be at work, if he had a job today. Or maybe out with Brenna, or whoever else he'd decided to start spending his time with since we broke up. Part of me ached to know . . . part of me wanted to crumble just thinking about it.

I looked over to my jar. I picked it up and felt the penny slide around, so lonely.

"Me, too," I whispered. "Me, too."

Was it stupid of me to keep this? I'd given back everything else, so why save one little penny? Would this be all I had left? A penny in a jar to show my daughter one day, to tell her about my first boyfriend—the one no one knew about?

I didn't have time to dwell on my worries. Maxon's firm knock came only minutes later. I found myself running to the door.

I drew it open in a big sweep, and Maxon looked surprised to see me.

"Where in the world are your maids?" he asked, surveying my room.

"Gone. I send them off when I come back from dinner."

"Every day?"

"Yes, of course. I can take my clothes off by myself, thank you."

Maxon raised his eyebrows and smiled. I blushed. I hadn't meant it to come out like that.

"Grab a wrap. It's chilly out."

We walked down the hall. I was still a little distracted by my thoughts, and I knew by now that Maxon wasn't great with starting conversations. I had looped my hand around his arm almost immediately, though. I was glad that there was a sort of familiarity there.

"If you insist on not keeping your maids around, I'm going to have to post a guard outside your door," he said.

"No! I don't like being babysat."

He chuckled. "He'd be *outside*. You wouldn't even know he was there."

"I would too," I complained. "I'd sense his presence."

Maxon made a playfully exhausted sigh. I was so busy arguing, I didn't hear the whispers until they were practically in front of us. Celeste, Emmica, and Tiny were heading past us toward their rooms.

"Ladies," Maxon said, and gave a small head nod.

I supposed it was foolish to think no one would see us together. I felt my face heat up, but I wasn't sure why.

The girls all curtsied and carried on their way. I looked over my shoulder at them as we went toward the stairs. Emmica and Tiny looked curious. Within minutes, they would be telling others about this. I would be cornered tomorrow for sure. Celeste was staring daggers at me. I was sure she thought I had personally wronged her.

I turned away and said the first thing that came to mind.

"I told you the girls who got nervous about the attack would end up staying." I didn't know exactly who had asked to leave, but rumors pointed to Tiny as being one. She had fainted. Someone else had said Bariel, but I knew that was a lie. You'd have to pry the crown out of her cold dead hands first.

"You can't imagine what a relief that was." He sounded sincere.

It took me a moment to think of how to respond, as that wasn't quite what I was expecting, and I was very focused on not falling. I didn't know how to take steps down very well while holding on to someone else. The heels didn't help. At least if I slipped, he would grab me.

"I would have thought it would be helpful in a way," I said as we made it to the first floor and I found my footing again. "I mean, it has to be complicated to pick one person out of all these girls. If the circumstances weeded some out for you, shouldn't that make it easier?"

Maxon shrugged. "I suppose it should. But it didn't feel that way at all, I assure you." He looked hurt. "Good evening, sirs," he greeted the guards, who opened the doors to the garden without the slightest hesitation. Maybe I would have to take Maxon up on that offer to have them know I liked to go outside. The idea of being able to escape so easily was appealing.

"I don't understand," I said as he led me to a bench—our bench—and let me sit facing the lights of the palace. He took a seat with his body facing the opposite direction, so that we were sort of turned in toward each other. It was an easy way to talk.

He looked hesitant about sharing, but he took a breath and spoke. "Maybe I was just flattering myself, thinking I'd be worth some sort of risk. Not that I'd wish that on anyone!" he clarified. "I don't mean that. It just . . . I don't know. Don't you all see everything *I'm* risking?"

"Umm, no. You're here with your family to give you advice, and we all live around your schedule. Everything about your life stays the same, and ours changed overnight. What in the world could you possibly be risking?"

Maxon looked shocked.

"America, I might have my family, but imagine how embarrassing it is to have your parents watch as you attempt to date for the first time. And not just your parents—the whole country! Worse than that, it's not even a normal style of dating.

"And living around my schedule? When I'm not with you all, I'm organizing troops, making laws, perfecting budgets . . . and all on my own these days, while my father watches me stumble in my own stupidity because I have none of his experience. And then, when I inevitably do things in a way he wouldn't, he goes and corrects my mistakes. And while I'm trying to do all this work, you—the girls, I mean—are all I can think about. I'm excited and terrified by the lot of you!"

He was using his hands more than I'd ever seen, whipping them in the air and running them through his hair.

"And you think my life isn't changing? What do you think my chances might be of finding a soul mate in the group of you? I'll be lucky if I can just find someone who'll be able to stand me for the rest of our lives. What if I've already sent her home because I was relying on some sort of spark I didn't feel? What if she's waiting to leave me at the first sign of adversity? What if I don't find anyone at all? What do I do then, America?"

His speech had started out angered and impassioned, but by the end his questions weren't rhetorical anymore. He really wanted to know: What was he going to do if no one here was even close to being someone he could love? Though that didn't even seem to be his main concern; he was more worried that no one would love him.

"Actually, Maxon, I think you will find your soul mate here. Honestly."

"Really?" His voice charged with hope at my prediction.

"Absolutely." I put a hand on his shoulder. He seemed to be comforted by that touch alone. I wondered how often people simply touched him. "If your life is as upside down as you say it is, then she has to be here somewhere. In my experience, true love is usually the most inconvenient kind." I smiled weakly.

He seemed happy to hear those words, and they consoled me as well. Because I believed them. And if I couldn't have love of my own, the best I could do was help Maxon find it himself.

"I hope you and Marlee hit it off. She's incredibly sweet."

Maxon made a strange face. "She seems so."

"What? Is something wrong with sweet?"

"No, no. Sweet is good."

He didn't elaborate.

"What do you keep looking for?" he asked suddenly.

"What?"

"You can't seem to keep your eyes in one place. I can tell that you're paying attention, but you seem to be looking for something."

I realized he was right. All through his little speech, I'd scanned the garden and the windows and even the towers along the walls. I was getting paranoid.

"People . . . cameras . . ." I shook my head as I looked into the night.

"We're alone. There's just the guard by the door." Maxon pointed to the lone figure in the palace lamplight. He was right, no one had followed us out, and the windows were all lit up but vacant. I'd seen that already through my scanning, but it helped to have it confirmed.

I felt my posture relax a little.

"You don't like people watching you, do you?" he asked.

"Not really. I prefer being below the radar. That's what I'm used to, you know?" I traced the patterns carved into the perfect block of stone beneath me, not meeting his eyes.

"You'll have to adjust to that. When you leave here, eyes will be on you for the rest of your life. My mom still talks to some of the women she was with when she went through the Selection. They're all viewed as important women. Still."

"Great," I moaned. "Just one more thing I can't wait to go home to."

Maxon's face was apologetic, but I had to look away. I was freshly reminded of how much this stupid competition was costing me, how my idea of normal was never coming back. It didn't seem fair. . . .

But I checked myself again. I shouldn't take it out on Maxon. He was as much a victim in this as the rest of us, though in a very different way. I sighed and looked back to him. I saw his face set as he decided something.

"America, could I ask you something personal?"

"Maybe," I hedged. He gave me a humorless smile.

"It's just . . . well, I can tell that you really don't like it here. You hate the rules and the competition and the attention and the clothes and the . . . well, no, you like the food." He smiled. I did, too. "You miss your home and your family . . .

and I suspect other people very, very much. Your feelings are incredibly close to the surface."

"Yeah." I rolled my eyes. "I know."

"But you're willing to be homesick and miserable *here* instead of going home. Why?"

I felt the lump rise in my throat, and I pushed it back down.

"I'm not miserable . . . and you know why."

"Well, sometimes you seem okay. I see you smiling when you talk to some of the other girls, and you seem very content at meals, I'll give you that. But other times you just look so sad. Would you tell me why? The whole story?"

"It's just another failed love story. It's nothing big or exciting. Trust me." *Please don't push me. I don't want to cry.*

"For better or for worse, I'd like to know one true love story besides my parents', one that was outside these walls and the rules and the structure. . . . Please?"

The truth was I'd carried the secret for so long, I couldn't imagine putting it into words. And it hurt so much to think of Aspen. Could I even say his name out loud? I took a deep breath. Maxon was my friend now. He tried so hard to be nice to me. And he'd been so honest with me. . . .

"In the world out there"—I pointed past the vast walls— "the castes take care of one another. Sometimes. Like my father has three families who buy at least one painting every year, and I have families that always pick me to sing at their Christmas parties. They're our patrons, see?

"Well, we were sort of patrons to his family. They're Sixes.

When we could afford to have someone help clean or if we needed help with the inventory, we always called his mother. I knew him when we were kids, but he was older than me, closer to my brother's age. They always played rough, so I avoided them.

"My older brother, Kota, he's an artist like my dad. A few years back this one metal sculpture piece that he'd been working on for years sold for a massive amount of money. You may have heard of him."

Maxon mouthed the words *Kota Singer*. The seconds passed, and I saw the connection click in his brain.

I brushed my hair off my shoulders and braced myself.

"We were really excited for Kota; he'd worked really hard on that piece. And we needed that money so badly at the time, the whole family was elated. But Kota kept almost all the money for himself. That one sculpture catapulted him; people started calling for his work every day. Now he has a waiting list a mile long and charges through the roof because he can. I think he might be a little addicted to the fame. Fives rarely get that kind of notice."

Our eyes met in a very significant moment, and I thought again of how I was past ever going unnoticed again, whether I wanted to be or not.

"Anyway, after the calls started coming, Kota decided to detach himself from the family. My older sister had just gotten married, so we lost her income. Then Kota starts making real money, and he up and leaves us." I put my hands on Maxon's chest to emphasize my point. "You don't do that.

You don't just leave your family. Sticking together . . . it's the only way to survive."

I saw the understanding in Maxon's eyes. "He kept it all for himself. Trying to buy his way up?"

I nodded. "He's got his heart set on being a Two. If he was happy being a Three or Four, he could have bought that title and helped us, but he's obsessed. It's stupid, really. He lives more than comfortably, but it's that damn label he wants. He won't stop until he gets it."

Maxon shook his head. "That could take a lifetime."

"As long as he dies with a Two on his gravestone, I guess he doesn't care."

"I take it you're not close anymore?"

I sighed. "Not now. But at first I thought that I'd just misunderstood something. I thought that Kota was moving out to be independent, not to separate himself from us. In the beginning, I was on his side. When Kota got his apartment and studio set up, I went to help him. And he called the same family of Sixes we always did and their eldest son was available and eager and worked with Kota a few days helping set things up."

I paused, remembering.

"So there I was, just pulling things out of boxes . . . and there he was. Our eyes met, and he didn't seem so old or rough anymore. It had been awhile since we'd seen each other, you know? We weren't kids anymore.

"The whole day I was there, we would *accidentally* touch each other as we moved things around. He would look at me or smile, and I felt like I was really alive for the first time. I just . . . I was crazy about him."

My voice finally broke, and some of the tears I'd been longing to shed came out.

"We lived pretty close to each other, so I'd take walks during the day just in case I might get to see him. Whenever his mother came by to help, sometimes he'd show up too. And we'd just watch each other—that's all we could do." I let out a tiny sob. "He's a Six and I'm a Five, and there are laws . . . and my mother! Oh, she would have been furious. No one could know."

I was moving my hands a little spastically, the stress of all the secret-keeping coming to the surface.

"Soon, there were little anonymous notes left taped to my window telling me I was beautiful or that I sang like an angel. And I knew they were from him.

"The night of my fifteenth birthday, my mom threw a party and his family was invited. He cornered me and gave me my birthday card and told me to read it when I was alone. When I finally got to it, it didn't have his name or even a 'Happy Birthday' on the inside. It just said, 'Tree house. Midnight.'"

Maxon's eyes widened. "Midnight? But—"

"You should know that I break Illéa curfew regularly."

"You could have landed yourself in jail, America." He shook his head.

I shrugged. "Back then, it seemed inconsequential. That first time, I felt like I was flying. Here he was, figuring out a way for us to be alone together. I just couldn't believe he wanted to be alone with *me*.

"That night I waited up in my room and watched the tree house in my backyard. Near midnight, I saw someone climb up. I remember I actually went to brush my teeth again, just in case. I crept out my window and up the tree. And he was there. I just . . . I couldn't believe it.

"I don't remember how it started, but soon we were confessing how we felt about each other, and we couldn't stop laughing because we were so happy the other one felt the same way. And I just couldn't be bothered to worry about breaking curfew or lying to my parents. And I didn't care that I was a Five and he was a Six. I didn't worry about the future. Because nothing could matter as much as him loving me . . .

"And he did, Maxon, he did. . . ."

More tears. I clutched my chest, feeling Aspen's absence like I never had. Saying it out loud only made it more real. There was nothing to do but finish the story.

"We dated in secret for two years. We were happy, but he was always worried about us sneaking around and how he couldn't give me what he thought I deserved. When we got the notice about the Selection, he insisted that I sign up."

Maxon's mouth dropped open.

"I know. It was so stupid. But it would have hung over him forever if I didn't try. And I honestly, *honestly* thought that I would never get chosen. How could I?"

I raised my hands in the air and let them fall. I was

still baffled by it all.

"I found out from his mom that he'd been saving up to marry some mystery girl. I was so excited. I made him a little surprise dinner, thinking I could coax the proposal out of him. I was so ready.

"But when he saw all the money that I'd spent on him, it upset him. He's very proud. He wanted to spoil me, not the other way around, and I guess he saw then that he'd never be able to. So he broke up with me instead. . . .

"One week later, my name got called."

I heard Maxon whisper something unintelligible.

"The last time I saw him was at my send-off," I choked. "He was with another girl."

"WHAT?" Maxon shouted.

I buried my head in my hands.

"The thing is, it drives me crazy because I know other girls are after him, they always were, and now he has no reason to turn them down. Maybe he's even with the girl from my send-off. I don't know. And I can't do anything about it. But the thought of going home and watching it . . . I just can't, Maxon. . . ."

I wept and wept, and Maxon didn't rush me. When the tears finally started to slow, I spoke.

"Maxon, I hope you find someone you can't live without. I really do. And I hope you never have to know what it's like to have to try and live without them."

Maxon's face was a shallow echo of my own pain. He looked absolutely brokenhearted for me. More than that, he looked angry.

"I'm sorry, America. I don't . . ." His face shifted a little. "Is this a good time to pat your shoulder?"

His uncertainty made me smile. "Yes. Now would be a great time."

He seemed as skeptical as he'd been the other day, but instead of just patting my shoulder, he leaned in and tentatively wrapped his arms around me.

"I only really ever hug my mother. Is this okay?" he asked.

I laughed. "It's hard to get a hug wrong."

After a minute, I spoke again. "I know what you mean, though. I don't really hug anyone besides my family."

I felt so drained after the long day of dressing and the *Report* and dinner and talking. It was nice to have Maxon just hold me, sometimes even patting my hair. He wasn't as lost as he seemed. He patiently waited for my breathing to slow, and when it did, he pulled back to look at me.

"America, I promise you I'll keep you here until the last possible moment. I understand that they want me to narrow the Elite down to three and then choose. But I swear to you, I'll make it to two and keep you here until then. I won't make you leave a moment before I have to. Or the moment you're ready. Whichever comes first."

I nodded.

"I know we just met, but I think you're wonderful. And it bothers me to see you hurt. If he were here, I'd . . . I'd . . ." Maxon shook with frustration, then sighed. "I'm so sorry, America."

He pulled me back in, and I rested my head on his broad shoulder. I knew Maxon would keep his promises. So I settled into perhaps the last place I ever thought I'd find genuine comfort.

CHAPTER 16

WHEN I WOKE THE NEXT MORNING, my eyelids felt heavy. As I rubbed the tiny ache out of them, I felt glad that I'd told Maxon everything. It seemed so funny that the palace—the beautiful cage—was the one place I could actually let myself be open about everything I'd been feeling.

Maxon's promise settled in during the night, and I felt sure that I'd be safe here. This whole process of Maxon whittling down thirty-five women to one was going to take weeks, maybe months. Time and space were just what I needed. I couldn't be sure I'd ever get over Aspen. I'd heard my mom talk about your first love being the one that sticks with you. But maybe I'd be able to just feel normal sooner rather than later with this time in between us.

My maids didn't ask about my puffy eyes, they just made them less swollen. They didn't question my mess of hair, they just smoothed it. And I appreciated that. It wasn't like home, where everyone saw that I was sad and didn't do anything about it. Here I could feel that they were all worried about me and whatever it was I was going through. In response they handled me with extreme care.

By midmorning I was ready to start my day. It was Saturday, so there was no routine or schedule, but it was the one day a week we were all required to stay in the Women's Room. The palace saw guests on Saturdays, and we had been warned that people might want to meet us. I wasn't too excited about it, but at least I got to wear my new jeans for the first time. Of course, they were the best-fitting pair of pants I'd ever owned. I hoped that since Maxon and I were on such good terms, he'd let me keep them after I left.

I went downstairs slowly, a little tired from a late night. Before I even got to the Women's Room, I heard the buzz of talking girls, and when I walked in, Marlee grabbed me and pulled me toward two chairs in the back of the room.

"There you are! I've been waiting for you," she said.

"Sorry, Marlee. I had a long night and slept in."

She turned to look at me, probably noting the leftover sadness in my voice, but sweetly decided to focus on my jeans. "Those look fantastic."

"I know. I've never felt anything like them." My voice lifted a bit. I decided to go back to my old rule: Aspen wasn't allowed here. I pushed him away and focused on my second-favorite person in the palace. "Sorry to keep you waiting. What did you want to talk about?"

Marlee hesitated. She bit her lip as we sat down. There was no one else around. She must have a secret.

"Actually, now that I think of it, maybe I shouldn't tell you. Sometimes I forget that we're competing against each other."

Oh. She had secrets of the Maxon variety. This I had to hear.

"I know just how you feel, Marlee. I think we could become really close friends. I can't bring myself to think of you as an enemy, you know?"

"Yeah. I think you're so sweet. And the people love you. I mean, you're probably going to win. . . ." She seemed a little defeated at the idea.

I had to will myself not to wince or laugh at those words.

"Marlee, can I tell you a secret?" My voice was full of gentle truth. I hoped she would believe my words.

"Of course, America. Anything."

"I don't know who will win this whole thing. Really, it could be anyone in this room. I guess everyone thinks that it'll be them, but I already know that if it can't be me, I'd want it to be you. You seem generous and fair. I think you'd be a great princess. Honestly." It was almost all the truth.

"I think you're smart and personable," she whispered. "You'd be great, too."

I bowed my head. It was sweet of her to think so highly of me. I felt a bit uncomfortable when people talked about me that way, though . . . May, Kenna, my maids . . . it was hard to believe how many people thought I'd be a good princess.

Was I the only one who saw how flawed I was? I was unrefined. I didn't have it in me to be bossy or overly organized. I was selfish and had a horrible temper, and I didn't like being in front of people. And I wasn't brave. You had to be brave to take this job. And that's what this was. Not just a marriage, but a position.

"I feel that way about a lot of the girls," she confessed. "Like everyone has some quality that I don't that would make them better than me."

"That's the thing, Marlee. You could probably find something special about everyone in this room. But who knows exactly what Maxon is looking for?"

She shook her head.

"So let's not worry about that. You can tell me anything you want to. I'll keep your secrets if you keep mine. I'll pull for you, and if you want to, you can pull for me. It's nice to have friends here."

She smiled, then looked around the room, checking to make sure no one could hear us.

"Maxon and I had our date," she whispered.

"Yeah?" I asked. I knew I seemed overly eager, but I couldn't help it. I wanted to know if he'd managed to be any less stiff around her. And I wanted to know if he liked her.

"He sent a letter to my maids and asked if he could see me on Thursday." I smiled as Marlee spoke and thought of how the day before he'd done that, Maxon and I had decided to eliminate those formalities. "I sent one back saying yes, of course, like I'd ever turn him down! He came to get me, and we walked around the palace. We got to talking about movies, and it turns out we like a bunch of the same ones. So we went downstairs to the basement. Have you seen the movie theater down there?"

"No." I'd never actually been in a movie theater, and I couldn't wait for her to describe it.

"Oh, it's perfect! The seats are wide and they recline and you can even pop some popcorn—they have a popper. Maxon stood there and made a batch just for us! It was so cute, America. He measured the oil wrong and the first batch burned. He had to call someone to come and clean it up and try again."

I rolled my eyes. Smooth, Maxon, real smooth. At least Marlee seemed to think it was endearing.

"So we watched the movie, and when we got to the romantic part at the end, he held my hand! I thought I'd faint. I mean, I'd taken his arm when we walked, but that's just what you're supposed to do. Here he was taking my hand. . . ." She sighed and fell back into her chair.

I giggled out loud. She looked completely smitten. Yes, yes, yes!

"I can't wait for him to visit me again. He's just so handsome, don't you think?" she asked.

I paused. "Yeah, he's cute."

"Come on, America! You have to have noticed those eyes and his voice. . . ."

"Except when he laughs!" Just remembering Maxon's laugh had me grinning. It was cute but awkward. He pushed his breaths out, and then made a jagged noise when he inhaled, almost like another laugh in itself.

"Yes, okay, he does have a funny laugh, but it's cute."

"Sure, if you like the lovable sound of an asthma attack in your ear every time you tell a joke."

Marlee lost it and doubled over in laughter.

"All right, all right," she said, coming up for air. "You have to think there's something attractive about him."

I opened my mouth and shut it two or three times. I was tempted to take another jab at Maxon, but I didn't want Marlee to see him in a negative light. So I thought about it.

What was attractive about Maxon?

"Well, when he lets his guard down, he's okay. Like when he just talks without checking his words or you catch him just looking at something like . . . like he's really looking for the beauty in it."

Marlee smiled, and I knew she'd seen that in him, too.

"And I like that he seems genuinely involved when he's there, you know? Like even though he's got a country to run and a thousand things to do, it's like he forgets it all when he's with you. He just dedicates himself to what's right in front of him. I like that.

"And . . . well, don't tell anyone this, but his arms. I like his arms."

I blushed at the end. Stupid . . . why hadn't I just stuck to the general good things about his personality? Luckily, Marlee was happy to pick up the conversation.

"Yes! You can really feel them under those thick suits,

can't you? He must be incredibly strong," Marlee gushed.

"I wonder why. I mean, what's the point of him being that strong? He does deskwork. It's weird."

"Maybe he likes to flex in front of the mirror," Marlee said, making a face and flexing her own tiny arms.

"Ha, ha! I bet that's it. I dare you to ask him!"

"No way!"

It sounded like Marlee had had a great time. I wondered why Maxon seemed so reluctant to mention that last night. Based on his reaction, it seemed like they hadn't been together at all. Maybe he was shy?

I looked around the room and saw that more than half the girls seemed tense or unhappy. Janelle, Emmica, and Zoe were listening intently to something Kriss was saying. Kriss was smiling and animated, but Janelle's face was tight with worry, and Zoe was biting her nails. Emmica was absently kneading a spot just below her ear, as if she was in pain. Beside them the mismatched pair of Celeste and Anna sat having another intense discussion. True to her usual form, Celeste looked incredibly smug as she spoke. Marlee noted my staring and clarified what was happening.

"The grumpy ones are the girls he hasn't been out with yet. He told me I was his second date on Thursday alone. He's trying to spend time with everyone."

"Really? You think that's it?"

"Yeah. I mean, look at you and me. We're fine, and it's because he's seen us both one-on-one. We know he liked us enough to see us and not kick us out right afterward. It's getting around who he's spent time with and who he hasn't. They're worried he's waiting on them because he isn't interested, and that once he does see them, he'll just let them go."

Why hadn't he told me any of this? Weren't we friends? A friend would talk about this. He'd seen at least a dozen girls based on their smiles. We'd spent the better part of the evening together last night, and all he did was make me cry. What kind of friend held those kinds of secrets while making me spill all my own?

Tuesday, who had been listening to Camille with an anxious expression on her face, got up from her seat and looked around the room. She found Marlee and me in the corner and quickly walked over.

"What did you guys do on your date?" she asked abruptly.

"Hi, Tuesday," Marlee said cheerfully.

"Oh, hush!" she cried, and turned back to me. "Come on, America, spill."

"I told you."

"No. The one last night!" A maid came to the corner and offered us tea, which I was prepared to take, but Tuesday shooed her away.

"How . . . ?"

"Tiny saw you together and told," Marlee said, trying to explain Tuesday's mood. "You're the only one he's been alone with twice. A lot of the girls who haven't seen him yet were complaining. They don't think it's right. But it's not your fault if he likes you."

"It's completely unfair," Tuesday whined. "I haven't seen

him outside of mealtimes, not even in passing. What in the world did you two do?"

"We . . . uh . . . we went back to the gardens. He knows I like it outside. And we just talked." I felt nervous, like I was in trouble. Tuesday's face was so intense, I looked away. When I did, I saw that a few girls at nearby tables were listening in.

"You just talked?" she asked skeptically.

I shrugged. "That's it."

Tuesday huffed and went to Kriss's table, urging her to tell her story over again, quite energetically. I, however, was stunned.

"Are you okay, America?" Marlee asked, snapping me back into reality.

"Yes. Why?"

"You just look upset." Marlee's brow furrowed in concern.

"Nope. Not upset. Everything's great."

Suddenly, in a move so swift I would have missed it if they weren't so close, Anna Farmer—a Four who worked land for a living—reached up and slapped Celeste across the face.

Several people gasped, including myself. Those who missed it turned around and asked what had happened, most notably Tiny, whose high voice pierced the quiet left in the room.

"Oh, Anna, no," Emmica said with a sigh.

The moment after it happened, Anna slowly comprehended what she'd just done. She would probably be sent home; we weren't supposed to physically assault another Selected. Emmica started tearing up while Anna sat in stunned silence. They were both farm girls and had bonded early on. I couldn't imagine how I'd feel if it was Marlee suddenly leaving.

Anna, who I'd only met in passing, had always struck me as an effervescent creature. I knew there was nothing in her that would naturally seek to harm another person. During a large part of the rebel attack, she'd been on her knees in prayer.

Undoubtedly, she had been provoked, but no one was sitting within earshot to prove that. It would be Anna's word against Celeste's as far as any exchange of words went, but Celeste would have a roomful of people who could back up that she'd been hit. Maxon would presumably be urged to send Anna home as an example to the others.

Tears welled in Anna's eyes as Celeste whispered something to her and swiftly left the room.

Anna was gone before dinner.

CHAPTER 17

"WHO WAS THE PRESIDENT OF the United States during the Third World War?" Silvia quizzed us.

This was one I didn't know, and I averted my eyes, hoping Silvia wouldn't call on me. Luckily, Amy raised her hand and answered. "President Wallis."

We were in the Great Room again, starting the week with a history lesson. Well, more like a history test. This was one of those areas where it always seemed that what people knew was varied, both as far as what was fact and just how informed they were. Mom always taught us orally when it came to history. We had pages and worksheets to master for English and math, but when it came to the stories that made up our past, there was very little that I knew for sure was truth.

"Correct. President Wallis was the president before the Chinese assault and continued leading the United States throughout the war," Silvia confirmed. I thought the name to myself. *Wallis, Wallis, Wallis.* I really wanted to remember this to tell May and Gerad when I went home, but we were learning so much, it was hard to keep it all straight. "What was their motivation for invading? Celeste?"

She smiled. "Money. The Americans owed them a lot of money and couldn't pay them back."

"Excellent, Celeste." Silvia gave her a doting smile. How did Celeste wrap people around her finger like that? It was so irritating. "When the United States couldn't repay their massive debt, the Chinese invaded. Unfortunately for them, this didn't get them any money, as the United States was beyond bankruptcy. However, it did gain them American labor. And when the Chinese took over, what did they rename the United States?"

I raised my hand, along with a few others. "Jenna?" Silvia called.

"The American State of China."

"Yes. The American State of China had the appearance of its original country, but was merely a facade. The Chinese were pulling strings behind the scenes, influencing any major political happenings, and steering legislation in their favor." Silvia walked through the desks slowly. I felt like a mouse in the sights of a hawk that was circling ever closer.

I looked around the room. A few people seemed confused. I thought that part was common knowledge.

"Does anyone have anything they'd like to add?" Silvia asked.

Bariel piped up. "The Chinese invasion prompted several countries, particularly those in Europe, to align themselves with one another and make alliances."

"Yes," Silvia replied. "However, the American State of China had no such friends at the time. It took them five years to regroup, and they could barely handle that, let alone trying to forge alliances." She tried to express the hardship through an exhausted look. "The ASC planned to fight back against China but was then faced with another invasion. What country attempted to occupy the ASC then?"

Lots of hands went up this time. "Russia," someone said without waiting to be called on. Silvia looked around for the offender, but couldn't pinpoint the source.

"Correct," she said, slightly unhappily. "Russia tried to expand in both directions and failed miserably, but this failure on their part provided the ASC with an opportunity to fight back. How?"

Kriss raised her hand and answered. "The entirety of what was North America banded together to fight Russia, since it seemed clear they had their eyes on more than just the ASC. And fighting Russia was easier because China was attacking them as well for attempting to steal their territory."

Silvia smiled proudly. "Yes. And who headed up the assault against Russia?"

The whole room shouted out the answer: "Gregory Illéa!" Some girls even clapped.

Silvia nodded. "And that led to the founding of the country. The alliances the ASC acquired had formed a united front, and the United States's reputation was so damaged, no one wanted to readopt that name. So a new nation was formed under Gregory Illéa's name and leadership. He saved this country."

Emmica raised her hand, and Silvia acknowledged her. "In some ways, we're kind of like him. I mean, we get to serve our country. He was just a private citizen who donated his money and knowledge. And he changed everything," she said with wonder.

"That is a beautiful point," Silvia said. "And exactly like him, one of you will be elevated to royalty. For Gregory Illéa, he became a king as his family married into a royal family, and for you, it will be marrying into this one." Silvia had moved herself to awe, so when Tuesday raised her hand, it took her a moment to acknowledge it.

"Umm, why is it that we don't have any of this in a book? So we could study?" There was a hint of irritation in her voice.

Silvia shook her head. "Dear girls, history isn't something you study. It's something you should just know."

Marlee turned to me and whispered, "But clearly we don't." She smiled at her own joke, and then focused again on Silvia.

I thought about that, how we all knew different things or had to guess at the truth. Why weren't we given history books?

I remembered a few years ago when I went into Mom and Dad's room, since Mom said I could choose what I wanted to read for English. As I went through my options, I spotted a thick, ratty book in the back corner and pulled it out. It was a U.S. history book. Dad came in a few minutes later, saw what I was reading, and said it was okay, so long as I never told anyone about it.

When Dad asked me to keep a secret, I did so without question, and I loved looking through all those pages. Well, the ones that were still legible. Lots had been torn out, and the edge of the book looked like it might have been burned, but that's where I saw a picture of the old White House and learned about the way holidays used to be.

I never thought to question the lack of truth until it had been placed in front of me. Why did the king just let us guess?

The flashbulbs went off again, capturing Maxon and Natalie smiling brightly.

"Natalie, bring your chin down just a touch, please. That's it." The photographer snapped another picture, filling the room with light. "I think that will do. Who's next?" he called.

Celeste came in from the side, a general group of maids still swarming around her before the photographer started up again. Natalie, still beside Maxon, said something and kicked up her foot flirtatiously behind her. He responded quietly, and she giggled as she walked away.

We'd been told after yesterday's history lesson that this photo shoot was merely for the amusement of the public, but

I couldn't help thinking that there was some actual weight to it. Someone had written an editorial in a magazine about the look of a princess. I didn't get to read the article myself, but Emmica and some of the others did. According to her, it was about Maxon needing to find someone who actually looked regal and photographed well with him, someone who would look nice on a stamp.

And now we were all lined up in identical cream-colored, cap-sleeved, drop-waist dresses with a heavy red sash across our shoulders, taking pictures with Maxon. The photos would be printed in the same magazine, and the magazine staff was going to make picks. I was kind of uncomfortable with it all. This was the thing I'd been bothered about since the beginning, that Maxon was looking for nothing more than a pretty face. Now that I'd met him, I was sure that wasn't true, but it got to me that people thought that Maxon was like that.

I sighed. Some of the girls were walking around, munching on no-drip foods and chatting, but the majority, including myself, were standing around the perimeter of the set erected in the Great Room. A huge golden tapestry that reminded me of the drop cloths Dad used at home was hung up against a wall and spilled across the floor. A small couch was off to one side and a pillar was on the other. In the middle the Illéan emblem stood, giving the whole silly thing an air of being patriotic. We watched as each Selected paraded across the space to be photographed, and many who watched were whispering things they liked and didn't or what they were planning for themselves.

Celeste walked up to Maxon with a sparkle in her eyes, and he smiled as she approached. The moment she reached him, she put her lips to his ear and whispered something. Whatever it was, Maxon leaned his head back with laughter and nodded, agreeing with her little secret. It was strange to see them like that. How could someone who got along so well with me do the same with someone like her?

"All right, miss, just face the camera and smile, please," the photographer called, and Celeste immediately complied.

She turned herself toward Maxon and placed a hand on his chest, tilted her head down, and gave an expert smile. She seemed to understand how to use the lighting and set to her best advantage and kept moving Maxon over a few inches or insisting on changing their pose. Where some of the girls took their time and made their turn with Maxon last—particularly those who still hadn't secured a date— Celeste appeared to want to show her efficiency instead.

In a bolt of speed, she was done, and the photographer called for the next girl. I was so busy watching Celeste run her fingers down Maxon's arm as she exited that a maid had to gently remind me it was my turn.

I gave my head a tiny shake and willed myself to focus. I gathered up my dress in my hands and walked toward Maxon. His eyes shifted from Celeste to me, and maybe I imagined it, but his face seemed to brighten a bit.

"Hello, my dear," he sang.

"Don't even start," I warned, but he merely chuckled and

reached his hands out.

"Hold on a moment. Your sash is crooked."

"Not surprised." The darn thing was so heavy, I could feel it shifting every time I stepped.

"I suppose that'll do," he said jokingly.

I fired back, "In the meantime, they ought to hang you up with the chandeliers." I poked at the glittering medals across his chest. His uniform, which looked almost like something the guards would wear, only far more elegant, also had golden things on his shoulders and a sword hanging off his hip. It was a bit much.

"Look at the camera, please," the photographer called. I looked up and saw not just his eyes but the faces of all the other girls watching, and my nerves shot up.

I wiped my moist hands on my dress and exhaled.

"Don't be nervous," Maxon whispered.

"I don't like everyone looking at me."

He pulled me very close and put his hand on my waist. I went to step back, but Maxon's arm held me securely to him. "Just look at me like you can't stand me." He squinted into a mock pout, which made me crack up.

The camera flashed at just that second, capturing us both laughing.

"See," Maxon said. "It's not so bad."

"I guess." I was still tense for a few minutes as the photographer shouted out instructions and Maxon shifted from a close embrace to a loose one, or turned me so my back was against his chest.

"Excellent," the photographer said. "Could we get a few on the lounge?"

I was feeling better now that it was half over, and I sat next to Maxon with the best posture I could muster. Every once in a while, he'd poke or tickle me, making my smile grow bigger until it burst into laughter. I hoped the photographer was catching the moments just before my face scrunched together, otherwise this whole thing was going to be a disaster.

From the corner of my eye, I noticed a waving hand, and a moment later Maxon turned as well. A man in a suit was standing there, and he clearly needed to speak to the prince. Maxon nodded, but the man hesitated, looking to him and then to me, evidently questioning my presence.

"She's fine," Maxon said, and the man came over and knelt before him.

"Rebel attack in Midston, Your Majesty," he said. Maxon sighed and dropped his head wearily. "They burned acres of crops and killed about a dozen people."

"Where in Midston?"

"The west, sir, near the border."

Maxon nodded slowly and looked as if he was adding this piece of information to others in his head. "What does my father say?"

"Actually, Your Majesty, he wanted your thoughts."

Maxon seemed taken aback for a split second, then spoke. "Localize troops in the southeast of Sota and all along Tammins. Don't go as far south as Midston, it'd be a waste. See if we can intercept them."

The man stood and bowed. "Excellent, sir." As swiftly as he'd come, he vanished.

I knew we were supposed to get back to the pictures, but Maxon didn't seem nearly so interested in it all now.

"Are you all right?" I asked.

He nodded somberly. "Just all those people."

"Maybe we should stop," I suggested.

He shook his head, straightened up, and smiled, placing my hand in his. "One thing you must master in this profession is the ability to appear calm when you feel anything but. Please smile, America."

I raised myself up and gave a shy smile to the camera as the photographer clicked away. In the middle of those last few frames, Maxon squeezed my hand tight, and I did the same to his. In that moment, it felt like we had a connection, something true and deep.

"Thank you very much. Next, please," the photographer sang.

As Maxon and I stood, he held on to my hand. "Please don't say anything. It's imperative you're discreet."

"Of course."

The click of a pair of heels coming toward us reminded me that we weren't alone, but I kind of wanted to stay. He gave my hand one last squeeze and released me, and as I walked away, I considered several things. How nice it felt that Maxon trusted me enough to let me know this secret, and how it had sort of felt like we were alone for a moment. Then I thought about the rebels, and how the king was usually quick to point out their sedition, but I was supposed to keep this news to myself. It didn't quite make sense.

"Janelle, my dear," Maxon said as the next girl approached. I smiled to myself at the tired endearment. He lowered his voice, but I still heard. "Before I forget, are you free this afternoon?"

Something kind of knotted in my stomach. I guessed it was a late batch of nerves.

"She must have done something terrible," Amy insisted.

"That's not what she made it sound like," Kriss countered.

Tuesday pulled on Kriss's arm. "What did she say again?"

Janelle had been sent home.

This particular elimination was crucial for us to understand, because it was the first one that was isolated and not caused by rule breaking. She had done something wrong, and we all wanted to know what it was.

Kriss, whose room was across from Janelle's, had seen her come in and was the only person she'd spoken to before she left. Kriss sighed and retold the story for the third time.

"She and Maxon had gone hunting, but you knew that," she said, waving her hand around like she was trying to clear her thoughts. Janelle's date really had been common knowledge. After the photo shoot yesterday, she gushed about their plans to anyone who would listen.

"That was her second date with Maxon. She's the only one who got two," Bariel said.

"No, she isn't," I mumbled. A few heads turned, acknowledging my statement. It was true, though. Janelle was the only girl to have two dates with Maxon besides me. Not that I was counting.

Kriss continued. "When she came back, she was crying. I asked her what was wrong, and she said she was leaving, that Maxon had told her to go. I gave her a hug because she was so upset and asked her what happened. She said she couldn't tell me about it. I don't understand that. Maybe we're not allowed to talk about why we're eliminated?"

"That wasn't in the rules, was it?" Tuesday asked.

"No one said anything to me about it," Amy replied, and several others shook their heads in confirmation.

"But what did she say then?" Celeste urged.

Kriss sighed again. "She said that I'd better be careful of what I say. Then she pulled away and slammed the door."

The room went quiet a moment, considering. "She must have insulted him," Elayna said.

"Well, if that's why she left, then it isn't fair, since Maxon said that *someone* in this room insulted him the first time they met," Celeste complained.

People started looking around the room, trying to discover the guilty party, perhaps in an effort to get them—me— kicked out as well. I gave a nervous glance to Marlee, and she sprang into action.

"Maybe she said something about the country? Like the policies or something?"

Bariel sucked her teeth. "Please. How boring must that date have been for them to start talking policy? Has anyone in here actually talked to Maxon about anything related to running the country?"

No one answered.

"Of course you haven't," Bariel said. "Maxon's not looking for a coworker, he's looking for a wife."

"Don't you think you're underestimating him?" Kriss objected. "Don't you think Maxon wants someone with ideas and opinions?"

Celeste threw her head back and laughed. "Maxon can run the country just fine. He's trained for it. Besides, he has teams of people to help him make decisions, so why would he want someone else trying to tell him what to do? If I were you, I'd start learning how to be quiet. At least until he marries you."

Bariel sidled up beside Celeste. "Which he won't."

"Exactly," Celeste said with a smile. "Why would Maxon bother with some brainiac Three when he could have a Two?"

"Hey!" Tuesday cried. "Maxon doesn't care about numbers."

"Of course he does," Celeste replied in a tone someone would use with a child. "Why do you think everyone below a Four is gone?"

"Still here," I said, raising my hand. "So if you think you've got him figured out, you're wrong."

"Oh, it's the girl who doesn't know when to shut up," Celeste said in mock amusement.

I balled my fist, trying to decide if it would be worth hitting her. Was that part of her plan? But before I could move at all, Silvia burst through the door.

"Mail, ladies!" she called out, and the tension in the room flew away.

We all stopped, eager to get our hands on what Silvia was carrying. We'd been at the palace nearly two weeks now, and with the exception of hearing from our families on the second day, this was our first real contact from home.

"Let's see," Silvia said, looking through stacks of letters, completely oblivious to the almost-argument that had taken place not seconds ago. "Lady Tiny?" she called as she looked around the room.

Tiny raised her hand and walked forward. "Lady Elizabeth? Lady America?"

I practically ran forward and snatched the letter out of her hand. I was so hungry for words from my family. As soon as it was in my clutches, I retreated to a corner for a few moments to myself.

> Dear America,
> I can't wait for Friday to come. I can't believe you're going to get to talk to Gavril Fadaye! You have all the luck.

I certainly didn't feel lucky. Tomorrow night we were all getting grilled by Gavril, and I had no idea what he would ask us. I felt sure I'd make an idiot out of myself.

> It'll be nice to hear your voice again. I miss you singing around the house. Mom doesn't

do it, and it's been so quiet since you left. Will you wave to me on the show?

How's the competition going? Do you have lots of friends there? Have you talked to any of the girls who left? Mom is saying all the time now that it's not a big deal if you lose anymore. Half those girls who went home are already engaged to the sons of mayors or celebrities. She says someone will take you if Maxon doesn't. Gerad is hoping you marry a basketball player instead of a boring old prince. But I don't care what anybody says. Maxon is so gorgeous!

Have you kissed him yet?

Kissed him? We'd only just met. And there'd be no reason for Maxon to kiss me anyway.

I bet he's the best kisser in the universe. I think if you're a prince, you have to be!

I have so much more to tell you, but Mom wants me to go paint. Write me a real letter soon. A long one! With lots and lots of details!

I love you! We all do.

May

So the eliminated girls were already getting snatched up by wealthy men. I didn't realize being the castoff of a future king made you a commodity. I walked around the perimeter of the room, thinking over May's words.

I wanted to know what was going on. I wondered what had really happened with Janelle and was curious if Maxon had another date tonight. I really wanted to see him.

My mind was racing, searching for a way to simply speak to him. As I thought, I stared at the paper in my hands.

The second page of May's letter was almost completely blank. I tore off a piece of it as I wandered. Some girls were still buried in pages of letters from their families, and others were sharing news. After a lap I stopped by the Women's Room guest book and picked up the pen.

I scribbled quickly on my scrap of paper.

Your Majesty—
Tugging my ear. Whenever.

I walked outside the room as if I were simply going to the bathroom and looked up and down the hall. It was empty. I stood there, waiting, until a maid rounded the corner with a tray of tea in her hands.

"Excuse me?" I called to her quietly. Voices carried in these great halls.

The girl curtsied in front of me. "Yes, miss?"

"Would you happen to be going to the prince with that?"

She smiled. "Yes, miss."

"Could you please take this to him for me?" I held out my little folded-up note.

"Of course, miss!"

She took it eagerly and walked away with a newfound

energy. No doubt she would unfold it as soon as she was out of sight, but I felt secure in its odd phrasing.

These hallways were captivating, each one more ornate than my entire house. The wallpaper, the gilt mirrors, the giant vases of fresh flowers all so beautiful. The carpets were lavish and immaculate, the windows were sparkling, and the paintings on the walls were lovely.

There were some paintings by artists I knew—van Gogh, Picasso—and some I didn't. There were photographs of buildings I had seen before. There was one of the legendary White House. Compared to the pictures and what I'd read in my old history book, the palace dwarfed it in size and luxury, but I still wished it was around to see.

I walked farther down the hall and came upon a portrait of the royal family. It looked old; Maxon was shorter than his mother in this picture. He towered over her now.

In the time I'd been at the palace, I had only ever seen them together at dinners and the *Illéa Capital Report* airing. Were they very private? Did they not like all these strange young girls in their house? Were they only all here because of blood and duty? I didn't know what to make of this invisible family.

"America?"

I turned at the sound of my name. Maxon was jogging down the hall toward me.

I felt like I was seeing him for the first time.

He had his suit coat off, and the sleeves were rolled up on his white shirt. His blue tie was loosened at the neck, and his hair that was always slicked back was bouncing around a bit as he moved. In stark contrast to the person in uniform yesterday, he looked more boyish, more real.

I froze. Maxon came up to me and grabbed my wrists.

"Are you okay? What's wrong?" he pressed.

Wrong?

"Nothing. I'm fine," I replied. Maxon let out a breath I didn't realize he was holding.

"Thank goodness. When I got your note, I thought you were sick or something happened to your family."

"Oh! Oh, no. Maxon, I'm so sorry. I knew that was a stupid idea. I just didn't know if you'd be at dinner, and I wanted to see you."

"Well, what for?" he asked. He was still looking me over with a furrowed brow, as if he was making sure nothing was broken.

"Just to see you."

Maxon stopped moving. He looked into my eyes with a kind of wonder.

"You just wanted to see me?" He looked happily surprised.

"Don't be so shocked. Friends usually spend time together." My tone added the *of course*.

"Ah, you're cross with me because I've been engaged all week, aren't you? I didn't mean to neglect our friendship, America." Now he was back to the businesslike Maxon.

"No, I'm not mad. I was just explaining myself. You look busy. Go back to work, and I'll see you when you're free." I noticed he was still holding on to my wrists.

"Actually, do you mind if I stay a few minutes? They're having a budget meeting upstairs, and I detest those things." Without waiting for an answer, Maxon pulled me over to a short, plush sofa halfway down the hall that rested underneath a window, and I giggled a little as we sat. "What's so funny?"

"Just you," I said, smiling. "It's cute to see that your job bugs you. What's so bad about the meetings, anyway?"

"Oh, America!" he said, facing me again. "They go round and round in circles. Father does a good job at calming the advisers, but it's so hard to push the committees in any given direction. Mom is always on Father to give more to the school systems—she thinks the more educated you are, the less likely you are to be a criminal, and I agree—but Father is never forceful enough to get them to take away from other areas that could manage perfectly with lower funds. It's infuriating! And it's not like I'm in command, so my opinion is easily overlooked." Maxon propped his elbows on his knees and rested his head in his hands. He looked tired.

So now I could see a bit of Maxon's world, but it was just as unimaginable as ever. How could you deny the voice of your future sovereign?

"I'm sorry. On the plus side, you'll have more of a say in the future." I rubbed his back, trying to encourage him.

"I know. I tell myself that. But it's so frustrating when we could change things now if they'd only listen." His voice was a little hard to hear when it was directed at the carpet.

"Well, don't be too discouraged. Your mom is on the

right path, but education alone won't fix anything."

Maxon raised his head. "What do you mean?" It almost sounded like an accusation. And rightly so. Here was an idea that he'd been championing, and I'd just squashed it. I tried to backpedal.

"Well, compared to the fancy-pants tutors someone like you has, the education system for Sixes and Sevens is terrible. I think getting better teachers or better facilities would do them a world of good. But then what about the Eights? Isn't that caste responsible for most of the crimes? They don't get any education. I think if they felt they had something, anything at all, it might encourage them.

"Besides . . ." I paused. I didn't know if this was something a boy who'd grown up with everything handed to him could grasp. "Have you ever been hungry, Maxon? Not just ready for dinner, but *starving*? If there was absolutely no food here, nothing for your mother or father, and you knew that if you just took something from people who had more in a day than you'd have in your whole life, you could eat . . . what would you do? If they were counting on you, what wouldn't you do for someone you loved?"

He was quiet for a moment. Once before—when we'd talked about my maids during the attack—we'd kind of acknowledged the wide gap between us. This was a far more controversial topic of discussion, and I could see him wanting to avoid it.

"America, I'm not saying that some people don't have it hard, but stealing is—"

"Close your eyes, Maxon."

"What?"

"Close your eyes."

He frowned at me but obeyed. I waited until his eyes were shut and his face looked relaxed before I started.

"Somewhere in this palace, there is a woman who will be your wife."

I saw his mouth twitch, the beginnings of a hopeful smile.

"Maybe you don't know which face it is yet, but think of the girls in that room. Imagine the one who loves you the most. Imagine your 'dear.'"

His hand was resting next to mine on the seat, and his fingers grazed mine for a second. I shied away from the touch.

"Sorry," he mumbled, looking my way.

"Keep 'em closed!"

He chuckled and went back to his original position.

"This girl? Imagine that she depends on you. She needs you to cherish her and make her feel like the Selection didn't even happen. Like if you were dropped on your own out in the middle of the country to wander around door to door, she's still the one you would have found. She was always the one you would have picked."

The hopeful smile began to settle. More than settle, it started to sag.

"She needs you to provide for her and protect her. And if it came to a point where there was absolutely nothing to eat, and you couldn't even fall asleep at night because the sound of her stomach growling kept you awake—"

"Stop it!" Maxon stood quickly. He walked across the hall and stayed there for a while, facing away from me.

I felt a little awkward. I hadn't realized this would make him so upset.

"Sorry," I whispered.

He nodded his head but continued to look at the wall. After a moment he turned around. His eyes were searching mine, sad and questioning.

"Is it really like that?" he asked.

"What?"

"Out there . . . does that happen? Are people hungry like that a lot?"

"Maxon, I—"

"Tell me the truth." His mouth settled into a firm line.

"Yes. That happens. I know of families where people give up their share for their children or siblings. I know of a boy who was whipped in the town square for stealing food. Sometimes you do crazy things when you're desperate."

"A boy? How old?"

"Nine," I breathed with a shiver. I could still remember the scars on Jemmy's tiny back, and Maxon stretched his own back as if he felt it all himself.

"Have you"—he cleared his throat—"have you ever been like that? Starving?"

I ducked my head, which was a giveaway. I really didn't want to tell him about that.

"How bad?"

"Maxon, it will only upset you more."

"Probably," he said with a grave nod. "But I'm only starting to realize how much I don't know about my own country. Please."

I sighed.

"We've been pretty bad. Most times if it gets to where we have to choose, we keep the food and lose electricity. The worst was when it happened near Christmas one year. It was very cold, so we were all wearing tons of clothes and watching our breath inside the house. May didn't understand why we couldn't exchange gifts. As a general rule, there are never any leftovers at my house. Someone always wants more."

I watched his face grow pale and realized I didn't want to see him upset. I needed to turn this around, make it positive.

"I know the checks we've gotten over the last few weeks have really helped, and my family is very smart about money. I'm sure they've already tucked it away so it'll stretch out for a long time. You've done so much for us, Maxon." I tried to smile at him again, but his expression remained unchanged.

"Good God. When you said you were only here for the food, you weren't kidding, were you?" he asked, shaking his head.

"Really, Maxon, we've been doing pretty well lately. I—" But I couldn't finish my sentence.

Maxon came over and kissed my forehead.

"I'll see you at dinner."

As he walked away, he straightened his tie.

CHAPTER 18

MAXON HAD SAID HE WOULD see me at dinner, but he wasn't there. The queen entered alone. We made our delicate bows as she took her seat, and then settled in ourselves.

I looked around the room to find the empty chair, assuming he was on a date, but everyone was here.

I had spent the afternoon replaying what I'd said to Maxon. No wonder I'd never had any friends. I was shockingly bad at it.

Just then Maxon and the king walked in. Maxon had his suit coat back on, but his hair was still a handsome mess. He and the king had their heads together as they walked. We hurried to stand. Their conversation was animated. Maxon was using his hands to express things and the king was nodding, acknowledging his son's words but looking a little put out. When they reached the head table, King Clarkson gave

Maxon a heavy pat on the back, his expression stern.

As the king turned to face us all, his face suddenly flooded with enthusiasm. "Oh, goodness, dear ladies, please sit." He kissed the queen on her head and sat himself.

But Maxon remained standing.

"Ladies, I have an announcement." Every eye focused in. What could he possibly have for us?

"I know you were all promised compensation for your participation in the Selection." His voice was full of a ringing authority that I had only really heard once—the night he let me into the garden. He was much more attractive when he was using his status for a purpose. "However, there have been some new monetary allocations. If you are a natural Two or a Three, you will no longer be receiving financing. Fours and Fives will continue to receive compensation, but it will be slightly less than what it has been so far."

I could see some of the girls had their mouths open in shock. Money was part of the deal. Celeste, for example, was fuming. I guessed if you had a lot of money, you got used to the idea of collecting it. And the thought that someone like me would be getting anything she wasn't probably got under her skin.

"I do apologize for any inconvenience, but I will explain this all tomorrow night on the *Capital Report*. And this is a nonnegotiable situation. If anyone has a problem with this new arrangement and no longer wants to participate, you may leave after dinner."

He sat down and started talking again to the king, who seemed more interested in his dinner than Maxon's words. I was a little disheartened that my family would be receiving less money, but at least we were still getting some. I tried to focus on my dinner, but mostly I was wondering what this meant, and I wasn't alone. Murmurs went up around the room.

"What do you think that's about?" Tiny asked quietly.

"Maybe it's a test," Kriss offered. "I bet there are some people here who are only in it for the money."

As I listened to her, I saw Fiona nudge Olivia and nod her head toward me. I turned away so she wouldn't know I saw.

The girls offered up theories, and I kept watching Maxon. I tried to catch his attention so I could tug my ear, but he didn't look my way.

Mary and I were alone in my room. Tonight I'd face Gavril—and the rest of the nation—on the *Illéa Capital Report*. Not to mention the other girls would be right there the whole time, watching one another and mentally critiquing. Saying I was nervous was a gross understatement. I fidgeted while Mary listed some possible questions, things she thought the public would want to know.

How was I enjoying the palace? What was the most romantic thing Maxon had done for me? Did I miss my family? Had I kissed Maxon yet?

I eyed Mary when she asked me that one. I'd been throwing out answers to the questions, trying not to think too hard. But I could tell she'd asked that one out of genuine curiosity. The smile on her face proved it.

"No! For goodness' sake." I tried to sound mad, but it was too funny to be upset about. I ended up smirking. And that made Mary giggle. "Oh, just . . . why don't you clean something!"

She laughed outright, and before I could tell her to stop, Anne and Lucy burst through the doors with a garment bag.

Lucy was looking more excited than I'd seen her since the moment I'd walked in the first day, and Anne seemed quietly devious.

"What's this about?" I asked as Lucy stopped in front of me to give a buoyant curtsy.

"We finished your dress for the *Report*, miss," she replied.

My brow wrinkled together. "A new one? Why not the blue one in the closet? Didn't you just finish that one? I love it."

The three of them exchanged looks.

"What did you do?" I asked, pointing at the bag Anne was hanging up on the hook near the mirror.

"We talk to all the other maids, miss. We hear a lot of things," Anne began. "We know that you and Lady Janelle are the only two who got more than one date with His Majesty, and from what we understand, there might be a link between you two."

"How so?" I asked.

"From what we've heard," Anne continued, "the reason she was asked to leave is because she said some rather unkind things about you. The prince did not agree and dismissed her immediately."

"What?" I put a hand to my mouth, trying to hide my shock.

"We're sure you're his favorite, miss. Most everyone says so." Lucy sighed happily.

"I think you've been misinformed," I told them. Anne shrugged with a smile on her face, not concerned at all with my opinion.

Then I remembered where this had started. "What does any of this have to do with my dress?"

Mary came over to Anne and began unzipping the long bag, revealing a stunning red dress that shimmered in the fading light falling through the window.

"Oh, Anne," I said, absolutely awestruck. "You've outdone yourself."

She acknowledged my praise with a nod of her head. "Thank you, miss. We all worked on it, though."

"It's beautiful. But I still don't understand what this has to do with anything you said."

Mary pulled the dress out of the bag, airing it out, while Anne continued. "As I said, many people around the palace think you're the prince's favorite. He says kind things about you and prefers your company above the others'. And it seems the other girls have noticed."

"What do you mean?"

"We go down to a workroom to do most of the sewing on your dresses. There are stores of material and a place to make shoes, and the other maids are in there, too. Everyone requested a blue dress for tonight. All the maids think it's because you wear that color almost daily, and the others are trying to copy you."

"It's true," Lucy chimed in. "Lady Tuesday and Lady Natalie didn't put on any of their jewelry today. Just like you."

"And most of the ladies are requesting simpler dresses, like the ones you prefer," Mary stated.

"That still doesn't explain why you made me a red dress."

"To make you noticeable, of course," Mary answered. "Oh, Lady America, if he really likes you, you have to keep standing out. You've been so generous with us, especially Lucy." We all looked over to Lucy, who nodded in agreement and said, "You—you're good enough to be the princess. You'd be amazing."

I hunted for a way to get out of this. I hated being the center of attention.

"But what if everyone else is right? What if the reason Maxon likes me is because I'm not as over the top as everyone else, and then you go and put me in something like that and it ruins it all?"

"Every girl needs to shine once in a while. And we've known Maxon most of his life. He would love this." Anne spoke with such assurance that I felt there was nothing I could do.

I didn't know how to explain to them that the notes he sent me, the time he'd spent with me, meant nothing other than friendship between us. I couldn't tell them. It would deflate their happiness, and besides, I needed to keep up appearances if I wanted to stay. And I did. I needed to stay.

"Okay, let's try it on," I conceded with a sigh.

Lucy jumped up and down with excitement until Anne reminded her that it wasn't proper. I slid the silky dress over my head, and they stitched a handful of places they hadn't quite finished. Mary's skilled hands held my hair in various ways to see which looked best with the dress, and within half an hour, I was ready.

The set was arranged a little differently tonight for our special show. The thrones for the royal family were off to one side as always, and our seats were on the opposite side again. But the podium was off center, leaving the space focused on two tall chairs. A microphone was resting on one for us to take when we spoke to Gavril. I got queasy just thinking about it.

Sure enough, the room was full of dresses in every shade of blue. Some of them fell closer to green, others closer to purple, but it was clear there was a theme. I felt immediately uncomfortable. I caught Celeste's eye right away and decided to just stay away from her until I absolutely had to go over to the seats.

Kriss and Natalie walked past, having just checked their makeup one last time. They both looked a little unhappy, though sometimes it was hard to tell with Natalie. Kriss at least looked somewhat different from the crowd as well. Her blue dress was melting into white, like delicate strands of ice were weaving their way to the floor.

"You look stunning, America," she said in a way that was slightly more an accusation than praise.

"Thanks. That dress is gorgeous."

She ran her hands down her torso, straightening imaginary wrinkles. "Yeah, I liked it, too."

Natalie ran her hand across one of the capped sleeves on my dress. "What's that material? It's really going to shine under the lights."

"I have no idea, actually. We don't get a lot of the nice stuff as Fives," I said with a shrug. I looked down at the fabric. I'd had at least one other dress made from the same type of cloth, but I hadn't bothered learning the name.

"America!"

I looked up to see Celeste standing right beside me. Smiling.

"Celeste."

"Could you come with me for just one moment? I need some help."

Without waiting for an answer, she pulled me away from Kriss and Natalie and around the heavy blue curtain that was the backdrop of the *Report* studio.

"Take off your dress," she ordered as she started unzipping her own.

"What?"

"I want your dress. Take it off. Ugh! Damn hook," she said, still trying to get out of her clothes.

"I'm not taking off my dress," I said, and went to leave. I didn't get very far, though, as Celeste buried her nails into my arm and jerked me back.

"Ouch!" I cried, grabbing my arm. It looked like there would be marks but hopefully no blood.

"Shut up. Take off the dress. Now."

I stood there, my face set, refusing to budge. Celeste was just going to have to get over not being the center of Illéa.

"I could take it off for you," she offered coldly.

"I'm not afraid of you, Celeste," I said as I crossed my arms. "This dress was made for me, and I'm going to wear it. Next time you pick out your clothes, maybe you should try being yourself instead of me. Oh, wait, but maybe then Maxon would see what a brat you are and send you home, huh?"

Without a second of hesitation, she reached up and ripped one of my sleeves off and walked away. I gasped in outrage but was too stunned to do anything more. I looked down and saw a tattered scrap of fabric dangling pathetically in front of me. I heard Silvia calling for everyone to come to their seats, so I walked around the side of the curtain as bravely as I could manage.

Marlee had saved me a seat beside her, and I saw the shocked look on her face as I came into view.

"What happened to your dress?" she whispered.

"Celeste," I explained in disgust.

Emmica and Samantha, who were sitting in front of us, turned around.

"She tore your dress?" Emmica asked.

"Yes."

"Go to Maxon and turn her in," she pleaded. "That girl's a nightmare."

"I know," I said with a sigh. "I'll tell him next time I see him."

Samantha looked sad. "Who knows when that will be? I thought we'd get to spend more time with him."

"America, lift your arm," Marlee instructed. She expertly tucked my tattered sleeve into the side of my dress as Emmica plucked away a few stray threads. You couldn't even tell anything had happened to it. As for the nail marks, well, at least they were on my left arm and away from the camera.

It was almost time to start. Gavril was flipping through notes as the royal family came in at last. Maxon had on a dark blue suit with a pin of the national emblem on his lapel. He looked sharp and calm.

"Good evening, ladies," he sang with a smile.

A chorus of "Majesty" and "Highness" fell over him.

"Just so you know, I'll be giving one brief announcement and then introducing Gavril. It'll be a nice change; he's always introducing me!" He chuckled, and we all followed. "I know some of you are probably a little nervous, but you have no need to be. Please, just be yourselves. The people want to know you." Our eyes met a few times while he was talking, but nothing long enough for me to read him. He didn't seem to notice the dress. My maids would be disappointed.

He walked over to the podium, calling out "Good luck" over his shoulder.

I could tell something was going on. I assumed this announcement of his would be related to what he'd told us yesterday, but I still couldn't guess at what it all meant. Maxon's little mystery distracted me, and I wasn't so nervous anymore. I felt all right as the anthem played and the camera settled squarely on Maxon's face. I'd been watching the *Report* since I was a child. Maxon had never addressed the country before, not like this. I wished I could have told him good luck, too.

"Good evening, ladies and gentlemen of Illéa. I know that tonight is an exciting night for us all as the country gets to finally hear from the twenty-five remaining women in the Selection. I can't begin to express how excited I am for you to meet them. I'm sure you will all agree that any one of these amazing young ladies would be a wonderful leader and future princess.

"But before we get to that, I'd like to announce a new project I am working on that is of great importance to me. Having met these ladies, I've been exposed to the wide world outside our palace, a world that I rarely get to see. I've been told of its remarkable goodness and made aware of its unimaginable darkness. Through speaking to these women, I've embraced the importance of the masses outside these walls. I have been woken to the suffering of some of our lower castes, and I intend to do something about it."

What?

"It will be at least three months before we can set this up properly, but around the new year, there will be public

241

assistance for food in every Province Services Office. Any Five, Six, Seven, or Eight may go there any evening for a free, nutritious meal. Please know that these women before you have all sacrificed some or all of their compensation to help fund this important program. And while this assistance may not be able to last forever, we will keep it running as long as we can."

I kept trying to swallow up the gratitude, the awe, but a few tears leaked out. I was still aware enough of what was coming next to worry about my makeup but so appreciative that it was no longer the top priority.

"I feel that no good leader can let the masses go unfed. Most of Illéa is comprised of these lower castes, and we have overlooked these people far too long. That is why I am moving forward and why I am asking others to join me. Twos, Threes, Fours . . . the roads you drive on don't pave themselves. Your houses aren't cleaned by magic. Here is your opportunity to acknowledge that truth by donating at your local Province Services Office."

He paused. "By birth you have been blessed, and it is time to acknowledge that blessing. I will have further updates as this project progresses, and I thank you all for your attention. But now, let's get to the real reason you all tuned in tonight. Ladies and gentlemen, Mr. Gavril Fadaye!"

There was a smattering of applause from everyone in the room, though it was obvious not everyone was enthusiastic about Maxon's announcement. The king, for instance, was clapping but without excitement, though the queen was radiant with pride. The advisers also seemed torn about whether or not this was a good idea.

"Thank you so much for that introduction, Your Majesty!" Gavril announced as he ran onto the set. "Very well done! If this whole prince thing doesn't work out, you should consider a job in entertainment."

Maxon laughed out loud as he walked to his seat. The cameras were focused on Gavril now, but I watched Maxon and his parents. I didn't understand why their reactions were mixed.

"People of Illéa, do we have a treat for you! This evening we'll be getting the inside scoop from each of these young women. We know you've been dying to meet them and hear how things are coming along with our Prince Maxon, so tonight . . . we're just going to ask! Let's get started with"— Gavril looked at his note cards—"Miss Celeste Newsome of Clermont!"

Celeste moved sinuously from her seat in the top row and down the steps. She actually kissed Gavril on both cheeks before she sat down. Her interview was predictable, and so was Bariel's. They tried to be sexy, bending forward a lot to get clear shots down their dresses. It looked fake. I watched their faces in the monitors as they kept glancing at Maxon and winking. Every once in a while, like when Bariel tried to smoothly lick her lips, Marlee and I made brief eye contact and then had to look away so we wouldn't laugh.

Others were more composed. Tiny's voice matched her name, and she seemed to fold in on herself as the interview progressed. But I knew she was sweet and hoped that Maxon wouldn't count her out just because she wasn't a great public speaker. Emmica was poised, as was Marlee, the main difference being that Marlee's voice was so full of excitement and enthusiasm it flew higher and higher as she talked.

Gavril asked a variety of questions, but there were two that seemed to pop up with everyone: "What do you think of Prince Maxon?" and "Are you the girl who yelled at him?" I wasn't looking forward to telling the country that I had chided the future king. Thank goodness that, as far as anyone knew, I'd behaved that way only once.

Everyone was proud to say they weren't the girl who'd yelled at him. Then every single girl thought that Maxon was nice. That was almost always the word: nice. Celeste said that he was handsome. Bariel said he was quietly powerful, which I thought sounded creepy. A few girls were asked if Maxon had kissed them yet. They all blushed and said no. After the third or fourth no, Gavril turned on Maxon.

"Haven't you kissed any of them yet?" he asked, shocked.

"They've only been here two weeks! What kind of man do you think I am?" Maxon replied. He said it lightheartedly but seemed to squirm in his seat a little. I wondered if he'd ever kissed anyone.

Samantha had just finished saying she was having a wonderful time, and then Gavril called me. The other girls applauded as I stood, like we had for everyone. I gave Marlee a nervous smile. I focused on my feet as I walked over, but once I got into the chair, I found it was easy to look right past Gavril's shoulder at Maxon. He gave me a little wink as I picked up the microphone. I felt instantly calmer. I didn't have to win anyone over.

I shook Gavril's hand and sat down across from him. Up close, I could finally see the pin on his lapel. It obviously lost its detail through the camera, but now I saw that it wasn't just the lines and curls of a forte sign, but a small X was engraved in the middle, making the whole thing look almost like a star. It was beautiful.

"America Singer. That's an interesting name you have there. Is there a story behind it?" Gavril asked.

I sighed in relief. This was an easy one.

"Yes, actually. While my mom was pregnant with me, I kicked a lot. She said she had a fighter on her hands, so she named me after the country that fought so hard to keep this land together. It's odd, but to her credit, she was right— we've been fighting ever since."

Gavril laughed. "She sounds like a feisty woman herself."

"She is. I get a lot of my stubbornness from her."

"So you're stubborn, then? Have a bit of a temper?"

I saw Maxon covering his mouth with his hands, laughing.

"Sometimes."

"If you have a temper, would you happen to be the one who yelled at our prince?"

I sighed. "Yes, it was me. And right now, my mother is having a heart attack."

Maxon called out to Gavril, "Get her to tell the whole story!"

Gavril whipped his head back and forth quickly. "Oh! What's the whole story?"

I tried to glare at Maxon, but the whole situation was so silly, it didn't quite work.

"I got a little . . . claustrophobic the first night, and I was desperate to get outside. The guards wouldn't let me through the doors. I was actually about to faint in this one guard's arms, but Prince Maxon was walking by and made them open the doors for me."

"Aw," Gavril said, tilting his head to one side.

"Yes, and then he followed to make sure I was all right. . . . But I was stressed out, so when he spoke to me, I basically ended up accusing him of being stuck-up and shallow."

Gavril chuckled deeply at this. I looked past him to Maxon, who was shaking with laughter. But the more embarrassing thing was that the king and queen were laughing along with him. I didn't turn to look at the girls, but I heard some of them giggling, too. Well, good. Maybe now they would finally stop seeing me as any sort of threat. I was just someone Maxon found entertaining.

"And he forgave you?" Gavril asked in a slightly more sober tone.

"Oddly enough." I shrugged.

"Well, since the two of you are on good terms again, what sort of activities have you been doing together?" Gavril was back to business.

"We usually just go for walks around the garden. He knows I like it outside. And we talk." It sounded pathetic after what some of the other girls had said. Trips to the theater, going hunting, horseback riding—those were impressive next to my story.

But I suddenly understood why he had been speed dating over the last week. The girls needed something to tell Gavril, so he had to provide it. It still seemed weird that he hadn't mentioned any of it to me, but at least I knew why he had been away.

"That sounds very relaxing. Would you say the garden is your favorite thing about the palace?"

I smiled. "Maybe. But the food is exquisite, so . . ."

Gavril laughed again.

"You are the last Five left in the competition, yes? Do you think that hurts your chances of becoming the princess?"

The word sprang from my lips without thought. "No!"

"Oh, my! You do have a spirit there!" Gavril seemed pleased to have gotten such an enthusiastic response. "So you think you'll beat out all the others, then? Make it to the end?"

I thought better of myself. "No, no. It's not like that. I don't think I'm better than any of the other girls; they're all amazing. It's just . . . I don't think Maxon would do that, just discount someone because of their caste."

I heard a collective gasp. I ran over the sentence in my head. It took me a minute to catch my mistake: I'd called him Maxon. Saying that to another girl behind closed doors was one thing, but to say his name without the word "Prince" in front of it was incredibly informal in public.

And I'd said it on live television.

I looked to see if Maxon was angry. He had a calm smile on his face. So he wasn't mad . . . but I was embarrassed. I blushed fiercely.

"Ah, so it seems you really have gotten to know our prince. Tell me, what do you think of *Maxon*?"

I had thought of several answers while I was waiting for my turn. I was going to make fun of his laugh or talk about the pet name he wanted his wife to call him. It seemed like the only way to save the situation was to get back the comedy. But as I lifted my eyes to make one of my comments, I saw Maxon's face.

He really wanted to know.

And I couldn't poke fun at him, not when I had a chance to say what I'd really started to think now that he was my friend. I couldn't joke about the person who'd saved me from facing absolute heartbreak at home, who fed my family boxes of sweets, who ran to me worried that I was hurt if I asked for him.

A month ago, I had looked at the TV and seen a stiff, distant, boring person—someone I couldn't imagine anyone loving. And while he wasn't anything close to the person I did love, he was worthy of having someone to love in his life.

"Maxon Schreave is the epitome of all things good. He is going to be a phenomenal king. He lets girls who are supposed to be wearing dresses wear jeans and doesn't get mad when someone who doesn't know him clearly mislabels him." I gave Gavril a keen look, and he smiled. And behind him, Maxon looked intrigued. "Whoever he marries will be a lucky girl. And whatever happens to me, I will be honored to be his subject."

I saw Maxon swallow, and I lowered my eyes.

"America Singer, thank you so much." Gavril went to shake my hand. "Up next is Miss Tallulah Bell."

I didn't hear what any of the girls said after me, though I stared at the two seats. That interview had become way more personal than I'd intended it to be. I couldn't bring myself to look at Maxon. Instead I sat there replaying my words again and again in my head.

The knock on my door came around ten. I flung it open, and Maxon rolled his eyes.

"You really ought to have a maid in here at night."

"Maxon! Oh, I'm so sorry. I didn't mean to call you that in front of everyone. It was so stupid."

"Do you think I'm mad at you?" he asked as he walked in and shut the door. "America, you call me by my name so often, it was bound to slip out. I wish it had been in a slightly more private setting," he said with a sly smile, "but I don't hold that against you at all."

"Really?"

"Of course, really."

"Ugh! I felt like such an idiot tonight. I can't believe you made me tell that story!" I slapped him on the side gently.

"That was the best part of the whole night! Mom was

really amused. In her day the girls were more reserved than even Tiny, and here you are calling me shallow . . . she couldn't get over it."

Great. Now the queen thought I was a misfit, too. We walked across my room and ended up on the balcony. There was a small, warm breeze blowing the scent of the thousands of flowers in the garden toward us. A full moon shone down on us, adding to the lights around the palace, and it gave Maxon's face a mysterious glow.

"Well, I'm glad you're so amused," I said, running my fingers across the railing.

Maxon hopped up to sit on the railing, looking very relaxed. "You're always amusing. Get used to it."

Hmm. He was almost being funny.

"So . . . about what you said . . . ," he started tentatively.

"Which part? The part about me calling you names or fighting with my mom or saying food was my motivation?" I rolled my eyes.

He laughed once. "The part about me being good . . ."

"Oh. What about it?" Those few sentences suddenly seemed more embarrassing than anything else I'd said. I ducked my head down and twisted a piece of my dress.

"I appreciate you making things look authentic, but you didn't need to go that far."

My head snapped up. How could he think that?

"Maxon, that wasn't for the sake of the show. If you had asked me a month ago what my honest opinion of you was, it would have been very different. But now I know you, and

I know the truth, and you are everything I said you were. And more."

He was quiet, but there was a small smile on his face.

"Thank you," he finally said.

"Anytime."

Maxon cleared his throat. "He'll be lucky, too." He got down from his makeshift seat and walked to my side of the balcony.

"Huh?"

"Your boyfriend. When he comes to his senses and begs you to take him back," Maxon said matter-of-factly.

I had to laugh. No such thing would happen in my world.

"He's not my boyfriend anymore. And he made it pretty clear he was done with me." Even I could hear the tiny bit of hope in my voice.

"Not possible. He'll have seen you on TV by now and fallen for you all over again. Though, in my opinion, you're still much too good for the dog." Maxon spoke almost as if he was bored, like he'd seen this happen a million times.

"Speaking of which!" he said a bit louder. "If you don't want me to be in love with you, you're going to have to stop looking so lovely. First thing tomorrow I'm having your maids sew some potato sacks together for you."

I hit his arm. "Shut up, Maxon."

"I'm not kidding. You're too beautiful for your own good. Once you leave, we'll have to send some of the guards with you. You'll never survive on your own, poor thing." He said all this with mock pity.

"I can't help it." I sighed. "One can never help being born into perfection." I fanned my face as if being so pretty was exhausting.

"No, I don't suppose you can help it."

I giggled. I didn't notice for a moment that Maxon didn't seem to think it was funny.

I stared out at the garden and saw out of the corner of my eye that Maxon was looking at me. His face was incredibly close to mine. When I turned to ask just what he was looking at, I was surprised to see that he was close enough to kiss me.

I was even more surprised when he did.

I pulled away quickly, taking a step. Maxon stepped back as well.

"Sorry," he mumbled, blushing.

"What are you doing?" I asked in a shocked whisper.

"Sorry." He was slightly turned away, obviously embarrassed.

"Why did you do that?" I put my hand to my mouth.

"It's just . . . with what you said earlier, and then seeking me out yesterday . . . just the way you acted . . . I thought maybe your feelings had changed. And I like you, I thought you could tell." He turned to face me. "And . . . Oh, was it terrible? You don't look happy at all."

I tried to wipe whatever expression I had off my face. Maxon looked mortified.

"I'm so sorry. I've never kissed anyone before. I don't know what I'm doing. I'm just . . . I'm sorry, America." He breathed a heavy sigh and ran his hand through his hair a few times, leaning against the railing.

I didn't expect it, but a warmth filled me.

He'd wanted his first kiss to be with me.

I thought about the Maxon I knew now—the man full of compliments, the man prepared to give me the winnings of a bet I lost, the man who forgave me when I hurt him both physically and emotionally—and discovered that I didn't mind that at all.

Yes, I still had feelings for Aspen. I couldn't undo that. But if I couldn't be with him, then what was holding me back from being with Maxon? Nothing more than my preconceived ideas of him, which were nothing close to who he was.

I stepped up to him and rubbed my hand across his forehead.

"What are you doing?"

"I'm erasing that memory. I think we can do better." I pulled my hand down and propped myself up beside him, facing toward my room. Maxon didn't move . . . but he did smile.

"America, I don't think you can change history." All the same, his expression looked hopeful.

"Sure we can. Besides, who'd ever know about it but you and me?"

Maxon looked at me for a moment, clearly wondering if this was really okay. Slowly, I saw a cautious confidence creep into his face as he looked into my eyes. We stayed that way for a moment before I could remember just what I had said.

"One can never help being born into perfection," I whispered.

He came close, wrapping an arm around my waist so that we faced each other. His nose tickled mine. He ran his fingers across my cheek so gently it seemed he was afraid I would break.

"No, I don't suppose you can," he breathed.

With his hand holding my face toward his, Maxon lowered his lips to mine and gave me the faintest whisper of a kiss.

Something about the tentativeness of it made me feel beautiful. Without a word, I could understand how excited he was to have this moment, but then afraid at the same time. And deeper than any of that, I sensed that he adored me.

So this was what it felt like to be a lady.

After a moment, he pulled back and asked, "Was that better?"

I could only nod. Maxon looked like he was on the verge of doing a backflip. There was a similar feeling in my chest. That was so unexpected. This was all too quick, too strange. The confusion must have shown on my face, because Maxon got serious.

"May I say something?"

I nodded again.

"I'm not so stupid as to believe that you've completely forgotten about your former boyfriend. I know what you've gone through and that you're not exactly here under the normal circumstances. I know you think there are others here more suited for me and this life, and I wouldn't want you to rush into trying to be happy with any of this. I just . . . I just want to know if it's possible . . ."

It was a hard question to answer. Would I be willing to live a life I'd never wanted? Would I be willing to watch as he kindly tried to date the others to be sure he wasn't making a mistake? Would I be willing to take on the responsibility that he had as a prince? Would I be willing to love him?

"Yes, Maxon," I whispered. "It's possible."

CHAPTER 19

I TOLD NO ONE WHAT had happened between Maxon and me, not even Marlee or my maids. It felt like a wonderful secret that I could revisit in the middle of one of Silvia's boring lessons or another long day in the Women's Room. And to be honest, I thought about our kisses—both the awkward and the sweet—more often than I expected I would.

I knew I wasn't just going to fall in love with Maxon overnight. I knew my heart wouldn't let me. But I suddenly found myself in a place where that was something I might want. So I thought about the possibility quietly in my head, though I was tempted to blurt out my secret more than once.

Particularly three days later when Olivia announced to the half-full Women's Room that Maxon had kissed her.

I couldn't believe how shattered I felt. I caught myself looking at Olivia and wondering what was so special about her.

"Tell us everything!" Marlee insisted.

Most of the other girls were curious as well, but Marlee was the most enthusiastic. In the short time since she and Maxon had their last date, her interest in everyone else's progress seemed to be growing. I couldn't tell what was behind the shift, and I wasn't quite brave enough to ask.

Olivia didn't need encouragement. She sat down on one of the couches and fanned out her dress. It looked like she was practicing to be the princess. I felt like telling her that one kiss didn't mean she was winning.

"I don't want to go into all the details, but it was quite romantic," she gushed, tucking her chin into her chest. "He took me to the roof. There's this place that's kind of like a balcony, but it looks like it's used for the guards. I couldn't tell. We could look out over the wall, and the whole city was just glittering as far as we could see. He didn't really say anything. He just pulled me in and kissed me." Her whole body contracted with joy.

Marlee sighed. Celeste looked like she was ready to break something. I sat there.

I kept telling myself that I shouldn't care so much, that this was all part of the Selection. And who's to say that I'd really want to end up with Maxon anyway? Honestly, I ought to consider myself lucky. It was clear Celeste's malice had a new target, and after that whole episode with my dress—which I realized I'd forgotten to mention to Maxon—I was glad to see her move on.

"Do you think she's the only one he's kissed?" Tuesday

whispered in my ear. Kriss, who was standing beside me, heard her concerns and piped in.

"He wouldn't just kiss anyone. She must be doing something right," Kriss lamented.

"What if he's kissed half the room and people are keeping quiet about it? Maybe it's part of their strategy," Tuesday wondered.

"I don't think anyone who kept quiet would necessarily consider that a strategy," I countered. "Maybe they're just private."

Kriss sucked in a breath. "What if Olivia telling us all this is just some game? Now we're all worried, and it's not as if any of us would actually ask Maxon if he'd kissed her. There's no way to tell if she's lying or not."

"Do you think she would do that?" I asked.

"If she did, I wish I'd thought of it first," Tuesday said longingly.

Kriss sighed. "This is much more complicated than I thought it would be."

"Tell me about it," I mumbled.

"I like almost everyone in this room, but when I hear about Maxon doing something with someone else, I just want to figure out how I can do one better than her," she confessed. "I don't like feeling competitive toward you all."

"It's kind of like what I was telling Tiny the other day," Tuesday said. "I know she's a little on the timid side, but she's very ladylike and I think she'd make a great princess. I can't be mad at her if she has more dates than me, even if

I want the crown myself."

Kriss and I met eyes for a second, and I could tell we were both thinking the same thing. She said *crown*, not *him*. But I let it drop, because the other part of her little speech struck on something familiar. "Marlee and I talk about that all the time. How we can see great qualities in each other."

We all exchanged looks, and something felt different. Suddenly I didn't feel so jealous of Olivia or even so at odds with Celeste. We were all going through this in a different way, and maybe even for different reasons, but we were at least going through it together.

"Maybe Queen Amberly was right," I said. "The only thing to do is be yourself. I'd rather have Maxon send me home for being myself than keep me for being like someone else."

"That's true," Kriss said. "And in the end, thirty-four people have to go. If I was the last one standing, I'd want to know I had everyone else's support, so we should try to be supportive, too."

I nodded, knowing she was right. I was confident that I could do that.

Just then Elise burst into the room, followed by Zoe and Emmica. She was usually very slow and calm, and never raised her voice. Today, however, she turned her head and squealed at us.

"Look at these combs!" she cried, pointing to two beautiful hair ornaments that were covered in what looked like thousands of dollars' worth of precious stones. "Maxon gave them to me. Aren't they beautiful?"

This set the room into a new flurry of excitement and disappointment, and my newborn confidence disappeared.

I tried not to be disappointed. After all, hadn't I received gifts? Hadn't I been kissed? But as the room filled with girls and the stories were retold, I found myself wanting to just go hide. Maybe today would be a good day to spend with my maids.

As I was considering leaving the room, Silvia came in, looking slightly frazzled and excited at the same time.

"Ladies!" she called out, attempting to quiet us. "Ladies, are you all here?"

We sang our yeses back to her.

"Thank goodness for that," she said, settling down. "I know this is very late notice, but we've just learned the king and queen of Swendway are coming to visit in three days, and as you all know, we have relations in their royal family. Also, the queen's extended family will be coming in to meet you at the same time, so we're going to have quite a full house. We have very little time to get ready, so clear your afternoons. Lessons in the Great Room immediately after lunch," she said, and turned to leave.

You would have thought the palace staff had months to plan. Giant tented pavilions were set up in the gardens, with food and wine stations scattered about the lawn. The number of guards out was higher than usual, and they were joined by several Swendish soldiers the king and queen had brought with them. I guess even they knew how at risk the palace was.

There was a tent with thrones set up for the king, queen, and Maxon as well as the king and queen of Swendway. The Swendish queen—whose name I couldn't pronounce to save my life—was almost as beautiful as Queen Amberly and seemed to be a dear friend to her. They were all settled comfortably under that tent except for Maxon, who was busy making rounds with all the girls and the extended members of his family.

Maxon looked thrilled to see his cousins, even the little ones who kept tugging on his suit coat and running away. He had one of his many cameras out and was chasing the children with it, snapping away. Nearly all the Selected girls were watching him in adoration.

"America," someone called. I turned to my right to see Elayna and Leah talking to a woman who looked almost identical to the queen. "Come and meet the queen's sister." There was something in Elayna's tone that I couldn't quite name but made me nervous about joining them.

I walked over and curtsied to the lady, who cackled and said, "Stop that, honey. I'm not the queen here. I'm Adele, Amberly's older sister." She extended a hand, which I took, and she hiccuped as we shook. The woman had a slight accent, and something about her was comforting in the way that coming home feels. She was curvaceous and held a near-empty glass of wine that, based on the heavy look in her eyes, was not her first.

"Where are you from? I love your accent," I said. Some of the other girls from the South sounded similar, and their voices seemed incredibly romantic to me.

"Honduragua. Right by the coast. We grew up in the tiniest house," she said, making a space the size of an inch between her finger and thumb. "And look at her now. Look at me," she said, motioning down to her dress. "Such a change."

"I live in Carolina, and my parents took me to the coast once. I loved it," I replied.

"Oh, no, no, no, child," she said, waving her hand about. Elayna and Leah looked like they were holding in laughter. Clearly they didn't think the queen's sister should be quite so familiar. "The beaches in middle Illéa are trash compared to the ones down south. You have to go see one day."

I smiled and nodded, thinking that I'd love to see more of the country, but it was doubtful I ever would. Shortly after, one of Adele's many children came up to her and pulled her away, and Elayna and Leah burst into laughter.

"Isn't she hilarious?" Leah said.

"I don't know. She seems friendly," I replied with a shrug.

"She's vulgar," Elayna replied. "You should have heard all the things she said before you came up."

"What was so bad about her?"

"You'd think she'd have picked up a few lessons in decorum over the years. How did Silvia not get ahold of her?" Leah said with a sneer.

"Need I remind you, she was raised as a Four. Same as you," I shot back.

Her smug expression faltered, and she seemed to remember that she and Adele weren't so different. Elayna, however, was a natural Three and kept on talking.

"You can bet, if I win, my family will either be trained or deported. I wouldn't let any of them embarrass me like that."

"What was so embarrassing?" I asked.

Elayna sucked her teeth. "She's drunk. The queen and king of Swendway are here. She ought to be caged."

I decided that was enough and walked away to get some wine of my own. Once I had a glass, I looked around and honestly couldn't find a single place I wanted to settle. The whole reception was beautiful and interesting and completely aggravating.

I thought about what Elayna had said. If I ended up living in the palace, would I expect my family to change? I looked at the children running around, the people huddled together catching up. Wouldn't I want Kenna to be exactly who she was, want her children enjoying all this no matter how they behaved?

How much would living at the palace change me?

Would Maxon want me to change? Was that why he was off kissing other girls? Because there was something not quite right about me?

Was the rest of the Selection going to feel this irritating?

"Smile."

I turned, and Maxon snapped a picture of me. I bounced back in surprise. That unexpected picture wore out the last of my patience, and I turned away.

"Something wrong?" Maxon asked, lowering the camera.
I shrugged.

"What's going on?"

"I just don't feel like being a part of the Selection today," I answered curtly.

Unfazed, Maxon stepped closer and lowered his voice. "Need someone to talk to? I could tug my ear right now," he offered.

I sighed and tried to put a polite smile on my face. "No, I just need to think." I went to leave.

"America," he said quietly. I stopped and turned. "Have I done something?"

I hesitated. Should I ask about him kissing Olivia? Should I tell him how tense I was feeling around the girls now that things had changed between us? Should I tell him how I didn't want to change myself or my family to be a part of this? I was about to let everything spill out when a shrill voice called from behind us.

"Prince Maxon?"

We turned, and Celeste was standing there, talking to the queen of Swendway. It was clear she wanted to have this conversation with Maxon on her arm. She waved, inviting him over.

"Why don't you run along?" I said, my annoyance leaking into my voice again.

Maxon looked at me. The expression on his face reminded me that this was part of the deal. I was expected to share.

"Careful with that one." I gave Maxon a quick curtsy and walked away.

I made my way toward the palace, and along the way noticed Marlee sitting alone. I didn't even want to be with her right now, but I noticed she was parked on a bench near the back wall of the palace in the brutally hot sun, her closest companion a young, silent guard stationed just a few yards away.

"Marlee, what are you doing? Get under a tent before you burn your skin."

She gave me a polite smile. "I'm happy here."

"No, really," I said, putting a hand around her arm. "You'll look like my hair. You should—"

Marlee jerked her hand out of my grip, but spoke gently. "I want to stay here, America. I prefer it."

There was a tension in her face she was trying to mask. I was sure she wasn't upset with me, but something was going on.

"Fine. Try to get some shade soon, though. Sunburns hurt," I said, attempting to cover my frustration, and walked toward the palace.

Once inside, I decided to go to the Women's Room. I couldn't be gone for too long, and at least that room would be empty. But when I went in, I found Adele sitting near the window and watching the scene unfold outside. She turned when I entered and gave me a small smile.

I walked over and sat next to her. "Hiding?"

She smiled. "Kind of. I wanted to meet you all and see my

sister again, but I hate it when these things turn into state functions. They make me tense."

"I'm not such a fan myself. I couldn't imagine doing things like this all the time."

"I bet," she said lazily. "You're the Five, right?"

The way she said it, it wasn't an insult. More like she was asking if I was in the club. "Yeah, that's me."

"I remembered your face. You were sweet at the airport. It's the kind of thing she would have done," she said, nodding out the window toward the queen. She sighed. "I don't know how she does it. She's stronger than most people know." I watched her pick up a wineglass and sip away.

"She does seem strong, but ladylike, too."

Adele beamed. "Yes, but it's more than that. Look at her now."

I watched the queen. I noticed her eyes were trained across the lawn. I followed her gaze, and she was watching Maxon. He was speaking to the queen of Swendway next to Celeste while one of his cousins clung to his leg.

"He would have been a great brother," she said. "Amberly had three miscarriages. Two before him, one after. She still thinks about it, she tells me so. And then I have six kids. I feel guilty every time I show up."

"I'm sure she doesn't think of it that way. I'll bet she's excited every time you visit," I assured her.

She turned. "You know what makes her happy? You do. Do you know what she sees out there? A daughter. She knows that when this is all over, she'll have two children."

I turned from Adele to look at the queen again. "You think so? She seems a little distant. I haven't even spoken to her yet."

Adele nodded. "Just you wait. She's terrified of becoming attached to all of you just to watch you leave. Once it's a smaller group, you'll see."

I looked at the queen again. And then at Maxon. Back to the king. And then to Adele.

So much went through my head. How families are families, no matter their castes. How mothers all have their own worries to bear. How I really didn't hate any of the girls here, no matter how wrong they might be. How everyone out there must be putting on a brave face for some reason or another. And finally, how Maxon had made me a promise.

"Excuse me. I have someone I need to talk to."

She sipped her wine and happily waved me away. I ran out of the room, and back into the blinding sun of the gardens. I searched around for a moment and found that Maxon's young cousin had begun chasing him around a shrub. I smiled and approached slowly.

Finally Maxon stopped, waving his hands in the air, admitting his defeat. As he laughed, he turned and saw me, his smile still wide on his face. When our eyes met, his smile faded. He searched my face, looking for a sign of my mood.

I bit my lip and looked down. It was clear that caring about what happened to me as a member of the Selection would mean processing a lot of other feelings that I hadn't been prepared for. However I took them in, I had to try not to force them out on other people, especially Maxon.

I thought about the queen—hosting visiting leaders, family members, a gaggle of girls all at once. She managed events and backed causes. She assisted her husband, her son, and the country. And underneath it all, she was a Four who held her own heartbreaks and never let her former rank or current aches keep her from doing it all.

I looked beneath my eyelashes at Maxon and smiled. He slowly smiled back, and whispered something to the little boy, who immediately turned and ran away. He reached up and tugged his ear. And I did the same.

CHAPTER 20

THE QUEEN'S FAMILY STAYED A few days, and the visitors from Swendway an entire week. They did a segment on the *Report* discussing international relations and movements toward more peace for both nations.

It was now a month into my stay at the palace, and I was completely at home. My body was comfortable in the new climate. The warmth of the palace was heavenly, like a holiday. September was almost over, and it got very cool in the evenings, but it was much warmer than home. The sights of this giant space were no longer a mystery. The sounds of heeled shoes on marble, crystal glasses clinking, guards marching—they were starting to become as normal as the refrigerator humming or Gerad kicking a soccer ball up against the house.

Meals with the royal family and times in the Women's

Room were staples in my routine, but the middle moments of my days were always new. I spent a lot of time working on music; the instruments at the palace were far superior to the ones I had at home. I had to admit, they were making me spoiled. The quality of the sound was unimaginably better. And the Women's Room had gotten a little more exciting, as the queen had shown up at least twice now. She hadn't really spoken to anyone yet, but she sat in a comfortable chair with her maids at her side, watching as we read or conversed.

In general, the animosity had settled as well. We were getting used to one another. We finally found out the magazine's top picks for our photographs. I was shocked to see I was one of the front-runners. Marlee was in the top spot, with Kriss, Tallulah, and Bariel close behind. Celeste didn't talk to Bariel for days upon hearing this, but eventually everyone let it pass.

What still seemed to bring the most tension were the bits of information tossed around. Whoever had been with Maxon recently couldn't help but gush about their little interlude. The way everyone spoke, it seemed as if Maxon was going to be choosing six or seven wives. But not everyone was shining in this experience.

For instance, Marlee had more than a few dates with Maxon, which put everyone on edge. Still, she never came across as excited as she had after their very first one.

"America, if I tell you this, you have to swear not to tell a soul," she said as we walked in the garden. I knew it was something serious. She'd waited until we got away from the listening ears in the Women's Room and far beyond the eyes of the guards.

"Of course, Marlee. Are you all right?"

"Yes, I'm fine. I just . . . I need your opinion on something." Her face was heavy with worry.

"What's wrong?"

She bit her lip. "It's Maxon. I'm not sure it's going to work out." She looked down.

"What makes you think that?" I asked, concerned.

"Well, for starters, I don't . . . I don't *feel* anything, you know? No spark, no connection."

"Maxon can be a little shy is all. You have to give him time." This was true. I was surprised she didn't know that about him.

"No, I mean, I don't think *I* like *him*."

"Oh." That was something very different. "Have you tried?" What a stupid question.

"Yes! So hard! I keep waiting for a moment to come when he'll say or do something to make me feel like we have something in common, but it never happens. I think he's handsome, but that's not enough to build a whole relationship on. I don't even know if he's attracted to me. Do you have any idea what kind of things he, you know, likes?"

I thought about it. "No, actually. We've never talked about what he's looking for in the physical department."

"And that's another thing! We never talk. He talks on and on to you, but we never seem to have anything to say. We spend a lot of our time quietly watching something or playing cards."

She looked more worried by the minute.

"Sometimes we're quiet together, too. Sometimes we just sit and say nothing. Besides, feelings like that don't always happen overnight. Maybe you're both just taking it slow." I tried to sound reassuring—Marlee looked like she was on the verge of tears.

"Honestly, America, I think the only reason I'm still here is because the people like me so much. I think their opinions matter to him."

That thought hadn't occurred to me, but it sounded plausible. Long ago, I'd dismissed their opinion, but Maxon loved his people. They'd have more of a hand in choosing the next princess than they would know.

"And besides," she whispered, "everything between us feels so . . . empty."

Then the tears came.

I sighed and hugged her. Truthfully, I wanted her to stay, to be here with me, but if she didn't love Maxon . . .

"Marlee, if you don't want to be with Maxon, I think you need to tell him."

"Oh, no, I don't think I can."

"You have to. He doesn't want to marry someone who doesn't love him. If you don't have any feelings for him, he needs to know."

She shook her head. "I can't just ask to leave! I need to stay. I couldn't go home . . . not now."

"Why, Marlee? What's keeping you here?"

For a moment, I wondered if Marlee and I shared the same dark secret. Maybe there was someone she needed distance from, too. The only difference in our situations was that Maxon knew about mine. I wanted her to say it! I wanted to know I wasn't the only one who'd ended up here out of some ridiculous circumstances.

But Marlee's tears stopped almost as quickly as they started. She sniffed a few times and straightened up. She smoothed out her day dress, squared her shoulders, and turned to face me. She pulled a strong, warm smile to her face and spoke.

"You know what? I bet you're right." She started to back away. "I'm sure if I just give it some time, it'll all work out. I have to go. Tiny's expecting me."

Marlee half ran back to the palace. What in the world had come over her?

The next day, Marlee avoided me. The day after that, too. I made a point of sitting in the Women's Room at a safe distance and making sure to acknowledge her whenever we crossed paths. I wanted her to know that she could trust me; I wouldn't make her talk.

It took four days for her to give me a sad, knowing smile. I just nodded. It seemed that would be all there was to say about whatever was going on in Marlee's heart.

That same day, while I was sitting in the Women's Room, Maxon called for me. It would be a lie to say I wasn't absolutely giddy when I ran out the door and into his arms.

"Maxon!" I breathed, falling into him. When I stepped

back, he sort of fumbled a moment, and I knew why. The day we'd left the Swendway reception and went inside to talk, I confessed what a hard time I was having dealing with the way I felt. And I asked him not to kiss me until I was more certain. I could tell he was hurt, but he nodded and hadn't broken his promise yet. It was just too hard to decipher those feelings when he acted like he was my boyfriend, but clearly wasn't.

There were still twenty-two girls here after Camille, Mikaela, and Laila had been sent home. Camille and Laila were simply incompatible and left with very little fanfare. Mikaela got so homesick she burst into heaving sobs during breakfast two days later. Maxon escorted her from the room, patting her shoulder the whole way. He seemed fine with letting them go, and was happy to focus on his other prospects, myself included. But he and I both knew it would be foolish of him to invest his heart completely in me when even I wasn't sure where mine was.

"How are you today?" he asked, stepping back.

"Perfect, of course. What are you doing here? Aren't you supposed to be working?"

"The president of the Infrastructure Committee is sick, so the meeting was postponed. I'm free as a bird all afternoon." His eyes were gleaming. "What do you want to do?" he asked, holding his arm out for me.

"Anything! There's so much of the palace I still haven't seen. There are horses here, right? And the movie theater. You still haven't taken me there."

"Let's do that. I could use something relaxing. What kinds of movies do you like best?" he asked as we started walking toward where I guessed the stairwell to the basement was.

"Honestly, I don't know. I don't get to watch a lot of movies. But I like romantic books. And comedies, too!"

"Romance, you say?" He raised his eyebrows like he was up to no good. I had to laugh.

We turned a corner and continued to talk. As we approached, a mass of the palace guard pulled to the side of the hall and saluted. There had to be more than a dozen men standing in the hallway. I was used to them by now. Even the sight of a collection that big couldn't distract me from the fun time I was about to have with Maxon.

What did stop me was when I heard the gasp that escaped someone's mouth as we passed. Maxon and I both turned.

And there was Aspen.

I gasped, too.

A few weeks ago, I'd heard some administrator in the palace talk about the draft in passing. I had wondered about Aspen, but seeing as I was running late to one of Silvia's many lessons, I didn't really have a chance to speculate much.

So he'd been taken by the draft after all. Of all the places he could have gone . . .

Maxon caught on. "America, do you know this young man?"

It had been more than a month since I'd seen Aspen, but this was the person I'd spent years committing to memory, the person who still visited my dreams. I would know him anywhere. He looked a little bigger, like he'd been fed, really fed, and was working out a lot. His scraggly hair had been cut short, practically all gone. And I was used to seeing him in secondhand clothes that were barely being held together by threads, and here he was in one of the brilliant, fitted uniforms of the palace guard.

He was alien and familiar at once. So many of the things around him seemed wrong. But those eyes . . . those were Aspen's eyes.

My eyes fell to the name tag on his uniform: OFFICER LEGER.

I doubted a second had passed.

I kept myself composed enough that no one saw the storm raging inside—a miracle in and of itself. I wanted to touch him, kiss him, scream at him, demand he leave my sanctuary. I wanted to melt away and disappear, but I felt so very *here*.

None of it made sense.

I cleared my throat. "Yes. Officer Leger comes from Carolina. He's actually from my hometown." I smiled at Maxon.

No doubt Aspen would have heard us laughing as we rounded the corner, would have noted that my arm was still draped on the prince's. Let him make of that what he would.

Maxon seemed excited for me. "Well, how about that! Welcome, Officer Leger. You must be happy to see your Champion Girl again." Maxon held his hand out, and Aspen shook it.

Aspen's face was like a stone. "Yes, Your Majesty. Very much so."

What did that mean?

"I'm sure you're pulling for her, too," Maxon encouraged as he winked at me.

"Of course, Your Majesty." Aspen bowed his head a bit.

And what did *that* mean?

"Excellent. Since America is from your home province, I can't think of a better man in the palace to leave her with. I'll make sure you're put on her guard rotation. This girl of yours refuses to keep a maid in her room at night. I've tried to tell her. . . ." Maxon shook his head at me.

Aspen finally seemed to relax a bit. "I'm not surprised by that, Your Majesty."

Maxon smiled. "Well, I'm sure you all have a busy day ahead of you. We'll just be off. Good day, officers." Maxon gave a quick nod and pulled me away.

It took all the strength in my body not to look back.

In the dark of the theater, I tried to figure out what to do. Maxon had made it clear from the night I'd told him about Aspen that he hated anyone who would treat me with so little care. If I told Maxon that the man he'd just assigned to watch over me was that very person, would he punish him somehow? I wouldn't put it past him. He'd invented an entire support system for the country based on my stories of being hungry.

So I couldn't tell him. I wouldn't tell him. Because as mad as I was, I loved Aspen. And I couldn't bear him being hurt.

Then should I leave? The ambivalence pulled at my heart. I could escape Aspen, get away from his face—a face that would torture me every day when I saw it and knew it was no longer mine. But if I left, I'd have to leave Maxon, too. And Maxon was my closest friend, maybe even more. I couldn't just go. Besides, how would I explain it without telling him Aspen was here?

And my family. Maybe the checks they got were smaller, but at least they were getting them. May had written saying that Dad was promising our best Christmas ever this year, but I was sure that came with the stipulation that another Christmas might never be as good. If I left, who could say how much money my past fame would bring for my family? We had to save up as much as we could now.

"You didn't like that one, did you?" Maxon asked nearly two hours later.

"Huh?"

"The movie. You didn't laugh or anything."

"Oh." I tried to remember one little piece of information, a single scene that I could say I'd enjoyed. Nothing registered. "I think I'm just a little out of it today. Sorry you wasted your afternoon."

"Nonsense." Maxon waved away my lackluster attitude. "I just enjoy your company. Though perhaps you should take a nap before dinner. You're looking a little pale."

I nodded. I was considering going to my room and never coming back out.

CHAPTER 21

IN THE END, I DECIDED against hiding in my room. Instead I chose the Women's Room. Usually I darted in and out all day, visiting libraries, taking walks with Marlee, or even heading back upstairs to visit my maids. But now I was using the Women's Room like a cave. No men, not even guards, were allowed inside without the queen's express permission. It was perfect.

Well, it was perfect for three days. With this many girls, it was only a matter of time until someone had a birthday. Kriss's was on Thursday. I guessed she'd mentioned it to Maxon— who seemed to never pass up an opportunity to give someone something—and the outcome was a mandatory party for all the Selected. As a result, Thursday was a mad rush of girls in and out of one another's rooms, asking what they were wearing or guessing at how grand it would be.

It didn't appear that gifts were required, but I figured I'd do something nice for her all the same.

On the day of the party, I donned one of my favorite day dresses and grabbed my violin. I crept down to the Great Room, looking around corners before I committed to walking on. Once I made it to the room, I did another sweep, surveying the guards who lined the walls. Mercifully, Aspen was nowhere to be seen, and I had to chuckle at the presence of so many men in uniform. Were they expecting a riot or something?

The Great Room was decorated beautifully. Special vases hung on the wall, displaying huge arrangements of yellow and white flowers, and similar bouquets sat in bowls around the room. Windows, stretches of wall, and pretty much anything that didn't move was draped in garlands. A few small tables had been set out, and they were covered with bright linens. Little bits of glittering confetti sparkled on the tabletops. Ornate bows adorned the backs of chairs.

In one corner, a massive cake that matched the colors of the room waited to be cut. Next to it, a small table held a few gifts for the birthday girl.

A string quartet was set up against the wall, effectively making my attempt at a gift meaningless, and a photographer wandered the room, capturing moments for the public eye.

The mood in the room was playful. Tiny—who had so far only managed to get close to Marlee—was talking to Emmica and Jenna and looking more animated than I'd ever seen her. Marlee hovered near a window, looking like one of the many guards dotting the wall. She made no effort to leave her chosen spot but stopped anyone who passed by to chat. A group of Threes—Kayleigh, Elizabeth, and Emily—all turned and waved and smiled. I returned the gesture. Everyone seemed so friendly and happy today.

Except for Celeste and Bariel. Usually they were inseparable, but today they were on opposite ends of the room, with Bariel speaking to Samantha, and Celeste sitting alone at a table, clutching a crystal glass of deep red liquid. I'd obviously missed something between yesterday's dinner and this afternoon.

I gripped my violin case again and walked toward the back of the room to see Marlee.

"Hi, Marlee. This is something, isn't it?" I asked, setting down the violin.

"It sure is." She hugged me. "I hear Maxon's coming by later to wish Kriss a happy birthday in person. Isn't that sweet? I'll bet he has a present, too."

Marlee went on in her typical enthusiastic way. I still wondered what her secret was, but I trusted her enough to bring up the subject if she really needed to talk about it. We spoke of little nothings for a few minutes until we heard a general clamor at the front end of the room.

Marlee and I both turned, and while she remained calm, I was completely deflated.

Kriss's dress choice had been incredibly strategic. Here we all were in day dresses—short, girlish things—and she was in a floor-length gown. But the length meant little. It was that her dress was a creamy, almost white color. Her hair was done up with a row of yellow jewels pinned into a line across the front in a very subtle resemblance to a crown. She looked mature, regal, bridal.

Even though I wasn't entirely sure where my heart was, I felt a pang of jealousy. None of us would ever get a similar moment. No matter how many parties or dinners came and went, it would be rather pathetic to try to copy Kriss's look. I saw Celeste's hand—the one that wasn't clutching her drink—ball into a fist.

"She looks really pretty," Marlee commented wistfully.

"Better than pretty," I replied.

The party continued on, and Marlee and I mostly crowd-watched. Surprisingly—and suspiciously—Celeste clung to Kriss, talking up a storm as Kriss circled the room, thanking everyone for coming, even though we really had no choice.

Eventually she made it to the back corner where Marlee and I were standing, soaking up the warm sun from the windows. Marlee, true to form, threw her arms around Kriss.

"Happy birthday!" she squealed.

"Thank you!" Kriss replied, returning Marlee's affection and enthusiasm.

"So you're nineteen today, right?" Marlee asked.

"Yes. I couldn't think of a better way to celebrate. I'm so glad they're taking pictures. My mother will love this! Even though we do pretty well, we've never had money to have something like this. It's so beautiful!" she gushed.

Kriss was a Three. There weren't nearly as many limits to her life as mine, but I'd imagine anything close to this scale would be hard to justify.

"It is impressive," Celeste commented. "For my birthday last year, I had a black and white party. Any trace of color, and you weren't even allowed in the door."

"Wow," Marlee whispered, obvious envy in the tiny word.

"It was fantastic. Gourmet food, dramatic lighting, and the music! Well, we flew in Tessa Tamble. You've heard of her?"

It was impossible not to know Tessa Tamble. She had at least a dozen hit songs. Sometimes we saw videos of hers on TV, though that was frowned on by Mom. She thought we were infinitely more talented than anyone like Tessa, and it irked her to no end that she had fame and money when we didn't for doing essentially the same thing.

"She's my favorite!" Kriss exclaimed.

"Well, Tessa's a dear friend of the family, so she came in and did a concert for my party. I mean, we couldn't have a bunch of dreary Fives sucking all the life out of the room."

Marlee gave me a quick sideways glance. I could tell she was feeling embarrassed for me.

"Oops," Celeste added, looking at me. "I forgot. I meant no offense."

The sticky sweetness of her voice was infuriating. Once again I was tempted to hit her. . . . Better not to push it.

"None taken," I replied, as composed as I possibly could. "Exactly what do you do as a Two, Celeste? I mean, I've never heard your music on the radio."

"I model," she answered in a tone that implied I should have known that. "Haven't you seen my ads?"

"Can't say I have."

"Oh, well, you are a Five. I guess you can't afford the magazines anyway."

It hurt because it was true. May loved to sneak peeks at magazines when we managed to go by a store, but there was absolutely no reason for us to buy them.

Kriss, taking on the role of host again, switched directions.

"You know, America, I've been meaning to ask what your focus was as a Five."

"Music."

"You should play for us sometime!"

I sighed. "Actually, I brought my violin to play for you today. I thought it would make a nice gift, but you've already got a quartet, so I figured—"

"Oh, play for us!" Marlee begged.

"Please, America, it's my birthday!" Kriss echoed.

"But they've already given you a—" It didn't matter how I protested. Kriss and Marlee had already shushed the quartet and made everyone come to the back of the room. Some girls fanned their dresses out and sat on the floor, while others pulled a few chairs toward the corner. Kriss stood in the middle of the crowd, clutching her hands with excitement, as Celeste stood by, holding the crystal glass she had yet to take a sip from.

As the girls settled themselves, I prepped the violin. The quartet of young men who had been playing walked over to support me, and the few waitstaff who had been buzzing about the room became still.

I took a deep breath and brought the violin to my chin. "For you," I said, looking at Kriss.

I let the bow hover above the strings for a moment, closed my eyes, and then let the music come.

For a while, there was no wicked Celeste, no Aspen lurking in the palace, no rebels trying to invade. There wasn't anything but one perfect note stringing itself to the next in such a way they seemed afraid they might get lost in time without one another. But they did hold together, and as they floated on, this gift that was meant to be something for Kriss became something for me.

I might be a Five, but I wasn't worthless.

I played the song—as familiar as my father's voice or the smell of my room—for a few brief, beautiful moments, and then let it come to its unavoidable end. I gave the bow one last sweep across the strings and lifted it into the air.

I turned to find Kriss, hoping she'd enjoyed her gift, but I didn't even see her face. Behind the crowd of girls, Maxon had walked in. He was in a gray suit with a box under his arm for Kriss. The girls were kindly applauding, but I couldn't register the sound. All I saw was that Maxon wore a handsome, awestruck expression, which slowly turned into a smile, a smile for no one but me.

"Your Majesty," I said with a curtsy.

The other girls all clambered to their feet to greet Maxon. In the midst of this, I heard a shocked squeal.

"Oh, no! Kriss, I'm so sorry."

A few girls had gasped in the same direction, and as Kriss turned my way I saw why. Her beautiful dress was stained down the front from Celeste's punch. It looked like Kriss had been stabbed.

"I'm sorry, I just turned too fast. I didn't mean to, Kriss. Let me help you." To the average person, Celeste's tone probably sounded sincere, but I could see through it.

Kriss covered her mouth as she started to cry, then ran from the room, which ended the party. To his credit, Maxon went after her, though I really wished he had stayed.

Celeste was pleading her case to anyone who would listen, saying it was a complete accident. Tuesday was nodding, saying she saw the whole thing, but there were so many rolling eyes and sagging shoulders from the rest that her support was pointless. I quietly put my violin away and went to leave.

Marlee grabbed my arm. "Someone should do something about her."

If Celeste could move someone as lovely as Anna to violence, or think it was acceptable to try and take the dress off my back, or make someone as good as Marlee come close to anger, then she really was too much for the Selection.

I had to get that girl out of the palace.

CHAPTER 22

"I'm TELLING YOU, MAXON, IT wasn't an accident." We were in the garden again, passing time until the *Report*. It had taken me a whole day to get a chance to speak with him.

"But she looked mortified, and she was so apologetic," he countered. "How could it not have been an accident?"

I sighed. "I'm telling you. I see Celeste every day, and that was her sneaky way of ruining Kriss's moment in the spotlight. She's so competitive."

"Well, if she was trying to take my attention from Kriss, she failed. I spent nearly an hour with the girl. Rather pleasant time I had, too."

I didn't want to hear about that. I knew that there was something small and tenuous between us, and I didn't want to deal with anything that might change it. Not until I knew how I felt about it myself.

"Then what about Anna?" I asked.

"Who?"

"Anna Farmer? She hit Celeste, and you kicked her out, remember? I know Anna had to have been provoked."

"Did you hear Celeste say something?" He sounded skeptical.

"Well . . . no. But I knew Anna, *and* I know Celeste. I'm telling you, Anna was not the type of person to head straight to violence. Celeste must have said something heartless to her for her to have reacted that way."

"America, I'm aware that you spend more time with the girls than I do, but how well can you really know them? You like to hide in your room or the libraries. I daresay you're more familiar with your maids' personalities than any of the Selected."

He was probably right, but I wouldn't back down. "That's not fair. I was right about Marlee, wasn't I? Don't you think she's nice?"

He made a face. "Yes . . . she is nice, I suppose."

"Then why won't you believe me when I say that what Celeste did was a calculated move?"

"America, it's not that I think you're lying. I'm sure, to you, it seemed that way. But Celeste was sorry. And she's been nothing but gracious with me."

"I'll bet she has," I muttered under my breath.

"That's enough," Maxon said with a sigh. "I don't want to talk about the others right now."

"She tried to take my dress, Maxon," I complained.

"I said I don't want to talk about her," he said fiercely.

That was all I was going to take. I huffed and lifted my arms in the air just to drop them with a thud against my legs. I was so frustrated I wanted to scream.

"If you're going to act this way, I'm going to find someone who does want my company." He walked off.

"Hey!" I called.

"No!" He turned back on me and spoke more forcefully than I'd ever imagined he could. "You forget yourself, Lady America. It would do you well to remember that I am the crown prince of Illéa. For all intents and purposes, I am lord and master of this country, and I'll be damned if you think you can treat me like this in my own home. You don't have to agree with my decisions, but you *will* abide by them."

He turned and left, either not seeing or caring that I had tears in my eyes.

I didn't look his way through dinner, but it was difficult to do during the *Report*. I caught him looking at me twice, and both times he tugged his ear. I didn't return the action. I didn't want to talk to him right now. I could only assume I'd be scolded more anyway, and I didn't need that.

I walked up to my room afterward so upset with Maxon I couldn't think clearly. Why wouldn't he listen to me? Did he think I was a liar? Even worse, did he think Celeste was above lying?

Maybe Maxon was just a typical guy, and Celeste was a beautiful girl, and in the end that would be what won out. For all his talk about wanting a soul mate, maybe all he wanted was a bedmate.

And if that was the kind of person he was, why was I even bothering with this? Stupid, stupid, stupid! I kissed him! I told him I'd be patient! And for what? I just—

I turned the corner to my room, and there was Aspen, waiting outside my door. All my rage melted away into a strange uncertainty. Guards, as a rule, kept their eyes forward and stayed at attention, but he was looking at me with an unreadable expression.

"Lady America," he whispered.

"Officer Leger."

Though it wasn't his job, he leaned over to open my door for me. I walked past slowly, almost afraid to turn my back on him, almost afraid he wasn't real. As much as I'd tried to keep him out of my head and my heart, I just wanted him to be with me in that moment. As I passed, I heard him inhale just next to my hair. It gave me a chill.

He fixed me with another stare and slowly closed the door.

Sleep was pointless. I tossed for hours as thoughts of Maxon's stupidity and Aspen's closeness battled in my head. I didn't know what to do about anything. My reflections were so consuming, I didn't even realize that I'd been mulling them over until well past two in the morning.

I sighed. My maids were going to have to work extra hard to make me look good tomorrow.

Suddenly I saw a light from the hallway. So quietly it felt like I was dreaming it, Aspen cracked open the door, walked in, and shut it behind him.

"Aspen, what are you doing?" I whispered as he crossed the room. "You'll be in so much trouble if you're caught in here!"

He continued to walk silently.

"Aspen?"

He stopped in front of my bed and quietly laid the staff he was holding on the ground. "Do you love him?"

I looked into Aspen's deep eyes, barely visible in the dark. For a split second, I didn't know what to say.

"No."

He ripped back my blankets in a move both graceful and violent. I should have protested, but I didn't. His hand was behind my head, pushing my face to his. He kissed me feverishly, and every good thing in the world fell into place. He didn't smell like his homemade soap anymore, and he was stronger than he used to be, but every move, every touch was familiar.

"They'll kill you for doing this," I breathed in a brief moment when his lips traveled to my neck.

"If I don't, I'll die anyway."

I tried to work up the will to tell him to stop, but I knew any attempts would be halfhearted. A thousand things about this moment felt wrong—that we were breaking so many rules, that as far as I knew Aspen had another girlfriend, that Maxon and I had some sort of feelings for each other—but I couldn't care. I was so angry with Maxon, and Aspen felt so comforting, I just let his hands travel up and down my legs.

I marveled at how different it felt. We'd never had so much space before.

Even with the distraction, I could feel everything else swarming in my head. I was angry with Maxon, angry with Celeste, even angry with Aspen. Hell, I was angry with Illéa. As we kissed on and on, I started crying.

Aspen kissed me through it, and soon some of the tears were his, too.

"I hate you, you know?" I said.

"I know, Mer. I know."

Mer. When he touched me like that, called me that name, I felt like I was a world away. Upset as I was, Aspen felt like home.

We went on for nearly fifteen minutes before he remembered himself.

"I have to get back, the guard doing rounds will be expecting me."

"What?"

"There are guards who do rounds at random. I might have twenty minutes, I might have an hour. If it's a short round, I have less than five minutes."

"Hurry!" I urged, hopping up with him to help him straighten his hair.

He grabbed his staff, and we ran across the floor together. Before he opened the door, he pulled me in to kiss me again. It felt like pure sunlight was traveling down my veins.

"I can't believe you're here," I said. "How did you end up on the palace guard?"

He shrugged. "Turns out I'm a natural. They fly everyone to this training place in Whites. America, it was covered in snow! Nothing like the flurries we get back home. All the new guards are fed and trained and tested. There are shots, too. Don't know what's in them, but I grew really fast. I'm a solid fighter, and I'm smart. I tested the highest in our class."

I smiled with pride. "Not surprised by that at all." I kissed him again. Aspen had always been too good to lead the life of a Six.

He opened the door and checked the hallway. It looked empty.

"I have so much to tell you. We need to talk," I whispered.

"I know. And we will. It's going to take some time, but I'll be back. Not tonight. I don't know when, but soon." He kissed me again, so hard it almost hurt.

"I missed you," he whispered into my mouth, and went back to his post.

I walked back to my bed in a daze. I couldn't believe what I'd just done. Part of me—a very upset part—felt like Maxon deserved this. If he wanted to spare Celeste and humiliate me, then I certainly wouldn't be a part of the Selection much longer. If she could find a way around the rules, there was nothing to stop me anymore. Problem solved.

Suddenly worn out, I fell asleep in moments.

CHAPTER 23

THE NEXT MORNING, I WOKE feeling a little guilty. Frightened even. Just because I didn't return Maxon's ear tug didn't mean he couldn't come to my room any time he wanted. We so easily could have been caught. If anyone had any idea what I'd done . . .

It was treason. And there was only one way the palace dealt with treason.

But another part of me didn't care. In the hazy moments of waking, I relived every look in Aspen's eyes, every touch, every kiss. I missed that so badly.

I wished we'd had more time to talk. I really needed to know what Aspen was thinking, though last night had given me some clues. It was just so unbelievable—after trying so hard to not want him—that *he* might still want *me*.

It was Saturday, and I was supposed to go to the Women's

Room, but I just couldn't stand it. I needed to think, and I knew that wouldn't happen in the endless chatter floating downstairs. When my maids came, I told them I had a headache and would be staying in bed.

They were so helpful, bringing me food and cleaning the room as quietly as possible, that I almost felt bad for lying to them. I had to, though. I couldn't face the queen and the girls and possibly Maxon while my mind was so solidly fixated on Aspen.

I closed my eyes but did not sleep. I tried to clear up just how I felt. Before I got very far, though, there was a knock at the door. I rolled over, catching Anne's face as she silently asked if she should answer it. I sat up quickly, straightened my hair, and gave her a nod.

I prayed that it wouldn't be Maxon— I was afraid he'd be able to read my crimes on my face—but I wasn't prepared to see Aspen's face walking through my door. I felt myself sit up taller and hoped my maids didn't notice.

"Pardon me, miss," he said to Anne. "I'm Officer Leger. I'm here to speak to Lady America about some security measures."

"Of course," she said, smiling brighter than usual and gesturing for Aspen to enter. In the corner I saw Mary nudge Lucy, who let out a tiny giggle.

When he heard the sound, Aspen turned toward them and tipped his hat. "Ladies."

Lucy ducked her head and Mary's cheeks looked redder than my hair, but they didn't answer. Anne, though she also seemed taken by Aspen's good looks, was put together enough to speak at least.

"Shall we leave, miss?"

I considered this. I didn't want to seem too obvious, but some privacy would be nice.

"Only for a moment. I'm sure Officer Leger won't need me for long," I decided, and they whisked right out of the room.

Once they had disappeared behind the door, Aspen spoke. "You're wrong, I'm afraid. I'm going to be needing you for a very long time." He winked at me.

I shook my head. "I still can't believe you're here."

Wasting no time, Aspen took off his hat and sat on the edge of my bed, setting his hands so our fingers just barely touched. "I never thought I'd count the draft as a blessing, but if it gives me the chance to apologize to you, I'll be forever grateful."

I was stunned into silence.

Aspen looked deep into my eyes. "Please forgive me, Mer. I was so, so stupid, and I've regretted that night in the tree house since the second I climbed down the ladder. I was too stubborn to say anything and then your name got called . . . I didn't know what to do." He stopped for a second. It looked like he had tears in his eyes. Was it possible that Aspen had been crying for me the way I'd been crying for him? "I'm still so in love with you."

I bit my lip, holding back my tears. I needed to be sure of one thing before I could even think about this.

"What about Brenna?"

His face fell. "What?"

I gave an unsteady breath. "I saw you two together in the square when I was leaving. Is that over?"

Aspen squinted his face in concentration then burst into laughter. He covered his mouth with his hands and fell backward on the bed before popping up and asking, "Is that what you think? Oh, Mer, she fell. She tripped and I caught her."

"Tripped?"

"Yeah, the square was so full, people were standing on top of one another. She fell into me and made a joke about being a klutz, which you know is true for Brenna even on a good day." I thought about the time she seemed to just fall off the sidewalk for no apparent reason. Why hadn't this occurred to me before? "As soon as I could get free, I was rushing to the stage."

I remembered those moments, Aspen's desperate attempt to get close to me. He hadn't been faking at all. I smiled. "And just what were you planning on doing once you got there?"

He shrugged. "I didn't actually think it out that far. I was considering begging you to stay. I was prepared to make an idiot out of myself if it meant you wouldn't get in that car. But then you looked so mad . . . and I get why you were." He let out a sigh. "I just couldn't do it. Besides, maybe you'd be happy here." He looked around the room at all the beautiful things that were temporarily considered mine. I could see how he would think that.

"Then," he continued, "I thought that I could win you

over once you came home." His voice seemed suddenly tinged with worry. "I was sure you'd want out and come home as soon as you could. But . . . you didn't."

He paused to look at me, but mercifully, didn't ask just how close Maxon and I were. He'd seen some of it already, but he didn't know that we kissed or had secret signals, and I didn't want to have to explain that.

"Then there was the draft, and I figured it would be unfair to even think about writing. I could die out here. I didn't want to try to make you love me again and then . . ."

"Love you again?" I asked incredulously. "Aspen, I never stopped."

In a swift but gentle move, Aspen leaned in and kissed me. He put his hand to my cheek, holding me to him, and every minute of the last two years flooded my body. I was so grateful they weren't lost.

"I'm so sorry," he mumbled between kisses. "I'm so sorry, Mer."

He pulled away to look at me, a small smile on his perfect face, his eyes asking exactly what I was thinking: What do we do now?

Just then, the door opened, and I was horror-struck as my maids took in Aspen's closeness.

"Thank goodness you're back!" he said to them as he pushed his hand more firmly against my cheek before moving it to my forehead. "I don't think you have a temperature, miss."

"What's wrong?" Anne asked, worry falling over her

face as she raced to my bedside.

Aspen stood. "She started saying that she felt funny, something about her head."

"Is your headache worse, miss?" Mary asked. "You look so pale!"

I bet I did. No doubt every drop of blood had dashed away from my face the moment they saw us together. But Aspen, so cool under pressure, had fixed it in a split second.

"I'll get the medicine," Lucy piped in, scurrying to the bathroom.

"Forgive me, miss," Aspen said as my maids went to work. "I don't wish to disturb you any more. I'll come back when you're feeling better."

In his eyes I could see the same face I'd kissed a thousand times in the tree house. The world around us was completely new, but our connection was the same as ever.

"Thank you, officer," I said weakly.

He went to leave, giving me a small bow.

Soon my maids were all stirring around me, trying to heal a sickness that wasn't even there.

My head didn't ache, but my heart did. The longing for Aspen's arms was so familiar, it was like it never left.

I woke to a hard shake on my shoulders from Anne in the middle of the night.

"Wha—?"

"Please, miss, you have to get up!" Her voice was frantic, worn with terror.

"What's wrong? Are you hurt?"

"We're under attack. We have to get you to the basement."

My mind was groggy; I couldn't be sure I was hearing her right. But I noticed behind her that Lucy was already crying.

"They're inside?" I asked in disbelief.

Lucy's fearful wail was all the confirmation I needed.

"What do we do?" I asked. A sudden adrenaline spike woke me up, and I jumped out of bed. As soon as I was standing, Mary was pushing my feet into shoes and Anne was putting a robe on me. All I could think was *North or South? North or South?*

"There's a passage here in the corner. It'll take you straight to the safe room in the basement. The guards are there waiting. The royal family should already be there and most of the girls, too. Hurry, miss." Anne pulled me out into the hallway and pushed on a section of wall. It turned, like a hidden passage from some mystery novel. Sure enough, behind the wall, a stairwell awaited me. As I stood there, Tiny bolted from her room and scurried down the passage.

"Okay, let's go," I said. Anne and Mary gaped at me. Lucy was shaking to the point she could barely stand. "Let's go," I repeated.

"No, miss. We go somewhere else. You have to hurry before they get here. Please!"

I knew at best they'd be injured if they were found; at worst they'd die. I couldn't bear them being hurt. Maybe I was a little cocky, but if Maxon had gone out of his way to do everything he'd done thus far, maybe they would matter to him if they mattered to me. Even if we were fighting. Perhaps it was too much generosity to bank on, but I wasn't leaving them here. The fear made me move faster. I grabbed Anne's arm and pushed her in. She stumbled and couldn't stop me as I grabbed Mary and Lucy.

"Move!" I told them.

They started walking, but Anne was protesting the whole way. "They won't let us in, miss! This place is just for the family. . . . They'll just make us leave!" But I didn't care what she said. Whatever their hiding place was, there was no way it would be as safe as wherever the royal family was staying.

The stairwell was lit every few yards, but even so I nearly fell a few times in my haste to move. My mind was blinded with worry. How far had the rebels penetrated before? Did they know these pathways to safety existed? Lucy was half-paralyzed, and I tugged her down to keep us together.

I couldn't tell how long it took for us to reach the bottom, but finally the tiny pathway opened up to a man-made cavern. I could see other stairways and other girls, everyone running behind what looked to be a two-foot-thick door. We ran up to our safe place.

"Thank you for delivering this girl. You can leave," a guard said to my maids.

"No! They're with me. They're staying," I said with authority.

"Miss, they have their own places to be," he countered.

"Fine. They don't go in, I don't go in. I'm sure Prince Maxon will appreciate knowing that my absence is your doing. Let's go, ladies." I pulled on Mary and Lucy's hands. Anne was shocked into stillness.

"Wait! Wait! Fine, go inside. But if anyone has an issue with it, it's on your hands."

"Not a problem," I said. I turned the girls and walked into the safe room with my head held high.

There was a clamor of activity inside. Some girls were huddled together crying, others were in prayer. I saw the king and queen sitting alone, surrounded by more guards. Beside them, Maxon was holding Elayna's hand. She looked a little shaken but obviously felt calmer with him touching her. I looked at the royal family's position . . . so close to the door. I wondered if it was like a captain going down with his ship. They'd do everything to keep this place afloat, but if it went down, they'd be the first ones to drown.

Their little group saw my entrance and noted the company I was keeping. I took in the confused expressions on their faces, nodded once, and continued to walk with my head high. I figured so long as I looked sure of myself, no one would question me.

I was wrong.

I took three more steps and Silvia walked up. She looked incredibly calm. This was all obviously old news for her.

"Good. Some help. Girls, you will immediately get to the water stores in the back and begin serving refreshments to the royal family and the ladies. Get going, now," she commanded.

"No." I turned to Anne and gave her my first real order. "Anne, please take some refreshments to the king, queen, and prince and then come join me." I faced Silvia. "The rest can fend for themselves. They chose to leave their maids alone, they can get their own damn water. Mine will be sitting with me. Come, ladies."

I knew we were close enough to the royals that they would have heard me. In my quest to have a level of authority, I'd spoken a little too loudly. But I didn't care if they thought I was rude. Lucy was more frightened than most of the people in this room. She was trembling head to foot, and there was no way I'd have her serving people half her equal in goodness in her state.

Perhaps it was all my years as a big sister, but I just had to keep these girls safe.

We found a little space in the back of the room. Whoever usually kept this place ready must not have been prepared for the influx the Selection would cause, because there weren't nearly enough chairs in here. But I saw the stores of food and water and could tell they would get us through months down here, if the need arose.

It was a funny little array of people. Obviously, several officials had been up working through the night, and they were in suits. Maxon himself was still dressed. But nearly all the girls were in their thin nightgowns that helped you sleep in the warmth of the rooms upstairs. Not all of them had been able to get a robe on in their haste to leave. I was even a little chilly under mine.

Many of the girls had piled themselves toward the front of the room. Obviously, they'd be the first to die if someone got through the door. But if they didn't, think of all the time spent right in front of Maxon! A few were closer to where we were, and most of them were in a similar state as Lucy— shaking, tearful, and petrified with worry.

I pulled Lucy under an arm and Mary cuddled her from the other side. There wasn't anything to say about the situation that was pleasant, so we stayed quiet, listening to the clamor of the room. The jangle of voices reminded me of the first day here, when they were giving us makeovers. I closed my eyes and pictured that action with the sound in an attempt to make myself as calm as I appeared.

"Are you okay?"

I looked up and there was Aspen, glorious in his uniform. His tone was very official, and he didn't seem shaken by the situation at all. I sighed.

"Yes, thank you."

We were quiet for a moment, watching people get settled in the room. Mary had obviously been exhausted—she was already asleep and leaning heavily on Lucy's side. Lucy was fairly calm, all things considered. She'd stopped crying and just sat there looking at Aspen with a kind of wonder in her eyes.

"It was good of you to bring your maids. Not everyone would be so kind to people considered beneath them," he said.

"Castes never meant that much to me," I said quietly. He

gave me the smallest smile.

Lucy took in a breath like she was going to ask Aspen a question, but a loud yelling coursed through the chamber. A guard on the far end of the room was barking instructions for us to all silence ourselves.

Aspen walked away, which was good. I feared someone would be able to see something.

"That was the same guard from earlier, wasn't it?" Lucy asked.

"Yes, it was."

"I've seen him guarding your door lately. He's awfully friendly," she commented.

I was sure Aspen would speak to my maids as kindly as he spoke to me when they crossed his path. They were Sixes, after all.

"He's very handsome," she added.

I smiled and contemplated saying something, but that same guard instructed us to be quiet. After a few jagged edges of conversation dulled away, an eerie hush fell over the room.

The silence was worse than any sound. Without a single sense to guide me, my imagination took over, producing horrific scenes in my head: rooms demolished, a string of bodies, a merciless army only feet from the door. I found myself clutching the girls nearer to me, as if we could protect one another from whatever would come.

The only stirring was Maxon walking around to check on each of the girls. When he got to our corner, only Lucy was awake with me, and every once in a while, we'd have a quick conversation in breathed words, reading each other's lips. As Maxon approached, he smiled at the pile of people leaning on me. In that moment, I could see no anger left from our argument, though I really wanted to resolve it. Instead, I saw his grateful smile, simply happy that I was okay. A wave of guilt went through me. . . . What had I gotten myself into?

"Are you well?" he asked.

I nodded. He looked at Lucy and leaned across me to speak to her. I inhaled. Maxon didn't smell like anything that could be bottled. Not like cinnamon or vanilla or even, I remembered quickly, like homemade soap. He had his own smell, a mix of chemicals that burned out from him.

"And you?" he asked Lucy.

She nodded, too.

"Are you surprised to find yourself down here?" He smiled at Lucy, making light of what was an unimaginable situation.

"No, Your Majesty. Not with her." Lucy nodded in my direction.

Maxon turned to look at me, and his face was incredibly close. I felt uncomfortable. Too many people could see us; Aspen included. But the moment passed quickly, and he turned back to Lucy.

"I know what you mean." Maxon smiled again. He looked like he might say more, but then changed his mind and moved to stand.

I quickly grabbed his arm and whispered, "North or South?"

"Do you remember the photo shoot?" he breathed.

Shocked, I nodded. These rebels were making their way northwest, burning crops and slaughtering people along the way. *Intercept them*, he'd said. These rebels, these murderers, had been slowly coming for us all this time, and we couldn't stop them. They were killers. They were Southerners.

"Tell no one." He left, moving on to Fiona, who was holding herself and crying quietly.

I practiced breathing slowly, trying to imagine ways I could escape if they got to us, but I was fooling myself. If the rebels managed to get down here, it was all over. There was nothing to do but wait.

The hours crept on. I had no idea what time it was, but people who had dozed off had woken up, and those of us who had powered through the time were starting to wilt.

Finally, the door opened as some guards left to investigate. More time passed as the palace was swept, and eventually they returned.

"Ladies and gentlemen," one of the guards called, "the rebels have been subdued. We are asking that everyone please return to their rooms via the back stairs. There's quite a mess and scores of injured guards. It's better if you all bypass the main rooms and halls until they can be cleared. If you are a member of the Selection, please proceed to your room and stay there until further notice. I've spoken with the cooks, and food will be brought to you within the hour. I'm going to need all medical personnel to report with me to the hospital wing."

With that, people stood and started moving like nothing had happened. Some people even looked bored. Except for the faces of people like Lucy, it seemed everyone took the attack in stride, as if it were to be expected.

My room had been ransacked. Mattress on the floor, dresses pulled out of the closet, the pictures of my family torn up on the ground. I looked around for my jar, and it was still intact with its penny inside, just hidden under the bed. I tried not to cry, but my eyes kept welling up. It wasn't that I was afraid, though I was. I just didn't like that an enemy had put their hands all over my things, had ruined them.

It took quite a while to set things right, since we were all so tired. We managed, though. Anne even found some tape so I could put my pictures back together. I sent my maids to bed the moment I got my tape. Anne protested, but I wouldn't have any of it. Now that I'd found my ability to command, I wasn't afraid to use it.

Once I was alone, I let myself cry. The fear, even though it had mostly passed, still had a hold on me.

I pulled out the jeans that Maxon had given me and my one shirt from home and put them on. I felt a little more normal this way. My hair was messy from the events of the night and most of the morning, so I pulled it up into a casual little bun on the top of my head, pieces falling down around my face.

I set the fragments of pictures on the bed, trying to figure out which ones went together. It was like having four puzzles' worth of pieces all in the same box. I had managed to put only one together when there was a knock at the door.

Maxon, I thought. *Please be Maxon*. I threw the door open hopefully.

"Hello, dearie." It was Silvia. She had a little pout on her face that I supposed was meant to be a consolation. She scuttled right past me into my room, then turned and took in what I was wearing.

"Oh, don't tell me you're leaving, too," she whined. "Honestly, it was nothing." She wiped the whole incident away with her hand.

I wouldn't call it nothing. Couldn't she tell I'd been crying?

"I'm not leaving," I said, tucking a hair behind my ear. "Are others going home?"

She sighed. "Yes, three so far. And Maxon, dear boy, told me to let anyone who wants to leave go home. Arrangements are being made as we speak. It's so funny. It was as if he knew girls would be leaving. If I were in your position, I'd think twice before leaving over all this nonsense."

Silvia started walking around my room, taking in the decor. Nonsense? What was wrong with this woman?

"Did they take anything?" she asked casually.

"No, ma'am. They made a mess, but nothing's missing as far as I can tell."

"Very good." She walked over to me and handed me a tiny portable phone. "This is the safest line in the palace.

You need to call your family and tell them you're fine. Don't take too long, now. I still have a few girls to see."

I marveled at the tiny object. I'd never actually held a portable phone. I'd seen them before in the hands of Twos and Threes, but I never thought I'd get to use one. My hands trembled with excitement. I was going to hear their voices!

I dialed the number eagerly. After everything that had happened, it actually brought a smile to my face. Mom picked up after two rings.

"Hello?"

"Mom?"

"America! Is that you? Are you okay? Some guard called to tell us we might not be able to get ahold of you for a few days, and we knew those damn rebels had gotten through. We've been so scared." She started crying.

"Oh, don't cry, Mom. I'm safe." I looked over at Silvia. She looked bored.

"Hold on." There was a bit of movement.

"America?" May's voice was thick with tears. She must have had the worst day.

"May! Oh, May, I miss you so much!" I felt the tears rising again.

"I thought you were dead! America, I love you. Promise me you won't die," she wailed.

"I promise." I had to smile at such a vow.

"Will you come home? Can't you? I don't want you there anymore." May was practically begging.

"Come home?" I asked.

I felt so many things. I missed my family, and I was tired of hiding from rebels. I was getting more and more confused over my feelings for Aspen and Maxon, and I didn't know how to handle them. The easiest thing to do would be to leave. But still.

"No, May, I can't come home. I have to stay here."

"Why?" May moaned.

"Because," I said simply.

"Because why?"

"Just . . . because."

May was quiet for a moment, thinking. "Are you in love with Maxon?" For a minute I heard the boy-crazy May that I was used to. She'd be fine.

"Umm, I don't know about that, but—"

"America! You're in love with Maxon! Oh my gosh!" I heard Dad yelling, "What?" in the background and then Mom's "Yes, yes, yes!"

"May, I never said—"

"I knew it!" May just laughed and laughed. Just like that, all her fears of losing me vanished.

"May, I have to go. The others need the phone. But I just wanted you all to know that I'm okay. I'll write you soon, I promise."

"Okay, okay. Tell me about Maxon! And send more treats! I love you!" she yelled.

"I love you, too. Bye."

I hung up the phone before she could ask for anything

else. The moment her voice was gone, though, I missed her more than I had before.

Silvia was swift. She had the phone out of my hand in a matter of seconds and was walking to the door.

"There's a good girl," she said, and disappeared down the hall.

I certainly didn't feel good. But I knew that once I figured out how to set things right with Aspen and Maxon, I would.

CHAPTER 24

AMY, FIONA, AND TALLULAH were gone within hours. I wasn't sure if the speed was due to the efficiency of Silvia or the nerves of the girls. We dropped to nineteen, and it suddenly felt like this was all moving quickly. Still, I couldn't have predicted how much faster it would become.

The Monday after the attacks, we returned to our routine. Breakfast was as delicious as ever, and I wondered if there would come a time when I wouldn't appreciate these amazing meals.

"Kriss, isn't this divine?" I asked as I bit into a piece of star-shaped fruit. I'd never seen it before I came to the palace. Kriss's mouth was full, but she nodded in agreement. I felt a warm sense of sisterhood this morning. Now that we had survived a major rebel attack together, it felt like these small bonds had sealed into something unbreakable. Beside

Kriss, Emily was passing me honey. Next to me, Tiny was asking where my songbird necklace came from with admiration in her eyes. The atmosphere was that of my family dinners a few years ago, before Kota turned into a jerk and we lost Kenna to a husband: full, bright, chatty.

I suddenly knew, just as Maxon had said his mother had done, that I would contact these girls down the road. I would want to know who everyone married and send them Christmas cards. And in twenty-some-odd years, if Maxon had a son, I'd call to ask them about their favorite girls in the new Selection. And we'd remember everything we'd gone through and laugh about it as if it had been an adventure, not a competition.

Oddly enough, the only person in the room who appeared to be distressed was Maxon. He didn't touch his food but instead gazed up and down the rows of girls with a clear look of concentration on his face. Every once in a while, he paused midthought and seemed to debate with himself over something, and then moved on.

When he came to my row, he caught me looking at him and gave me a weak smile. Except for the quick interlude last night, we hadn't spoken since our argument, and there were things that needed to be said. This time, I needed to be the initiator. With an expression that said it was a request, not a demand, I tugged my ear. His expression remained strained, but he tugged his ear, too.

I sighed with relief and found my eyes moving toward the doors of the massive room. As I'd suspected, another pair of eyes was looking my way. I'd noticed Aspen when I entered, but I tried not to acknowledge him. I supposed it was impossible to ignore someone you've loved that much.

Maxon stood up. The sudden movement made his chair screech in a way that drew our collective attention. As we all turned toward him, he looked like he wished he could sit back down unnoticed. Realizing that wasn't an option, he spoke instead.

"Ladies," he said with a bow of his head. He looked genuinely pained. "I'm afraid that after yesterday's attack, I've been forced to seriously reconsider the operation of the Selection. As you know, three ladies asked to leave yesterday, and I obliged. I wouldn't want anyone here against their will. Furthermore, I don't feel comfortable keeping anyone in the palace, facing this constant threat of danger, when I feel confident that we don't have any sort of future together."

Around the room, the confusion changed to a clear and unhappy understanding.

"He's not . . . ," Tiny whispered.

"Yes, he is," I replied.

"Though it grieves me to do this, I have discussed the matter with my family and a few close advisers and have decided to go ahead and narrow the Selection down to the Elite. However, instead of ten, I've decided to send all but six of you home," Maxon stated in a businesslike tone.

"Six?" Kriss gasped.

"That's not fair," Tiny breathed, already starting to cry.

I looked around the room as the hum of complaints rose

and fell. Celeste braced herself, as if she could fight for a spot. Bariel had closed her eyes and crossed her fingers, perhaps hoping that image would garner her some sympathy. Marlee, who had admitted that she didn't care for Maxon, looked incredibly tense. Why did she want to stay so badly?

"I don't wish to draw this out unnecessarily, so only the following ladies will be staying. Lady Marlee and Lady Kriss."

Marlee breathed out a sigh of relief and put a hand to her chest. Kriss did a happy, fidgety dance in her chair and looked at the girls around her, expecting us to be happy. And I was until I realized that two of the six spots were already gone. With a disagreement hanging between Maxon and me, would he send me home? Did he not see any future with me? Did I want him to? What would I do if I had to go?

This whole time, the power had been in my hands as to when I would leave. I was abruptly aware of how important it was to me to stay.

"Lady Natalie and Lady Celeste," he continued, looking at them both in turn. I cringed at Celeste's name. He couldn't keep her and not me. I could hardly believe he was keeping her at all. But was that a sign I was going? We'd fought about her very presence here.

"Lady Elise," he said, and the room inhaled a breath, awaiting the final name. I realized Tiny and I were squeezing each other's hands.

"And Lady America." Maxon looked over at me, and I felt every muscle in my body relax. Tiny started bawling immediately, and she wasn't alone. Maxon let out a long sigh.

"To everyone else, I'm incredibly sorry, but I hope you all trust me when I say that I meant this to be a good thing for you. I don't want to raise anyone's hopes for no reason and risk your life in the process. If anyone who is leaving wants to speak to me, I'll be in the library down the hall, and you may visit me as soon as you've finished eating."

Maxon walked out of the room as quickly as he could without running. I watched him until he crossed in front of Aspen, and then my attention was diverted. Aspen's face was confused, and I knew why. I'd told him I didn't love Maxon, so he would have assumed I meant next to nothing to Maxon as well. So why would I be so tense about staying or going? And why would Maxon want to keep me around?

Before a second had passed, Emmica and Tuesday were running after Maxon, no doubt looking for an explanation. Some girls were in tears, obviously heartbroken, and it fell on those of us remaining to comfort them.

It was unbearably awkward. Tiny ended up swatting away my hands and running out of the room. I hoped she wouldn't hold any bitter feelings against me.

People left within minutes, no longer hungry. I didn't linger myself, unable to handle the outpouring of emotion. As I passed Aspen, he whispered "tonight." I gave a tiny nod and went on my way.

The rest of the morning was odd. I'd never really had friends that I would miss. All the occupied rooms on the second floor were open, and girls scurried in and out, passing notes and gathering addresses. We cried together and laughed together, and by the afternoon, the palace had turned into a far more serious place than it was when we came.

No one was left in my little wing of the hall, so there was no sound of maids rushing to and fro, or of doors closing. I sat at my table, reading a book as my maids dusted. I wondered if the palace always felt this lonely. The emptiness made me miss my family.

Suddenly a knock came at the door. Anne rushed to get it, looking at me to make sure I was prepared for a visitor. I gave her a small nod.

When Maxon came into the room, I jumped to my feet.

"Ladies," he said, looking to my maids. "We meet again."

They curtsied and giggled. He acknowledged them and turned his eyes to me. I hadn't realized how eager I was to see him. I stood by the table in a daze.

"Do forgive me, but I need to speak with Lady America. Would you give us a moment?"

There was more curtsying and giggling, and Anne asked—with a tone that implied near worship of the prince—if she could bring him anything. Maxon declined, and they left us. He had his hands in his pockets. We were silent for a while.

"I thought you might not keep me," I finally admitted.

"Why?" he asked, sounding honestly confused.

"Because we fought. Because everything between us is weird. Because . . ." *Because even though you're dating five other women, I think I'm cheating on you*, I thought.

Maxon closed the distance between us slowly, choosing

his words as he walked. When he finally reached me, he picked up my hands in his and explained everything.

"First, let me say I'm sorry. I shouldn't have yelled at you." His voice was completely sincere. "It's just that some of the committees and my father are already pressuring me in this, and I truly want to be able to make the decision for myself. It was frustrating to run into another situation where my opinion wasn't being taken seriously."

"Another situation?" I asked.

"Well, you've seen my choices. Marlee is a favorite with the people, and that cannot be overlooked. Celeste is a very powerful young woman, and she comes from an excellent family to align ourselves with. Natalie and Kriss are charming girls, both very agreeable and favorites of some in my family. Elise happens to have relations in New Asia. Since we're trying to end this damn war, that is something to take into consideration. I've been debated down and cornered from every side on this decision."

There was no explanation for me, and I almost didn't ask for it. I knew that we were friends first and that I had no political uses at all. But I needed to hear the words so I could make the decision for myself. I couldn't look him in the eye.

"And why am I still here?" My voice was barely above a whisper. I was sure this was going to hurt. In the pit of my stomach I was sure I was only still here because he was too good to break his promise.

"America, I thought I'd made myself clear," Maxon said

calmly. He let out a patient sigh and used his hand to nudge up my chin. When I was finally looking into his eyes, he confessed.

"If this were a simpler matter, I'd have eliminated everyone else by now. I know how I feel about you. Maybe it's impulsive of me to think I could be so sure, but I'm certain I would be happy with you."

I blushed. I could feel tears rising, but I blinked them away. The expression on his face was so adoring, I didn't want to miss it.

"There are moments when I feel like you and I have broken down every last wall, and then others when I think you only want to stay for convenience. If I knew for sure that I, and I alone, was your motivation . . ."

He paused and shook his head, as if the end of his sentence was something he couldn't let himself want.

"Would I be wrong in saying that you're still unsure of me?"

I didn't want to hurt him, but I had to be honest. "No."

"Then I have to hedge my bets. You may decide to leave, and I will let you go if you do. In the meantime, I have to find a wife. I'm trying to make the best decision I can within the boundaries I've been given, but please, don't doubt for a moment that I care for you. Deeply."

I couldn't hold back the tears anymore. I thought about Aspen and what I'd done, and I felt so ashamed.

"Maxon?" I sniffed. "Can you . . . can you ever forgive—?" I didn't get to finish my confession. He came even closer and started sweeping the tears off my face with his strong fingers.

"Forgive what? Our stupid little fight? It's already forgotten. Your feelings being a little slower than mine? I'm prepared to wait," he said with a shrug. "I don't think there's anything you could do that I couldn't forgive. Need I remind you of the knee to my groin?"

I couldn't help but laugh. Maxon chuckled once, then became suddenly serious.

"What's wrong?" I asked.

He shook his head. "They were so fast this time." Maxon's voice was full of an aggravated wonder at the talents of the rebels. I suddenly wondered how close to disaster I had come by trying to save my maids.

"I'm getting more and more worried, America. North or South, they're getting exceptionally determined. It seems they won't stop until they get what they want, and we haven't the faintest clue what it is." Maxon looked confused and sad. "I feel like it's only a matter of time until they destroy someone important to me."

He looked into my eyes.

"You know, you still have a choice in this. If you're afraid to stay, you should say so." He paused, thinking. "Or if you don't think you can love me at all, it would be kinder to tell me now. I'll let you go on your way, and we can part as friends."

I wrapped my arms around him, resting my head against his chest. Maxon seemed both comforted and surprised by the gesture. It took only a second for him to wrap his arms securely around me.

"Maxon, I'm not completely sure what we are, but we're definitely more than friends."

He let out a sigh. With my head there against his chest, I could faintly make out the sound of his heart beating through his suit coat. It seemed to be rushing. His hand, gentle as ever, reached to cup my cheek. As I looked into his eyes, I felt that unnameable feeling that was growing between us.

With his eyes, Maxon asked for something we'd both agreed to wait on. I was glad he didn't want to wait anymore. I gave him a tiny nod, and he bridged the small gap between us, kissing me with unimaginable tenderness.

I felt a smile underneath his lips, and it lingered for a long time after.

CHAPTER 25

I FELT A NUDGE ON my arm. It was dark and either very late or very early. For a fraction of a second, I thought that there'd been yet another attack. Then I knew I was wrong because of the single word used to wake me.

"Mer?"

My back was to Aspen, and I took a moment to steady myself before I faced him. In my head, I knew that there were things that needed to be set right between us. I hoped my heart would let me say them.

I rolled over and caught Aspen's bright green eyes and knew this would be difficult. Then I noticed that he'd left the door to my room open.

"Aspen, are you crazy?" I whispered. "Close the door."

"No, I've thought this out. With the door open, I can tell anyone who comes by that I heard a noise and was checking on you, which is my job. No one would suspect a thing."

It was simple and brilliant. I nodded my head in under-standing. "Okay."

I turned on the small lamp on my bedside table to make it clear to any passersby that we weren't hiding anything. I noticed that the clock said it was past three in the morning.

Aspen was obviously pleased with himself. His smile, the same one that used to greet me in the tree house, was wide.

"You kept it," he said.

"Huh?"

Aspen pointed down to my bedside table, where the jar sat with its lone penny.

"Yeah," I said. "I just couldn't bring myself to get rid of it."

His expression grew more and more hopeful. He turned to look at the door, as if checking quickly that no one was there. Then he bent down to kiss me.

"No," I said quietly, pulling away. "You can't do that."

The look in his eyes warred between confusion and sad-ness, and I feared that everything I was about to say was only going to make things worse.

"Did I do something wrong?"

"No," I said adamantly. "You've been wonderful. I've been so happy to see you again and to know that you still love me. It's changed everything."

He smiled. "Good. Because I do love you, and I'm plan-ning on making sure you never have a reason to doubt it."

I squirmed. "Aspen, whatever we were, or are right now,

we can't be that here."

"What do you mean?" he asked, shifting his weight.

"I'm part of the Selection right now. I'm here for Maxon, and I can't date you or whatever this is while it's still going on." I started fidgeting with a bit of my comforter.

He thought a moment. "So were you lying to me? When you said you never stopped loving me?"

"No," I assured him. "You've been in my heart the whole time. You're the reason things have been going as slow as they are. Maxon likes me, but I can't let myself really care about him because of you."

"Well, great," he said sarcastically. "Glad to know you'd be fine dating him if I wasn't around."

Underneath the anger, I could see he was heartbroken, but it wasn't my fault it turned out this way.

"Aspen?" I asked quietly, getting him to look at me. "When you left me in the tree house, you crushed me."

"Mer, I said I—"

"Let me finish." He huffed, then was silent. "You took away my dreams, and the only reason I'm here is because you insisted I sign up."

He shook his head, irritated at the truth.

"I've been trying to put myself back together, and Maxon really cares about me. You mean so much to me, you know you do. But I'm part of this now, and I'd be stupid to not let myself see what happens."

"So you're choosing him over me?" he asked miserably.

"No, I'm not choosing him *or* you. I'm choosing me."

That was the truth at the core of everything. I didn't know what I wanted yet, and I couldn't let myself be swayed by what was easy or what someone else thought was right. I had to give myself time to decide what was best for me.

Aspen mulled this over for a moment, still not happy with what I was saying. Finally he smiled.

"You know I'm not giving up, right?" His tone was an obvious challenge, and I grinned in spite of myself. It was true that Aspen was not the type to admit defeat.

"This really isn't a good place to try to fight for me. Your determination is a dangerous trait here."

"I'm not afraid of that *suit*," he scoffed.

I rolled my eyes, amused at being on this end of the relationship. I'd always been worried about someone stealing Aspen. I felt guilty about how refreshing it was to see him worried about someone stealing me for a change.

"Okay. You said you didn't love him . . . but you must like him a little to be willing to stay, right?"

I ducked my head. "I do," I said with a tiny nod. "He's more than I ever imagined he was."

He considered that for a moment, soaking it in.

"I guess that means I'll have to fight harder than I thought," he said, heading for the hall. Then he turned and gave me another wink. "Goodnight, Lady America."

"Goodnight, Officer Leger."

The door clicked shut, and the sense of peace was overwhelming. Since the Selection had started, I'd been worrying that it was something that was going to ruin my life. But in this moment, I couldn't think of a time that felt more right.

Too soon, my maids bustled in. Anne pulled back the curtains, and as the light fell on me, it felt like this was truly my first day at the palace.

The Selection was no longer something that was simply happening to me, but something I was actively a part of. I was an Elite. I pulled back the covers and leaped into the morning.

END OF BOOK ONE

ACKNOWLEDGMENTS

OKAY, JUST IN CASE YOU'RE really busy or tired because you stayed up late finishing, I want to thank you first for reading my book. For reals, I love you. Thanks.

Now, to the people who made this happen. Well, actually, let's go back a bit more.

As always, I thank God for words. I'm so glad I don't have to try to communicate this story to you with my antennae or something. Words are so delicious, and I'll be forever happy they exist.

Callaway: Oat bananas! Thanks for supporting me and being generally awesome.

Guyden: Thank you for sharing Mommy with the friends in her head.

Loads of love to my mom, dad, and little brother for encouraging me to be strange. Also, hugs and love to my mom, dad, and little brother-in-law for being such incredible cheerleaders. Between the six of you, I've been engulfed in excitement, and I'm so grateful for all of you.

Thank you to the gang at [nlcf] and to the FTW Crew for celebrating with me along the way. Hugs!

Thanks to Mary—the first person to read *The Selection*

ever—for thinking it was cool, and to Liz and Michelle for being the thoughtful, rational, in-depth readers that I am not. The book is better because of you guys. Also, I think you are awesome.

Thank you to Ashley Brouillette for making a great video and earning her name a spot in the book. Bravo, miss! I also have to say thanks to Elizabeth O'Brien, Emily Arnold, and Kayleigh Poulin for hanging out with me when I was a nerd. Thanks for letting me use your names as well.

Other names I borrowed: Jenna, Elise, Mary, Lucy, Gerad, Amy, etc. Thanks for popping into my mind when I had no idea what to type. Yay!

Elana Roth: You are a rock goddess of an agent, and I cannot thank you enough for taking a chance on me even though I'm really, really awful on the phone. Still can't figure out what possessed you. Also, thanks for letting me hug you. Love!

To Caren and Colleen at JLA, thanks for being there and generally rocking.

Erica Sussman: You are so dang cool. For realzies. It's kind of amazing how well you get America and how fun you are to work with. I adore you and your purple pen. Thank you for never making this feel like work.

Tyler, you sassy girl, I feel your energy in everything. Thanks for all your work.

Dear Everyone at HarperTeen: Umm, THANK YOU! You were a dream I didn't dare speak aloud, and I'm honored to be one of your authors and appreciate all of your work for me. From cover art to marketing to just the way you communicate with me, everything has been better than I could have ever hoped for. Thank you. Truly.

Jeannette, Catherine, Kati, Ciara, Christina, the ladies at Guy's daycare, and anyone I might have missed: Thank you for watching Guyden at various times so I could work. It meant so much to me to know I wasn't alone in this.

And, if you made it all the way through this, thanks again to you! Some of you have been with me from the first time I sat in front of a camera and said "Hello Interwebs." Some of you read *The Siren* or found me on Twitter. Some of you just saw the pretty girl on the cover of the book and decided to pick it up. However and whenever you found me, thank you for reading my book. I hope it made you all kinds of happy.

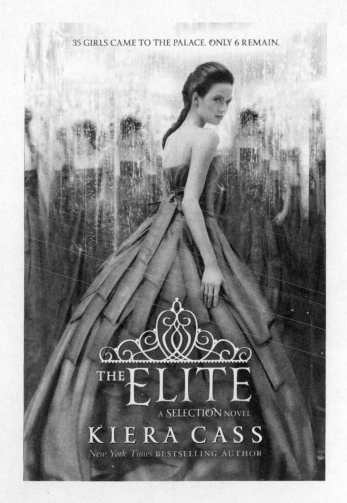

CHAPTER 1

THE ANGELES AIR WAS QUIET, and for a while I lay still, listening to the sound of Maxon's breathing. It was getting harder and harder to catch him in a truly calm and happy moment, and I soaked up the time, grateful that he seemed to be at his best when he and I were alone.

Ever since the Selection had been narrowed down to six girls, he'd been more anxious than he was when the thirty-five of us arrived in the first place. I guessed he thought he'd have more time to make his choices. And though it made me feel guilty to admit it, I knew I was the reason why he wished he did.

Prince Maxon, heir to the Illéa throne, liked me. He'd told me a week ago that if I could simply say that I cared for him the way he did for me, without anything holding me back, this whole competition would be over. And sometimes

I played with the idea, wondering how it would feel to be Maxon's alone.

But the thing was, Maxon wasn't really mine to begin with. There were five other girls here—girls he took on dates and whispered things to—and I didn't know what to make of that. And then there was the fact that if I accepted Maxon, it meant I had to accept a crown, a thought I tended to ignore if only because I wasn't sure what it would mean for me.

And, of course, there was Aspen.

He wasn't technically my boyfriend anymore—he'd broken up with me before my name was even drawn for the Selection—but when he showed up at the palace as one of the guards, all the feelings I'd been trying to let go of flooded my heart. Aspen was my first love; when I looked at him . . . I was his.

Maxon didn't know that Aspen was in the palace, but he did know that there was someone at home that I was trying to get over, and he was graciously giving me time to move on while attempting to find someone else he'd be happy with in the event I couldn't ever love him.

As he moved his head, inhaling just above my hairline, I considered it. What would it be like to simply love Maxon?

"Do you know the last time I really looked at the stars?" he asked.

I settled closer to him on our blanket, trying to keep warm in the cool Angeles night. "No idea."

"A tutor had me studying astronomy a few years ago. If

you look closely, you can tell that the stars are actually different colors."

"Wait, the last time you looked at the stars was to *study* them? What about for fun?"

He chuckled. "Fun. I'll have to pencil in some between the budget consultations and infrastructure committee meetings. Oh, and war strategizing, which, by the way, I am terrible at."

"What else are you terrible at?" I asked, running my hand across his starched shirt. Encouraged by the touch, Maxon drew circles on my shoulder with the hand he had wrapped behind my back.

"Why would you want to know that?" he asked in mock irritation.

"Because I still know so little about you. And you seem perfect all the time. It's nice to have proof you're not."

He propped himself up on an elbow, focusing on my face. "You *know* I'm not."

"Pretty close," I countered. Little flickers of touch ran between us. Knees, arms, fingers.

He shook his head, a small smile on his face. "Okay, then. I can't plan wars. I'm rotten at it. And I'm guessing I'd be a terrible cook. I've never tried, so—"

"Never?"

"You might have noticed the teams of people keeping you up to your neck in pastries? They happen to feed me as well."

I giggled. I helped cook practically every meal at home. "More," I demanded. "What else are you bad at?"

He held me close, his brown eyes bright with a secret. "Recently I've discovered this one thing. . . ."

"Tell."

"It turns out I'm absolutely terrible at staying away from you. It's a very serious problem."

I smiled. "Have you really tried?"

He pretended to think about it. "Well, no. And don't expect me to start."

We laughed quietly, holding on to each other. In these moments, it was so easy to picture this being the rest of my life.

The rustle of leaves and grass announced that someone was coming. Even though our date was completely acceptable, I felt a little embarrassed and sat up quickly. Maxon followed suit as a guard made his way around the hedge to us.

"Your Majesty," he said with a bow. "Sorry to intrude, sir, but it's really unwise to stay out this late for so long. The rebels could—"

"Understood," Maxon said with a sigh. "We'll be right in."

The guard left us alone, and Maxon turned back to me. "Another fault of mine: I'm losing patience with the rebels. I'm tired of dealing with them."

He stood and offered me his hand. I took it, watching the sad frustration in his eyes. We'd been attacked twice by the rebels since the start of the Selection—once by the simply disruptive Northerners and once by the deadly Southerners—and even with my brief experience, I could understand his exhaustion.

Maxon was picking up the blanket and shaking it out, clearly not happy that our night had been cut short.

"Hey," I said, urging him to face me. "I had fun."

He nodded.

"No, really," I said, walking over to him. He moved the blanket to one hand to wrap his free arm around me. "We should do it again sometime. You can tell me which stars are which colors, because I seriously can't tell."

Maxon gave me a sad smile. "I wish things were easier sometimes, normal."

I moved so I could wrap my arms around him, and as I did so, Maxon dropped the blanket to return the gesture. "I hate to break it to you, Your Majesty, but even without the guards, you're far from normal."

His expression lightened a bit but was still serious. "You'd like me more if I was."

"I know you find it hard to believe, but I really do like you the way you are. I just need more—"

"Time. I know. And I'm prepared to give you that. I only wish I knew that you'd actually want to be with me when that time was over."

I looked away. That wasn't something I could promise. I weighed Maxon and Aspen in my heart over and over, and neither of them ever had a true edge. Except, maybe, when I was alone with one of them. Because, at that moment, I was tempted to promise Maxon that I would be there for him in the end.

But I couldn't.

"Maxon," I whispered, seeing how dejected he looked at my lack of an answer. "I can't tell you that. But what I can tell you is that I *want* to be here. I *want* to know if there's a possibility for . . . for . . ." I stammered, not sure how to put it.

"Us?" Maxon guessed.

I smiled, happy at how easily he understood me. "Yes. I want to know if there's a possibility for us to be an us."

He moved a lock of hair behind my shoulder. "I think the odds are very high," he said matter-of-factly.

"I think so, too. Just . . . time, okay?"

He nodded, looking happier. This was how I wanted to end our night, with hope. Well, and maybe one more thing. I bit my lip and leaned into Maxon, asking with my eyes.

Without a second of hesitation, he bent to kiss me. It was warm and gentle, and it left me feeling adored and somehow aching for more. I could have stayed there for hours, just to see if I could get enough of that feeling; but too soon, Maxon backed away.

"Let's go," he said in a playful tone, pulling me toward the palace. "Better get inside before the guards come for us on horseback with spears drawn."

As Maxon left me at the stairs, the tiredness hit me like a wall. I was practically dragging myself up to the second floor and around the corner to my room when, suddenly, I was quite awake again.

"Oh!" Aspen said, surprised to see me, too. "I think it makes me the worst guard ever that I assumed you were in your room this whole time."

I giggled. The Elite were supposed to sleep with at least one of their maids on watch in the night. I really didn't like that, so Maxon insisted on stationing a guard by my room in case there was an emergency. The thing was, most of the time that guard was Aspen. It was a strange mix of exhilaration and terror knowing that nearly every night he was right outside my door.

The lightness of the moment faded quickly as Aspen grasped what it meant that I hadn't been safely tucked in my bed. He cleared his throat uncomfortably.

"Did you have a good time?"

"Aspen," I whispered, looking to make sure no one was around. "Don't be upset. I'm part of the Selection, and this is just how it is."

"How am I supposed to stand a chance, Mer? How can I compete when you only ever talk to one of us?" He made a good point, but what could I do?

"Please don't be mad at me, Aspen. I'm trying to figure all this out."

"No, Mer," he said, gentleness returning to his voice. "I'm not mad at you. I *miss* you." He didn't dare say the words aloud, but he mouthed them. *I love you.*

I melted.

"I know," I said, placing a hand on his chest, letting myself forget for a moment all that we were risking. "But that doesn't change where we are or that I'm an Elite now. I need time, Aspen."

He reached up to hold my hand in his and nodded. "I can give you that. Just . . . try to find some time for me, too."

I didn't want to bring up how complicated that would be, so I gave him a tiny smile before gently pulling my hand away. "I need to go."

He watched me as I walked into my room and shut the door behind me.

Time. I was asking for a lot of it these days. I hoped that if I had enough, everything would somehow fall into place.

CHAPTER 2

"No, no," Queen Amberly answered with a laugh. "I only had three bridesmaids, though Clarkson's mother suggested I have more. I just wanted my sisters and my best friend, who, coincidentally, I'd met during my Selection."

I peeked over at Marlee and was happy to find she was looking at me, too. Before I arrived at the palace, I had assumed that with this being such a high-stakes competition, there'd be no way any of the girls would be friendly. Marlee had embraced me the first time we met, and we'd been there for each other from that moment on. With a single almost-exception, we'd never even had an argument.

A few weeks ago, Marlee had mentioned that she didn't think she wanted to be with Maxon. When I'd pushed her to explain, she clammed up. She wasn't mad at me, I knew that, but those days of silence before we'd let it go were lonely.

"I want seven bridesmaids," Kriss said. "I mean, if Maxon chooses me and I get to have a big wedding."

"Well, I won't have bridesmaids," Celeste said, countering Kriss. "They're just distracting. And since it would be televised, I want all eyes on me."

I fumed. It was rare that we all got to sit and talk with Queen Amberly, and here Celeste was, being a brat and ruining it.

"I'd want to incorporate some of my culture's traditions into my wedding," Elise added quietly. "Girls back in New Asia use a lot of red in their ceremonies, and the groom has to bring gifts to the bride's friends to reward them for letting her marry him."

Kriss piped up. "Remind me to be in your wedding party. I love presents!"

"Me, too!" Marlee exclaimed.

"Lady America, you've been awfully quiet," Queen Amberly said. "What do you want at your wedding?"

I blushed because I was completely unprepared to comment.

There was only one wedding I'd ever imagined, and it was going to take place at the Province of Carolina Services Office after an exhausting amount of paperwork.

"Well, the one thing I've thought about is having my dad give me away. You know when he takes your hand and puts it in the hand of the person you marry? That's the only part

I've ever really wanted." Embarrassingly enough, it was true.

"But everyone does that," Celeste complained. "That's not even original."

I should have been mad that she called me out, but I merely shrugged. "I want to know that my dad completely approves of my choice on the day it really matters."

"That's nice," Natalie said, sipping her tea and looking out the window.

Queen Amberly laughed lightly. "I certainly hope he approves. No matter who it is." She added the last words quickly, catching herself in the middle of implying that Maxon would be my choice.

I wondered if she thought that, if Maxon had told her about us.

Shortly after, the wedding talk died down, and the queen left to go work in her room. Celeste parked herself in front of the large television embedded in the wall, and the others started a card game.

"That was fun," Marlee said as we settled in at a table together. "I'm not sure I've ever heard the queen talk so much."

"She's getting excited, I think." I hadn't mentioned to anyone what Maxon's aunt had told me about how Queen Amberley tried many times for another child and failed. Adele had predicted that her sister would warm up to us once the group was smaller, and she was right.

"Okay, you have to tell me: Do you honestly not have any other plans for your wedding or did you just not want to share?"

"I really don't," I promised. "I have a hard time picturing a big wedding, you know? I'm a Five."

Marlee shook her head. "You *were* a Five. You're a Three now."

"Right," I said, remembering my new label.

I was born into a family of Fives—artists and musicians who were generally poorly paid—and though I hated the caste system in general, I liked what I did for a living. It was strange to think of myself as a Three, to consider embracing teaching or writing as a profession.

"Stop stressing," Marlee said, reading my face. "You don't have anything to worry about yet."

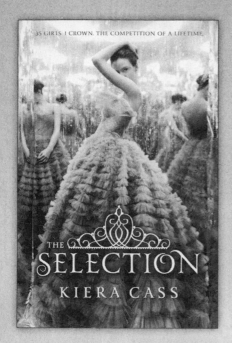